Your

what's the story?

NORTHERN IRELAND

Edited by Steve Twelvetree

First published in Great Britain in 2003 by
YOUNG WRITERS
Remus House,
Coltsfoot Drive,
Peterborough, PE2 9JX
Telephone (01733) 890066

SB ISBN 1 84460 278 8

FOREWORD

This year, Young Writers proudly presents a showcase of the best short stories and creative writing from today's up-and-coming writers.

We set the challenge of writing for one of our four themes - 'General Short Stories', 'Ghost Stories', 'Tales With A Twist' and 'A Day In The Life Of . . .'. The effort and imagination expressed by each individual writer was more than impressive and made selecting entries an enjoyable, yet demanding, task.

What's The Story? Northern Ireland is a collection that we feel you are sure to enjoy - featuring the very best young authors of the future. Their hard work and enthusiasm clearly shines within these pages, highlighting the achievement each story represents.

We hope you are as pleased with the final selection as we are and that you will continue to enjoy this special collection for many years to come.

CONTENTS

Camphill Primary School, Ballymena

Ryan Logan	30
Amy McCosh	31
Gemma Dennison	32
Amy Millar	33
Sara McMullan	34
Nicola Stewart	36
Courtney McGall	37
Zoë McQueen	38
Lauren Agnew	39
Christopher Shields	40
Samuel Scott	41
Hannah Craig	42
David McNeill	43
Matthew McBride	44
Bronwyn Hillis	45
Timothy Curry	46
Robert Workman	47

Churchill Primary School, Caledon

Shannon Read	48
James Murray	49
Rebecca Fitzsimons	50
Andrew Burns	51

Comber Primary School, Comber

Monique Zakhari	52
Ashleigh Halliday	53
Matthew Crooks	54
Glenn Martin	55
Sacha Ghionis	56
Rachel Carleton	58
Ross Hewitt	59
Lesley Bailie	60
Christopher Wallace	62
Shona Ayre	64

The Stories

GRAVEYARD PETE

Once upon a time, long ago, there lived a young boy called Joshua. He liked to tell stories and his favourite was about Graveyard Pete, who slept in the graveyard with all the dead bodies and stole children from their beds at night. All of his friends laughed at him and they thought he was silly. Even his best mate Jack got fed up with him.
'Stop telling that stupid story Joshua, don't you know that nobody believes you?'
Joshua wouldn't listen and he kept telling his spooky story about Graveyard Pete. 'It's the truth. Why won't anybody listen to me?'

One stormy, dark night, Jack was getting ready for bed when he thought he heard a noise outside his window. He hid under his blankets and stayed really still to see if he could hear the noise again . . . *yes, there is definitely someone out there,* thought Jack. He heard a scratching sound that grew louder and louder. Jack started to cry and was shaking like a leaf, then he remembered what Joshua told him to do. He shouted really loudly, 'Graveyard Pete, you can't hurt me, 'cause I've got smelly feet!'

All of a sudden, he felt a hand shaking him and someone saying, 'Get up lazy bones, it's time for school.' He was dreaming the whole time and was so happy to see his mummy, he gave her a big hug and she told him that he'd just had a nightmare. He squeezed her really tightly and looked over at his bedroom window. A shiver ran down his back, for there at his window was a big scratch mark, as if someone had been trying to get in!

Peter Vennard (9)
Aughnacloy Primary School, Aughnacloy

A Day In The Life Of The Scotland Vampire

One day, Karean, my friend, and I heard a ghost story from my uncle Paul. It was about a vampire that took you away if you disturbed its house. We didn't believe it at first, but one day we had to.

When we were both teenagers, we decided to go to Scotland as the vampire was supposed to live there. We asked four people where would be the best place to look for the vampire.
They all said, 'We're looking for the vampire as well. Why don't we all join up to look for the vampire in the haunted house?'
So we happily joined up with the two girls and two boys and went to the house. Karean and I slept with Jo and Sindy. The two boys, Adam and Timothy, slept in the opposite room.

'Lesabella,' said Sindy in my ear, 'it's here, the vampire.'
We quickly woke Jo and Karean up and got our guns. The boys came as they heard all the ghostly sounds and us talking. Sindy and I went together, Jo and Karean paired up and the boys went together.

We went upstairs, something moved, then we saw a skeleton. We ran downstairs and met the two boys being chased by a witch, the vampire was after Jo and Karean. So we put the guns side by side, which made a very big blast. We shot all of them, except the vampire. After five shots, we finally killed the vampire. At last our scary trip was over.

That's why we have to believe it, because we saw the vampire and the ghosts.

Naomi Galloway (9)
Aughnacloy Primary School, Aughnacloy

THE GIRL WHO FELL IN LOVE

One day at school (high school 6th class) a girl called Megan fell in love with a new boy. His name was Matthew and he was cute. He had short blond hair, handsome blue eyes and he was kind. She had long blonde hair, lovely blue eyes and was gentle. They both felt the same way, it was love.

Next thing you know, everyone was laughing and teasing. At breaktime, they went to the playground and sat on the swings. At first Megan was shy, but found Matt so easy to talk to, that she talked for ages about her family and her dreams. Matt was also able to talk and they found they had a lot in common, they both wanted to go to university to study and to work with animals.

After school, they met at the school gates and were happy to find that they were on the same bus. Matt asked Megan to go for a coffee at the restaurant and Megan happily agreed, even though all their friends shouted and laughed. Megan had never been so happy and hoped this was going to be okay, she rang her mum who said she could go for a while and would pick her up later.

Megan and Matt had a wonderful time and they finished it off with a kiss.

Katie Older (9)
Aughnacloy Primary School, Aughnacloy

A DAY IN A HAUNTED CASTLE

One day, in a small town, there lived two small children called Jack and James, who lived near a big castle.

One day Jack and James went for a walk up to the castle to see what was inside it. When they got there they had a look inside. When they were inside, it felt dark and spooky and very, very cold. Jack took a lollipop out of his pocket and threw the wrapper in the bin beside him. Suddenly, the bin spat the wrapper out at Jack, then they ran as fast as they could to another room.

In the room that they had run to, there was a big chimney. They heard something coming down the chimney and started to run.

They ran out of the castle, down to the village and locked the door of their small house and never went to the castle again.

Even though they heard very weird noises at night and sometimes they could not get to sleep, they still went out to play with their friends and family. When they were growing up, they still remembered that day, because it was so scary and they lived happily ever after.

Adam Clarke (9)
Aughnacloy Primary School, Aughnacloy

A Day In The Life Of Buttons

One afternoon on a beautiful summer's day, Sarah and David were playing games outside. Sarah looked at her watch and realised it was time to go home for tea. Her mother had made her promise that she would be home by 5 o'clock and it was nearly that.

They headed home chatting to each other about homework and what was on TV that night. As they passed an old empty house with broken windows, they heard a barking sound. They thought it might be a trapped dog. They followed the sound into the garden of the house. They saw two dark eyes shining out at them from under a bush. It was a little puppy and he was so happy to see them, that not only did he wag his tail, he wagged his whole body.

When they got home, their mother was glad to see them and to their surprise, she put up a sign to see if anyone had lost a puppy. The children were hoping no one had, because they might be allowed to keep it and they were already thinking up names.

Buttons, the puppy, was put to bed. At about midnight, they heard banging on the door. It was a man in a black cloak - he had seen the sign about the puppy. He said the puppy belonged to him. The children sadly went to get Buttons. They handed him over to the strange man.

A very unusual thing happened then. As they were walking down the drive, the puppy suddenly turned into a man and they walked off together, laughing.

Emma Williams (9)
Aughnacloy Primary School, Aughnacloy

THE HAUNTED HOUSE

Once upon a time, there was a girl called Janice. She had a fire at her house and her dad died, so that meant she had to move.

This house was a spooky house, that she moved into. Her room was covered in spider webs and bats. One night she went downstairs, there was a sound calling her name. She went into the front room. There was blood all over the floor.

She heard her dad calling her name. He said, 'Janice, Janice, I'm going to get you.'
Janice ran up the stairs to her mum, but her mum was not there. She started to cry and heard a voice again. This time it said, 'I've got your mum, I'm going to get you.'

She ran to the phone, the line was cut. She ran to the door, the door was locked. She ran up the stairs and got her mobile. She rang the police, but there was no answer. Then all she heard was *bang!* Someone banged the door and she heard them walking up the stairs. Soon she realised it was only her mum.

The next night she saw someone open the door. They cut her head off and she was never to be seen again.

Katie Bell (9)
Aughnacloy Primary School, Aughnacloy

A DAY IN THE LIFE OF THE HAUNTED HOUSE

A long, long time ago, there was a haunted house on a hill. The Grousess family lived there. It was in the year 1999.

One night, Diane out of Emmerdale, came to their house. Her car had broken down, so she went up to the house and asked if she could stay. The house was very creepy and spooky-looking, but she knocked the rusty knocker on the front door anyhow.

A tall, thin, bearded man, wearing a long, black coat came to the door, he looked rather strange. Diane spoke first, she asked if there was anyone who could fix her car.
Immediately the man said, 'No, but you would be welcome to stay the night.'

Inside the house, Diane could see no one else around, she became very scared and tried to get out through the front door, but it was locked. What was she going to do now? The man had left her in a very dark, spooky room, all alone, with just the dim light of a candle burning.

Suddenly, a woman dressed in a long gown entered the room. She gave Diane a drink, but when her back was turned, Diane poured the drink into her lap so that she didn't make a sound.

The strange sounds went on all night long and when morning came, Diane noticed a window with a very shaky latch. She climbed up onto the sill and after pushing the window open, jumped out and ran as fast as she could down the road.

Louise Gilmour (9)
Aughnacloy Primary School, Aughnacloy

THE ULTIMATE ADVENTURE

One Saturday (just the same as any other) I was playing Lego Racers on the computer. Suddenly, I whizzed through the screen and into a vortex. A galaxy of colours swam around me as I floated along. It was enchanting. I entered a fascinating new world, the Lego Drome, the place for all Lego lovers. Each of the seven sections had a unique landscape.

Amazingly, the Nitro team came along and transported me to the centre stadium. They gave me a special T-shirt and watch. I slipped into the T-shirt and fastened my watch. What a journey. I felt just like a jitterbug.

I arrived in time to see the only performance of the day. The commentator had just announced it. The Nitro Pulverizer performed its most famous trick, the 'lorry jump', which consists of ten lorries end to end. The mighty machine rose up powerfully and cleared the whole lot.

At the race track I saw the Nitro-Burner verses Slammer G-Force. It was a nail-biting race. My head pounded inside and Nitro-Burner roared past, winning by a hair's breadth.

In the steamy jungle section, the race included Jungle Monster and Raptor. Jungle Monster resembled a *giant* replica of my toy. I was so excited when the emerald shape of Jungle Monster flashed past me to win the race.

I dashed to the hot, dusty desert region. Nitro-Stunt Bike and X-treme Power Bike were in stiff competition. I checked my watch. It dazzled and I felt myself being catapulted again . . .

Stephen A R Colbert (8)
Aughnacloy Primary School, Aughnacloy

JOURNEY TO THE EDGE OF THE SEA

Halbared was strolling through the fair Mermish wood of Misminean, on duty, when he spotted a shining glint of golden metal. He walked over to the spot and picked up a golden flute. He knew immediately that it was the Golden Flute of Legendary Times, for he was an intelligent merman, learned in the lore of his people. He ran back to his home city of Gilga-Thoniel.

His masters decided to have it put back in the Magic Shell at the Edge of the Sea and set the merpeople free from all evil. So began the quest of the Flute, seeing Halbared and a score of his best warriors start off on their 1,000 league journey.

On their way, they had different skirmishes with lobards - evil, half-lizard, half-lobster creatures. Once the Company of the Flute was ambushed and four mermen lost their lives from evil lobard darts, fired from their underwater crossbows. At every encounter, Halbared fought bravely, slaying all the lobards he could, with his trusty sword, forged long ago in the Mermish kingdom of Wennellair.

On one such occasion, he picked up a lobard crossbow and two pouches of darts. When they were within three leagues of the Magic Shell, after a 40-day swim, they had to be extra careful, because of the increased lobard security. They kept working their way closer, until they knew it was make or break time.

Their strategy was for ten of the mermen to create a distraction. The enemy was drawn in and all the lobards raced across to fight the ten. Halbared lunged for the shell. There were a few lobards he had to slay on his way, but finally he made it and placed the Flute in the shell. All the lobards disappeared in clouds of bubbles. The mermen cheered. They were free! They swam home bearing the bodies of their fallen comrades in honour.

Peter Burton (11)
Ballymena Primary School, Ballymena

LOUDMOUTH LOUIS

Louis was telling John, who sits beside Louis in class, about the new movie that he had heard about the day before.

'I heard James Bond shoots somebody in the head!' exaggerated Louis.

'Cool! I want to see that movie!' replied John, sounding excited.

'Louis and John! Stop talking! That's the third time I've spoken to you boys! It's only nine-thirty and you haven't stopped talking since you came in!' shouted Mrs McCready.

'Sorry Mrs McCready,' said the boys.

'Now we can get started. Everyone take out their maths books,' said Mrs McCready.

Louis Bradshaw was a normal 11-year-old boy. He lived in Liverpool with his mum, dad and his two-year-old sister Jane. He wasn't the smartest in the class, but he had a good head on his shoulders. The only bad point about Louis was that he talked non-stop! His parents called him Loudmouth Louis. His sister would have called him that too, but all she could say was 'daddy' at the minute.

The bell had just rung and Louis was already out of the school gates. He was so excited to get home to play his new computer game. He ran all the way home. When he got there, his mum was gardening in the front garden.

'Where's the fire?' asked his mum, sarcastically.

'I'm excited about playing my new computer game, that's all!' explained Louis.

'Well, your computer game will still be there after you do your homework.'

'I don't have any, so I'm going to play the game!'

'Fine, but be quiet or you'll wake Jane!'

'OK. I'll be as quiet as I can!'

The next day at school, Mrs McCready wasn't there. They had a substitute for the rest of the week.

The week after that, an announcement was made in assembly.

'I'm sad to say that Mrs McCready had to leave, as she has been offered a job at Brookwalle Primary as vice-principal,' said Mrs Henderson, the principal, 'But I'm happy to announce that we have found a replacement. Please give a warm welcome to Mrs Bradshaw!'
Everyone clapped except Louis. He couldn't believe that his mum was his new teacher!
'It must be another Mrs Bradshaw,' said Louis.
But it wasn't. It was Louis' mum!

The next morning, before school, Louis asked his mum, 'Why didn't you tell me you were going to take Mrs McCready's place?'
'Because I wanted it to be a surprise!' said his mum.

When he arrived at school, there was only time for a quick chat with John before class.
'You're going to be teacher's pet now, Louis!' teased John, 'You'll have to stop talking in class or you'll get told off in school and at home!'
'I know,' said Louis, 'I'm going to have to be good.'

So from then on, for the rest of the year, Louis was teacher's pet, or should I say, mother's pet!

Kerry Kirk (11)
Ballymena Primary School, Ballymena

THE WOODEN DOG

Mary Marcus woke up with a fright. She had been woken by a noise coming from the living room. So, she got out of bed, got her dressing gown and went to the top of the stairs. She stopped for a moment. The noise was getting louder. But this time the noise was like a howl from a dog.

Mary knew that the only dog in the house was the big wooden statue, sitting behind the door. She took a deep breath and walked down the stairs and across to the living room door. The noise had stopped so she walked in.

Something caught the corner of Mary's eye. It was the shadow of a dog.

Mary was very smart you see, so she thought that the statue had come alive and that was its shadow. But how did it come alive?

When she turned around, it was gone.

Mary was so scared now that she didn't even turn around to walk out the door. So she walked out backwards. The next moment, the noise began again. Mary peeked in and the dog *jumped* out at her.

She screamed and ran up the stairs. She got into her bed, got under the covers and tried to pretend it was only a dream. She stopped screaming and started crying.

Mary had woken up her parents, who came into her room and asked her what was wrong. Mary told her parents what had happened in the living room and about the *scary* wooden dog. Her mother said it was just a dream and went back to bed.

A few minutes later, Mary heard a voice and it was saying, 'I am going to get you, I am going to get you.'

Was she dreaming or was she not?

Ruth Dornan (9)
Ballynahinch Primary School, Ballynahinch

HAUNTED HOUSE!

It was October 31st 1981. It was the day I moved into my new house. It was a pretty house with a rose-scented smell in every room. The village was pleasant and the people were nice. Even the stray animals were friendly. But there was only one problem - Hill House Mansion! It was a dark, creepy, dusty, haunted house. Nobody had lived there in centuries.

One day, my two new friends and I went to explore Hill House Mansion. We all thought the rumours about the creepy house were a lot of rubbish. So off we went to the creepy, old house.

First we knocked, but nobody answered.
Then I shouted, 'Is there anybody home?' There was no reply, so we just went on in.

Suddenly, we heard a noise saying, 'Danger! Get out!'
We all screamed and then . . . there it was. The ghost of Hill House Mansion.
It said, 'You heard about what has happened here, but no, you thought it was all a joke! Now be gone, or I will get you!'

With that I ran out of the house and never went there again, but one of my friends did and that was the end of her.

So be warned!

Rebecca Hughes (9)
Ballynahinch Primary School, Ballynahinch

STRANGE

Once, there were two girls named Mary and Jane. They lived in a crumbly, dusty, dirty and very old house in the middle of a wood named Green Tree Wood. They lived on their own because a strange kind of man killed their parents. These two children were trying to get their revenge on him.

Anyway. There they were, trying to find the monster for the fourth time. (Their mum and dad had died five days ago). The two children were arguing.
'We have to get some food,' said Jane.
'You can, but I care more about my parents,' said Mary.
'We're going to starve then,' said Jane.
'OK, we'll get some food then.'
So the two children went into the forest to find some food.

When they got into the forest, Jane heard something. They both turned around and something grabbed them both! The thing that grabbed them was tall, hooded and very spooky. They were dragged along for a long time.

'Where are we?' asked Jane, for the first time in ages.
'Don't know,' said Mary.
They were in a dark place in the middle of the forest. Then they saw their parents tied to a bit of rope.
'I thought they were dead,' said Mary.
'I thought they were too,' said Jane.

They untied them, gave them both a big kiss and hug and brought them home. They gave them something to eat and went to bed.

When they woke up they heard banging noises. Their dad had got the beast that had got them.
'It was a person dressed up,' said Dad.
'A famous murderer,' said Mum.

'Never mind that. We bought a house and tickets for Disneyland with all the money, £50,000, we got from catching the person.

Disneyland was brilliant, the house was lovely and they lived happily ever after.

Rebekah Davis (9)
Ballynahinch Primary School, Ballynahinch

THE HORRIBLE SHAKE

One dark and cold night, Sarah woke up from her sleep. She thought she had felt someone shake her. But who could it be? She lived with her gran, but her gran was still asleep.

Sarah got out of her bed. She lived in a dark country house. Sarah was scared. She looked forward, but all she saw was the landing. No one was there. At least, no one that she could see!

Sarah walked down the stairs. She looked out of the window. Sarah saw a dog running about, so she took another look, but the dog was gone. Everything felt strange. Sarah did not know what was happening, so she went back upstairs to her bed.

She lay down, but she could not sleep. Finally, she got to sleep. It happened again. Someone shook her. She was terribly scared, so she stayed in her bed.

After about three hours, her gran came up to her. Sarah was crying, so her gran asked her what was wrong. Sarah told her gran all about it and her gran said, 'Don't worry,' but she did.

Nobody knows, but Sarah can still feel shakes today.

Laura Montgomery (9)
Ballynahinch Primary School, Ballynahinch

HALLOWE'EN HORROR

On a dark night of October 21st, a girl named Alex got a surprising gift from her aunt. Her auntie and uncle came over for Hallowe'en. They got her a doll. It had blue eyes, ginger hair, wearing a pink frock and rosy-red lips. Alex collected dolls, she had about 29 all together. There was something about this one, so when she went to bed that night, she put it on the top of the pile.

Alex woke up and looked at the pile - there was only 28. She went into the hall and found ginger hair. She went into the kitchen and found a piece of pink material. She walked on. Then, she could not believe her eyes. The doll was walking about in the garden singing a song. It was a sound that made you want to scream. Alex made out the words, 'I am going to get you!'

Alex grabbed the doll and went to her mum's room. She was not there! Alex heard a cracking noise and then she saw her mum and dad as she looked down, out of the window, they walked past the sign 'Stray Park' which is what the house was called. Alex looked down at the doll and then threw it out of the window. As it flew through the air, a bright light hit her face!

Courtney Lyons (9)
Ballynahinch Primary School, Ballynahinch

THE MYSTERY OF THE MUMMY

One day in Ancient Egypt, a pharaoh was looking for a place for his pyramid, for when he died. He thought he would have a look inside some other pyramids.

There was a tour guide. The pharaoh thought he could handle it so he asked the tour guide to leave him. When he was walking around the pyramid he saw a shadow.

He went a little further and saw a coffin, lid open. He kept going on a little further and further. He kept seeing shadows everywhere he went. He felt very scared. He wished he had not said, 'I can handle it!'

At last, he found it was a mummy and it was in its second life.

When the pharaoh came out he was as white as a ghost. No one else knew what he saw or why he was as white as a ghost.

Hannah McMillan (9)
Ballynahinch Primary School, Ballynahinch

The Dolly Of Death

Once there was a girl and she always got porcelain dolls that she did not like, so she threw them down the stairs.

But one day, she was at the mall, there was a lady selling porcelain dolls.
The lady said, 'Don't hurt this doll or it will come and hurt you!'
So the girl went home and threw the doll down the stairs.

While she was watching TV, she kept getting the feeling that the doll was trying to move towards her. When she was eating her tea, she heard voices saying, 'Rachel, I'm coming to get you!'

That night, she couldn't get to sleep because of it and at 4am she heard someone saying, 'You shouldn't have hurt me!' Then, 'Dolly up one step, dolly up two steps, dolly up three steps, dolly up four steps, dolly up five steps, dolly on your landing, dolly at your door, dolly in your room, dolly on your bed and now you're *dead!*'

Craig Lockhart (9)
Ballynahinch Primary School, Ballynahinch

THE SKELETON MAN

I woke up suddenly! I went out of my bedroom, because this school isn't very big. My name is Alison and I have long, golden hair and green eyes. My parents died when I was a baby, so now I am an orphan. The small boarding school that I go to, is called Hilton House and my friends are called Kirsty and Naomi.

I went to see if my friends were in their room, but they weren't. I went a bit closer but nobody was there at all. I heard a window slamming, it was coming from Kirsty's room. I went to close it and that was when I saw a man. He had a skeleton body and had a coat to cover his skeleton body and a hat to cover his skull.

My feet were shaking and when I looked up again, he wasn't there. I ran outside to look for him, but he wasn't there at all, so I went back in.

The owner of the boarding school said, 'Alison, come here now!'
So then I ran into my bedroom and put the covers over me.

I woke up and it was all a dream.
My mum came in and said, 'What is all this screaming about?'
I said, 'I'm screaming because I had a nightmare and it was horrible.'

Eve Martin (9)
Ballynahinch Primary School, Ballynahinch

SARAH BLACK!

Sarah woke up. She looked around quickly. She could faintly hear the sounds from outside coming through her slightly open window. She tiptoed over the floor and suddenly stopped. Something had caught her eye. There, outside, behind a tree, a tall, dark figure stood glaring at Sarah. She ran as fast as she could to her mum's room.

When she got there, her mum wasn't about. She walked further in and tripped over something. Sarah screamed! Her mum was lying on the floor with blood gushing out of her. Who could have done this terrible deed? She looked out of the window again and it was her dad. The moon shone brightly on him and the silver of his knife glistened as he held it tightly. Sarah ran to the phone. She dialled nervously and then begged her aunt to come quickly, 'Please drive down the back road because something strange is out the front,' she said.

When her aunt arrived, she hugged her tightly. Suddenly, her aunt became very still. Sarah slowly looked up. She stepped back and saw something glistening in the moonlight, which streamed through the window. As she stepped back again, she suddenly realised it was a large, jagged knife. It was being held up to her aunt's neck. Sarah ran as fast as she could back to the window, to look to where her dad had been standing. He had vanished! She looked back to where her aunt stood, shivering with fear, the hand holding the knife belonged to her dad. She could not believe her eyes, was it really her dad who was going to kill her favourite aunt? It had been some years since he had died tragically. How could this be happening?

Sarah ran back to her room, in shock. She took deep breaths, when she listened, all she could hear was a deafening scream. She peered through her bedroom door and could see the shadow on the wall, the jagged knife through her aunt's heart!

Was this the revenge her father had promised before he died? Did he think it was her aunt who had killed him?

Amy Burtney (9)
Ballynahinch Primary School, Ballynahinch

KIDNAP!

One night, I heard a noise coming from my mummy's bedroom. I walked slowing into the dark and dull room, but my mum was not there! I ran into the garden and I saw a dark shadow behind a tree.

A man jumped out and he tried to grab me! I ran back into the house and I locked the door behind me and ran up the stairs.

I got into my bedroom and put the quilt over me. I tried to be quiet, but I was out of breath from sprinting up the stairs. The man threw a brick through the top window and I could hear him opening the door of the room beside me.

The man had a large figure and I swore that I had seen him somewhere before; he seemed strangely familiar. His face was round and he had a scar running down the side of his face. My thoughts were interrupted by the sound of the door opening and there he was, towering above the bed!

'You thought you could get away!' he said in a low growl. 'Come with me!'

He lifted me up and carried my limp body into the boot of his car.

'£25,000 is what I'll get for you!' he whispered into my ear.

I'll remember that grim voice for the rest of my life.

Kirsty Green (9)
Ballynahinch Primary School, Ballynahinch

JOHN AND THE GHOST

It was the middle of Monday night, but suddenly, John woke up! He sensed in his mind, that there was danger. He felt that something strange was going to happen. He spoke to his mum about this, but she told him that he was talking absolute nonsense. John then approached his dad, but he said the same thing.

John went on to school that morning. When he hung his coat up, he noticed something unusual. It was a hole in the roof of the cloakroom and he could hear funny noises coming from the bathrooms. He turned on one of the taps, but nothing happened. Suddenly, he heard a rumble and the floor cracked open! A hand came out of the crack and grabbed him, pulling him in, never to be seen again.

Robert Hunter (9)
Ballynahinch Primary School, Ballynahinch

THE MUMMIES

It was night-time and I suddenly heard a strange noise from the house beside us. I was sleeping at my friend's house. My friend Andrew Bennett was awake because of me. I kept waking him because I couldn't sleep.

The address I was at was 14 Henry Road. My name is Gareth Magill.
Andrew said, 'You woke me up Gareth!'
I said, 'I woke you up to tell you that I heard a strange noise outside. Let's look about outside.'
'The front door is locked,' said Andrew, 'so let's climb down the tree.'
(We were sleeping upstairs, you see.)

We climbed out of the window and down the tree.
'The noise sounds as if it's coming from the haunted house,' Andrew said, 'let's look.'

I turned the knob of next-door's front door. The door suddenly opened, noisily. Inside there was a lot of dust and a clock. The clock suddenly struck 12 midnight. There were some bandages on the floor. We looked up and shouted, 'Tutankamun and another mummy, blimey!' We ran for our lives.

What a dream! *Phew!* Then Andrew's mum came into the room and said, 'Are you boys alright?'
'Yep,' we both replied, by now Andrew was awake.
He had had the same dream.

Suddenly, we heard the chilling noise that was in the dream. I quickly pulled the covers over my head. I had had enough!

Gareth Magill (9)
Ballynahinch Primary School, Ballynahinch

THE STONE RABBIT

In a house by the country, there lived a girl called Ashleigh. She had lived there for quite a long time, but not much had happened to her. She had always longed for something exciting to happen, but she never believed that it would.

She woke up one morning and felt a tingle go all the way up her spine and she knew it was going to be a special day. She went down to the grassy bank beside her house. There was a path beside it, but her mother had told her not to go down it. She had turned 10 the week before, so she thought she would be allowed.

She strolled down the path and saw before her a long, sparkling stream and a little stone rabbit. As soon as she picked it up, it sprang to life. She was really surprised, I mean, wouldn't you be?

She knew her dad didn't like animals, but she took him home with her anyway. The big problem was, where was she going to put him? She decided he could stay in one of the cupboards under the sink.

During the next couple of months, she had to try her best to hide the rabbit from her mum and dad, but she enjoyed having him around. They spent the rest of the year playing by the stream and spent the summer at the seaside.

It was the night before Ashleigh's eleventh birthday and she had just given the rabbit his supper and was about to go to bed, when she heard him crying and took him from the cupboard into her bedroom. She asked him what the matter was, but he wouldn't tell her. She just told him to go to sleep and it would be okay in the morning.

The next morning Ashleigh went over to where the rabbit had slept, but he was no longer a real rabbit, he was just a normal stone one. She realised what had happened and went back to the stream and set him down.

She had the best day of her life.

Courtney Jackson (10)
Brooklands Primary School, Belfast

THE ADVENTURE

One day, it was very hot and a little mouse called Pete was being chased through a jungle by a falcon, then he came to a beach. There were a lot of people on the beach. Pete knew that if he joined the crowd, the falcon would not see him. So he did and just as he thought, the falcon could not see him, so he went away. Pete could swim, so he ran as fast as he could to the sea.

Under the sea was like a whole new world to him. There were fat fish, thin fish, flat fish, long fish, short fish, scary fish, sweet fish and spiky fish. There were even cat and dogfish. Pete thought it was a very nice place and wished that he lived there, but of course, he couldn't breathe underwater. He had to go to the surface every five minutes to get air. So, he explored more and saw some sea anemone. He saw a great big fish. It had sharp teeth and all the fish were swimming away fast. The fish then saw Pete and he treid to eat him, but another fish swooped him off his feet, it looked like a horse, his name was Paul.

Paul was light blue with green eyes. He had a curled up tail. He was very old, about 10-years-old. Pete thanked him, then Paul's mum and dad came, Pauline and Patrick. Pete told them what had happened. They were very happy. They had a little party, but Pete didn't eat anything because it was seafood.

After the party, Pete asked Paul to take him as close to the shore as possible. So he did. They said goodbye and Pete went away. Pete walked around and then came across a little boy called Jon. Jon was very fond of mice. He saw Pete and asked if he could keep him.
His mum said, 'No!' but then she said, 'Oh, all right then, but he is your responsibility.'

They took Pete home. Jon treated him like a brother. They played with each other every day and went every where together and lived happily ever after.

Danika Moffett (10)
Brooklands Primary School, Belfast

THE BABYSITTER FROM HELL

It all started when Mum and Dad got invited to a party. I was too young to attend the party, so Mum and Dad had to get me a babysitter. It was okay at first, because my friend was sleeping over.

On the night of the party, there was a loud *knock* at the door. My mum answered it and invited the man in. At last, my mum and dad left.

Well, the babysitter was okay at first. He let us watch TV and have pillow fights, everything. But when bedtime came, it was awful! He pulled us upstairs by our ears, forced us to have a bath in boiling water, then when we thought the horror was over, he walked into my room, took out a glass eye and said, 'I will be watching you all night. If you touch my glass eye, you will die tomorrow!' With a spine-chilling laugh, he trudged downstairs.

Now my friend, who was quite silly, got out of bed, picked up the glass eye and chucked it out of the window. Eventually we got to sleep.

We woke at 10 the next morning. We had our breakfast and went outside to play football. I kicked the ball too hard. It went over the road. My friend ran over to get it and just then a bus came and it was going too fast. She died.

Lauren Tumilson (9)
Brooklands Primary School, Belfast

THE GHOST HOUSE

Once upon a time, there was a gloomy, old house with broken windows and ivy growing up the walls at the end of a dark and quiet lane. No one had lived there for thousands of years and many people believed it to be haunted.

Now, one foggy, dark night, a young boy named Jack, was out walking and the rain came on and he was an awfully long way from home, so he thought maybe he could shelter in the old house. Across he went towards the old house. When he got there he found the door slightly ajar, so he went in.

Inside was a terrible sight. It was damp and full of cobwebs and it was dark, creepy and very eerie. Jack felt his body going cold and wanted to get out as he was really scared. A creak on the floorboard made him turn around and there, before him, was a ghost! It was translucent and it had an icy voice.
It said, 'Who are you?'
Jack froze. He wanted to run, but he felt rooted to the spot. The ghost looked as though he would kill Jack.
'Why are you here?' said the ghost.
'Getting shelter,' replied Jack.
'Well, not here you're not!' screeched the ghost.

The ghost went right through Jack and suddenly he went very cold again and his legs went like jelly and then he died.

Jennifer Gorman (9)
Brooklands Primary School, Belfast

YOU ARE CUTTING MY LIFE INTO PIECES!

This story all happened years ago. A storm came and covered the whole graveyard. I'm Mark, I just live across the street from the graveyard.

My best friend called Paul, was staying over the night it happened. I asked my mum if we could go out and play, but she said no because it was too dark. But there was another plan to get out of the house.

We climbed out of the window and we walked across the road to the graveyard. The road was very quiet! We were just playing, minding our own business, when we saw a man chopping up a body! He was wearing a black cloak and a tall hat and you couldn't see his face.

We tried to run but Paul stepped on a branch . . .

Leah Kelly (9)
Brooklands Primary School, Belfast

FOOTBALL

Hello, my name is Dave. I play for my school football team that doesn't do very well, but hey, it's just a game isn't it? Well, I'll tell you the story from the beginning.

We were halfway through a match and we were losing 2-0 against a team that you couldn't even say right. We kept on losing throughout the season but at least we drew our last match. Two of our top players were injured so they missed practising and the start of the season.

When I went home that night I was thinking of how to improve our team because, after all, I am the team captain. When the new season began I told all our players about my new plan.

Mike, our defender, thought it was a great idea, so in our next match we tried it and we won 2-1, but Mike thought we were too loose at the back. He told us some of his ideas and we tried them out. After all, we were one of the favourites to win our league because we only lost one match all season which was against the reigning champions.

By the end of the season we were even on points and on goal difference which meant it came down to the final game. This was a game that the other team's fans thought was over by half-time because they were 3-0 up. But we came back and won the match 5-3. Our fans went wild and so did our players.

Ryan Logan (11)
Camphill Primary School, Ballymena

MIGHTY BEANS

Hi, I'm doing a short story of mighty beans, they are a collectable. There are sixty altogether and they sell them in a double pack of two and a packet of four. They have just started the first series; they are going to start a second series soon. My friends are starting to design their own thoughts of what they would like the second series to be like.

The beans are all in different teams, there are twelve altogether. They are the Musician Beanz Team, the Fairy Tale Bean Team, Circus Bean Team, Wrestling Bean Team, Extreme Bean Team, Western Bean Team, Spooky Bean Team, Worker Bean Team, Jungle Bean Team, Prehistoric Bean Team, Freak Bean Team and Robotic Bean Team.

I have got all the Musician team. They are Rock And Roll Bean (we call it Elvis Presley), Heavy Metal Bean, Pop Star Bean, Deejay Bean, Rapper Bean (we call it Ali G). I have also got Prince Charming, Evil Queen Bean, Moto X Bean and Skating Bean. That is all I have so far. I only have ten at the minute as I have only started to collect. My favourite bean is Elephant Bean 'cause it is cool and funny-looking. The one I am not so keen on is Brawl Bean because it is ugly and boring-looking.

You also play games with the beans. You can play races and you can make them bounce on a piece of paper. You can trade them with your friends for a team or better bean. You can also battle with your friends!

Amy McCosh (11)
Camphill Primary School, Ballymena

THE MAGIC HAIRBRUSH

Once upon a time there was a town called Kattamonsington. It was a lovely place where everybody was friendly. The only downfall to this town was that people were bald!

'Not a hair on our heads have we seen
For we are all bald as a bean,
We have looked everywhere,
For a good bit of hair
But the wig shop owner is mean!'

Years passed and the wig shop owner died. As people were searching through his things, someone found a hairbrush.
'I only wish I could use this!' he said, rubbing it against his head.
The other people stared, for the man had grown hair down to his knees!

Soon everyone was growing hair. You may think that the people would have celebrated but they never got a chance to for the hair kept growing and soon the whole town was buried under hair!

Perhaps it's still out there somewhere. If you ever go there and you find a hairbrush I would advise you not to brush your hair with it!

Gemma Dennison (11)
Camphill Primary School, Ballymena

THE DEAD MAN'S PARTY

Once there was a girl called Becky. She was a normal girl, 13 years old, hobbies, good grades and best friends. Everything was going well until . . .

'Becky! I don't care if you stand on your head and burp 'Baa Baa Black Sheep' I'm not going to your house to pick a stupid Hallowe'en costume for you,' said Kate.
'But please,' begged Becky.
'Okay,' said Kate.
'Thank you so much,' said Becky gratefully.

When they eventually got to the party there were already a ton of people there and decorations that looked really life-like.
'*Wow!* Look at this place!' said Becky in amazement.
'It looks so cool!' Kate replied, totally gobsmacked.

Then suddenly there was a loud bang! Everyone looked around to see what had happened. Then they realised that the door had slammed shut and in front of it there stood a huge headless figure.
It shrieked, 'I am the man who has no head, I will not stop until you are all dead!'
Everyone screamed and shouted, then silence. Everyone was frozen in time.

The headless figure glided across the room, coming to a stop in front of Becky and laid his hands on her head. Becky fell to the floor instantly, her vampire cape covering her completely.

When she opened her eyes, she felt different. She got to her feet. What had happened? She looked around. Everyone was laughing, dancing and having a good time. She looked at Kate. Why did she suddenly have the need to *drink blood?*

Amy Millar (11)
Camphill Primary School, Ballymena

When I Grow Up . . .

When I grow up I want to become the Prime Minister. I'd make some major changes, like for instance . . .

Education:
Pupils at primary and secondary schools will all be given their own private laptops.
Children will be taught to wear arm pads and kneepads during cycling proficiency. (I'm the only one who wears them, it's dead embarrassing!) Head teachers won't be allowed to give lectures.

TV Media:
Football and other sports shall have a special channel of their own - so as not to interrupt programmes such as Emmerdale, Coronation Street, CBBC and so on.
If you do not like the presenter presenting the programme you should be able to switch and swap them until you find someone suitable.

Sport and Recreation:
Skateboards will be banned - anyone who does not conform to this rule will have to see their skateboard go *crunch*.
Football pitches will be out in the middle of nowhere.
Swimming teachers will have to come into the pool and get cold too.

Environment:
Any dog owners who do not dispose of the dog's waste will have their noses stuck in it.
Anyone caught chewing or spitting bubblegum onto the ground will instead of chewing gum have to chew paper.

Other:
No queues.
Free travelling for children.
Child allowance will be paid in three parts - into the child's savings account for CDs, clothes and accessories; child's savings accounts for a car when older; and a tiny proportion into the parents' account.

And those are just a few of my rules!

Sara McMullan (11)
Camphill Primary School, Ballymena

A NEW DOG FOR LUCY

Hi, my name is Lucy. I really wanted a dog about two months ago, so my mum took me to the kennels. Here is the story of me getting a dog.

Our story starts on the 28th of July at the kennels with my mum, dad and bratty little sister called Katie.

We pulled up at the kennels and hopped out. When we got inside we started to look around. Katie really liked a Yorkie called Sam, but Mum thought it looked like a rat. Dad liked an ugly crossbred called Missy but that's just Dad! Mum fell in love with an Old English Sheepdog. I liked it too but it was too big for our small townhouse. We walked around the last bend to see a Cocker Spaniel called Vanilla. We all loved her so we brought her home.

It all went very well and we still have her. She is extremely friendly, but not much of a guard dog. We have bought her a new collar and I take her for walks.

One day Katie left the gate open and Vanilla got out. It took us three days to find her! She was next door with our neighbours, Mr and Mrs Parker. That was a week ago. I really missed her. I don't know what I would do without her!

Nicola Stewart (11)
Camphill Primary School, Ballymena

POOR OLD PING

There was a dog who lived down the road from the Browns with his owner, Mr Beat. Mr Beat was a nasty man and had no friends. When the children were out playing he would come and shout at them and take their ball off them.

He neglected his dog and gave him no attention, he didn't even give him a name but the children called him Ping. When the children called on him he would come running to play.

The Brown children, Chris and Clare, would bring Ping home and feed him. In the morning they would find him lying on the doorstep waiting patiently for them. Sometimes they would sneak him in the house when their mum wasn't around.

One day, Mr Beat had to be rushed to hospital with a heart attack. The doctor said he would never be home again. Now Ping had no home. Chris and Clare let him sleep in their shed for a few nights until their mum found out and called the RSPCA. The children didn't see him go, but their mum explained to them he would get a new home.

The children were very upset and cried every night because they missed him so much. Ping was missing them too and wasn't eating. Chris and Clare persuaded their mum to go to the kennels and bring him home. Ping was delighted to see them and the children were overjoyed when they brought him home to start a new life.

Courtney McGall (11)
Camphill Primary School, Ballymena

THE PRETTY DUCKLING

Once upon a time, six little ducklings were sitting quietly in their nests. Suddenly one duckling boasted, 'I am the most beautiful duckling in the world and -'

'Sarah, stop boasting about your looks and get to sleep. We are all very tired and don't want to be disturbed, so *shh!'* grumbled her sisters.

Sarah got to sleep quite quietly and woke early the next morning, but when she got out of her nest, the other ducklings were laughing at her.

'Look at Sarah. She looks as if she's been attacked by a cat. I don't think she's the prettiest anymore!'

Sarah didn't know what they were talking about, so she waddled over to the pond and saw her reflection. She started to cry and wondered what had happened to her last night. 'Why am I not pretty anymore?' groaned Sarah.

'It doesn't matter about how you look, it's how you act,' said another voice.

Sarah looked around and saw a young gosling that looked about her own age. 'What would you know about it?' mumbled Sarah, starting to cry even more.

'Well, I've experienced it before. Last year in April I was just what you used to be, pretty and beautiful, until one night I changed! But I coped because my mum told me not to worry about it and get on with my life and so I did. You should do it too because you'd feel much better.'

'Thanks a lot. I think I will,' said Sarah, waddling back to her family.

From that day on, not only did Sarah change her looks, she also changed her personality.

Zoë McQueen (10)
Camphill Primary School, Ballymena

THE SECRET PASSAGE

It was the beginning of the summer holidays and James was sent to his great aunt's house, whilst his father and mother were visiting his sick grandma.

As soon as James set foot in his great aunt's house, he knew there was something mysterious about it. James couldn't get to sleep that night and decided to find out what time it was. He found a clock which read 12 o'clock and on his journey back to his room he came across an old grandfather clock which read 11 o'clock. Knowing it was 12 o'clock he twitched the hands around to twelve. Almost immediately after doing this, the old grandfather clock slid to one side to reveal a secret passage.

James followed the ascending passage until he found himself in a small room lit by candlelight. He went over to where the candle was sitting and found a diary of some sort with 'Herbert' written on the front, and started reading it.

Whilst reading it, James came across an old photo. It was a young boy with 'Herbert' written on the back. James decided to play cards and suddenly the ghost of Herbert appeared and started playing with him. James won, which made Herbert livid. James grabbed the diary and made a quick exit. He later found out from the diary that Herbert had never been beaten in a game of cards.

From then on, James never went up the secret passage again!

Lauren Agnew (11)
Camphill Primary School, Ballymena

RACE CAR DRIVER

In Texas there was a race, it was called the Texas 5000. The cars were just doing their warm-up lap around the track. One driver wasn't the very best but he tried hard. He was called Johnny Walker; his car was a Dodge Viper GTS-R Concept. There was a rival though, Enzo Pizzonia from Italy. He drove a Porsche 911 GT 3Turbo. The cars were ready to start the Texas 5000.

The loudspeaker shouted, 'And they're off!'
The cars were thundering up the track and taking the first corner.
'And Johnny is really trying to take Enzo up this straight!' said the commentator.
Johnny flew past Enzo in the Viper. Suddenly Enzo crashed into a Toyota, which smashed into a barrier. Enzo powered up the straight too. The cars were coming round another corner. Johnny spun on that turn and another car was coming straight towards him but just missed him! He turned the car around, zoomed to catch up with the other cars and put the pedal to the metal!

He drove around a corner faster than usual and caught up with the other cars. He was behind a Mustang on a corner and accelerated past. Enzo was two cars in front of Johnny, taking the next turn gently, and then Johnny went into the pit stop to have the tyres changed and refuelled. Enzo was there, also getting his car refuelled and tyres changed.

Both cars went out at the same time. Enzo was just in front of Johnny. All cars had reached the final lap of the Texas 5000. Johnny had had an engine problem with the transmission but got it sorted. Enzo was behind a Lotus which had had its bumper smashed off by Enzo earlier.

There was oil on the wide corner before the finish. Team members told their drivers to slow on that corner, but Enzo sped round the corner and *smash* into the barrier, but Johnny went slowly round the corner and *won!* The Dodge team was delighted with young Johnny.

Christopher Shields (11)
Camphill Primary School, Ballymena

IS IT 3.10 YET?

It's Monday, first day of school and always seems to be the longest. Anyway, I'm at the school gate and it's half-past eight and the bell will be ringing in fifteen minutes to open the school. The reason I'm in so early is because my mum's teaching today and had to drop me off early to get to her class in time. Well, I've spent too much time talking, the bell's ringing.

Playtime's over and we've sat down in class ready to do maths. Maths isn't my favourite subject, I like science, but maths is alright I suppose. We're doing some multiplying and dividing and I've finished sections A and B, but I'm bored. I lean over and ask Chrissy, 'Is it ten past three yet?'
I get the reply, 'It's only quarter to ten, nowhere near ten past three!'

We did maths until break time and got outside for ten minutes and now we're back in class to do English. I really don't like English that much but it's just nouns so it shouldn't take long. This English is longer than expected, four sections of nouns! I've finished A, B and C but it's pretty dull. I lean over and ask Matthew, 'Is it ten past three yet?'
I get the reply, 'It's only half-past twelve, better get outside for lunch.'

We've had our lunch and now we've got to do science. Finally, something I like. I think science is a lot better than maths and English. We're experimenting with seeds, the best way to grow them. Time seems to fly by and I'm about to ask the time when the home bell rings. Finally going home!

Samuel Scott (11)
Camphill Primary School, Ballymena

EVERY DOG HAS ITS DAY

Once upon a time there was a girl called Karla. She had fair, curly hair and blue eyes. Karla's dog, Spot, was a Dalmatian and it was a pup. Karla bought a cat called Socks, it was ginger and had white feet. Karla brought it back home and the dog was smelling it and made friends so the cat stayed in to play with the dog.

The next week, the cat got all the attention and it got presents like new dishes, a litter tray and all the other things cats need.
The dog called over Socks and they had a few words. 'Just because you're new to this house doesn't mean you have to get everything.'
Then suddenly the cat attacked the dog and the dog got to sleep with the owner.

The next day, the dog got new bowls and toys etc. The dog now received a lot of attention and got big dinners. It was treated really well just like the cat had been when Karla bought it. The cat asked the dog to make friends and they became best friends.

Karla now treats them the same and they are living happily ever after.

Hannah Craig (11)
Camphill Primary School, Ballymena

THE PRICKLY PROBLEM

One day there was a hedgehog who had many brothers, sisters and cousins that had all been squashed on the road. The hedgehog went to a very clever crow which he knew and asked how he could get across the road and be seen?

The crow thought, then said, 'Why don't you try a brightly coloured jacket?'

They headed to the nearby construction site and when a man sat down for his coffee break, *whooosh* they lifted his jacket!

When they got back to the hedgehog's house it was on fire so they called the fire brigade and as the house was smouldering into ashes, the fire brigade arrived. The hedgehog got very angry with the firefighters and just then a man came out of the house.

'Hey whazzap? Just doin' a scene for a movie called 'Man Jumps Out Of Third Floor Window When The House Is Blazing'.'

'But where will I live?' protested the hedgehog.

'Oh yeah, we'll build you a new one!'

'You what?' said the hedgehog. 'I mean, thank you!'

They went around and saw the new house and went inside.

This house is far nicer than my old one, thought the hedgehog, so the village rallied round and helped him move in properly.

He had only moved in one week and then he was crossing a road and then . . . *splat!*

David McNeill (11)
Camphill Primary School, Ballymena

CRAZY APES

'Bang! Crash! The crazy apes have landed; they're destroying everything! Buildings, cars, even people!' said the 'Prime At Eight' reporter.

Kong, Monking, Wildape and Wreakwrocket *were* destroying everything, of course these weren't your normal zoo apes. These apes were over 30 metres tall with 68942 style laser shotguns that when shot at you, would hit you at around 68942mph!

Wreakwrocket is the most agile and the fastest of the apes. Kong is a good climber and can take a lot of damage. Wildape is a bit eccentric, slow but very strong. Monking is the only ape to be part-monkey, making him fast, brainy and a good climber.

The army came in and started to attack Kong - not a good idea. They threw bombs at Wreakwrocket, also not a good idea. They tried to outwit Monking and tried to fire guns at Wildape which didn't work.

The crazy apes ate the army and then they decided to 'split up'. Each ape chose part of the world to destroy.

Kong took the northern part of the world, Monking the eastern, Wreakwrocket the southern and Wildape the western.

Kong wreaked terror on part of Asia, Europe and part of Africa. Monking obliterated the rest of Asia and Australia. Wildape conquered South and North America. Finally Wreckwrocket dissected Antarctica.

After dominating the world the apes took over the *whole* universe!

Matthew McBride (11)
Camphill Primary School, Ballymena

THE DOG THAT CLIMBED MOUNT EVEREST

One morning, a little dog called Lady woke up very early. The sun was shining bright and the birds were singing. Lady got out of bed and went into her mum and dad's room, but they were still sound asleep. As she looked outside at the beautiful green fields she noticed for the first time how tall the mountain was that they lived beside. As Lady looked closer she could see something on top of the mountain. It looked like a ball. lady wanted the ball so she left a note for her mum and dad and off she went.

As she climbed the mountain, she realised just how tall the mountain was. When she was halfway there she could see the ball, well, what she thought was a ball, was moving about a little. Just then she could hear her dad calling her but she couldn't turn back now, she had come too far, she needed to know what the object was. So off she went, she climbed and climbed and finally reached the top. She could see the object quite clearly now. It was Kitty, Lady's friend. She hadn't seen her for days. Kitty was scared to come back down the mountain so Lady helped her.

When Lady and Kitty reached the bottom, Lady's dad was very angry but yet he was very happy.

In the end, everyone threw a party for Kitty and Lady's safe return.

Bronwyn Hillis (11)
Camphill Primary School, Ballymena

BATTLE OF THE BEASTS

One day a portal to a different dimension opened and out came Rancor Ackley, the Reek, and all sorts of monster like Minotaurs and monsters. These monsters couldn't be controlled by anyone and the dragons were the worst because they burned down cities!

As this was happening, the army and even criminals joined together with the police. The army they had formed started to get rid of the easiest monsters, then tried a different tactic by going for the nests.

Now the world was in despair, but the army was ready for action in a secret base. The animals began to starve and kill each other, they even killed their babies. Now everything was twisted and going mad. The bull was going crazy, killing anything that moved and even took on a beast Godzilla who was also going mad!

The army couldn't do anything and were wasting away. They were eating anything in sight, like baby dragon eggs and some even turned into cannibals.

By now there were very little life forms there, so when the bull was weak, the small army came up with a plan to kill him with a trap of dynamite. The bull fell for this trap and got so many injuries he died and the army rejoiced with this news and started all over again in their lives.

After years, the population had returned to normal. Life was better than ever and the world was more advanced than in many years, so be very careful civilians.

Timothy Curry (11)
Camphill Primary School, Ballymena

THE GHOST CAR

One stormy night, Christopher was walking down the lane when he heard a noise. It sounded like an engine. Then from out of nowhere a car started to head towards him. He realised it had no driver and you could see through it. He started to run but he could not outrun a car, so he jumped into the hedge. After he did that it just disappeared.

Next day he told his best friend, Robert, who believed him. They both went back that night. The same thing happened, but this time they outran it by a second. The car turned and turned until it disappeared.

Next afternoon they were thinking about the car and why it was chasing them. Then they remembered there was an accident which they had caused by throwing stones at a car. They realised it was the same car but only as a ghost!

At night they did not go to the lane, but had a good night's sleep.

In the morning they went to school and that night they went to the hill where they saw the car. The same thing happened except they caught the car and asked it why it was hunting them.
It said, 'Because you killed my master!'
They said, 'No we did not.'
'But I saw you,' the car replied.
'No, he's not dead, he was just knocked out,' they pleaded.

The next night the car disappeared for good and was never seen again.

Robert Workman (11)
Camphill Primary School, Ballymena

THE HOUSE OF SPOOKS

One dark, stormy night, Ashley and Emma were coming home from shopping. Suddenly the car broke down.

'Look,' said Emma, 'there's a house.'

'You are going in *there?*'

'I'm only going to find a telephone. You stay here and try to fix the car.'

'O-O-O-K. Be careful!'

Emma went through the overgrown garden and knocked on the door. The door opened in thin air. As she walked, the door slammed! Emma felt scared. She looked for a telephone, but when she found one it was dead. Next she heard something coming towards her. She ran as fast as she could up the stairs and went into a bedroom. It was creepy. It had a lot of pictures. Eyes were moving on them. Emma jumped when she heard a picture fall. She ran into the next room. It was a small room filled with webs but on the wall she saw red writing. It said *Beware! Beware!* The writing was like blood. Then someone grabbed her.

Ashley heard the noise outside and ran in to help Emma. She ran up the stairs and into the small, dark bedroom. Emma wasn't there, only a zombie. She got a chair and broke the window. She climbed out, jumped down and ran through the trees. She saw car lights and waved. The car stopped. She was safe.

Does anyone know what happened to Emma? Nobody knows and nobody has dared to enter the house again!

Shannon Read (8)
Churchill Primary School, Caledon

ONE NIGHT TO NEVER FORGET

One Friday, two cops were heading to the police station when lightning started to strike. One blast shot down the chimney of Herman Hall and a giant came out through the gate and squeezed the jeep. James jumped out with a gun and tried to shoot it, but he couldn't. He called in Ian with his gun. Written on the wall in a spiderweb was: *You will pay for entering Herman Hall.*

Suddenly, a spider as big as a 14 rabbits appeared. It had 80 eyes and 8 mouths as big as rubbers. It was just about to bite us. We whistled and our motorbikes came in, but the spider pounced on them. That was not the only surprise, the spider shot its web around them. Andrew switched his jet pack on and blasted through the roof, of course, with his helmet on. So did the spider with his jet pack. Luckily we met Ryan in his lorry. We jumped in and he rode over it. It turned into millions of tiny spiders. Suddenly the spiders covered the cab. The windows started to break so we had to dig through the spiders with our hands. Ian had an idea. He jumped over a hole of wet cement and the spiders fell into it.

Luckily Ryan's helicopter arrived and picked us up and we flew away. When I looked in my bag for my phone, there was a dead man's hand on it!

James Murray (8)
Churchill Primary School, Caledon

SPOOKS

One stormy night, Hannah and I were in our house. Suddenly, just in a flash, there was thunder and lightning. The trees were scraping along the bedroom window. Hannah was scared stiff. The lightning had made the electric go out.

We went on our bikes to see. We were pedalling away but suddenly the handles were steering by themselves. We tried to stop but they started to pedal by themselves. We went into a garden but it wasn't just any garden. It was the garden of a haunted house.

We ran inside but it was too late. The door slammed tight. There was writing in blood and big skeletons. There were moans and groans. We went upstairs and looked in the bedrooms. We slammed the door tight because there was a great big monster with five eyes. He ran down the hall. Fire came out of the statues' mouths. The fire killed the monster for good.

Suddenly Hannah ran into the bathroom and she disappeared. A giant zombie had taken Hannah. I heard someone calling. I went to look. It was Hannah. We ran down the stairs and saw the zombie. Hannah found a bucket and poured water over him and ran outside. We grabbed our bikes and went back home. By the time we got home the electric was back on. We both jumped into bed.

Nobody knows what happened to the zombie. Some think he moved house and some think he is still there. Beware of the zombie!

Rebecca Fitzsimons (8)
Churchill Primary School, Caledon

SKELETONS IN THE CLOSET

One spooky night my car broke down beside a graveyard.

'Oh no!' said my friend, James.

James and I had to walk in the freezing cold night to a shattered, creepy, old mansion. I was scared because written on the door in blood was *Beware the ghost*. When I knocked at the door it opened in thin air! We ran inside because I thought I saw a pair of eyes in the bushes. When we got inside, the door slammed shut. We were trapped!

In the mansion was a machine that sold drinks for twenty-five pence. I was so thirsty that I put twenty-five pence in, but when I put my hand in to grab the can, it tore my skin off. Then we saw a mummy with glowing red eyes We took out our water guns and blasted the mummy to dust. I tried to phone someone, but the phone was dead.

Suddenly I heard someone coming behind me. I grabbed James, shoved the door and ran across the road, waved at a taxi and got in. What a lucky escape!

Andrew Burns (7)
Churchill Primary School, Caledon

THE HAUNTED HOUSE

It was a dark stormy night. The moon was full that night as the clouds
drifted across the sky. I was lying in my tent in the middle of nowhere
on a camping trip. I couldn't sleep. I was bored. I looked out to see,
directly above me, a house on top of a hill. A path swayed up to the
house. It had vines growing up the walls, dead plants and moss upon the
door. I rapped the door. A man answered. His skin was pale, his head
was bald.

He said, '*Guuuhhh,*' and he grabbed me by the wrist.

We walked up the stairs. I looked forward and in the back of his head
was an axe! I stayed silent. He pointed to a doorway. I turned around to
look and he was gone. I went in where he had shown me. It was the
study. I saw books. I picked out a purple one, it was dusty. As I opened
it, a key appeared.

The butler appeared again. He placed the key inside a green book. The
bookcase swerved round and opened to leave a dark blue hole . . . the
curtains swayed and the wind blew and the rain lashed down. The man
touched my shoulder almost as if he was comforting me . . . I was
wrong, he pushed me down. I landed on a bench, got up to see before
me . . . a corpse. It had been chewed up, spat out and left. I was
horrified, so scared . . . I froze.

And there I stand this very day. The wind still blows, the rain still falls
and I still stand. For the next poor kid who stumbles upon this house,
God help them.

Monique Zakhari (11)
Comber Primary School, Comber

TOO ILL FOR SCHOOL

At 7.30, the usual time, Megan's alarm clock went *ring, ring, ring.* Time to get up and go to school.

While Megan was in bed, she decided she didn't want to go to school because she was too cosy and outside it was always freezing. She got up and went over to her dressing table on which there was a pot of red ink and a fine paintbrush. She decided she would have the chickenpox. She picked up the paintbrush, dipped it into the ink and started putting wee dots on her face.

As soon as she got back into bed, her mother came up the stairs.
'Come on, time to get up for school.'
Megan said, 'But Mum, I don't feel well and I have little red dots all over my face.'
Megan's mum went over and saw that she did have little red dots all over her face and said, 'Oh you poor dear, you have chickenpox.' Secretly Megan's mum knew that she wasn't really sick.

When Megan's mum was gone, Megan got up and went to the window. Suddenly 3 of her friends came to the window and shouted, 'No school, power cut, we're off to the park!'

While she was at the window she heard her mum coming upstairs and as quickly and quietly as she could, she ran and got back into bed.
Megan's mum came into the room and said, 'Time for some medicine.'

Ashleigh Halliday (11)
Comber Primary School, Comber

GIZMO

Some time ago there was a boy called David who had received a cat from his mum and dad for his birthday. He called the cat Gizmo because he looked like one. David invited his neighbour, Mr Clever, over to see his new pet and Mr Clever thought Gizmo was just lovely.

One day, David sat playing with Gizmo, they were playing with a ball of string. Then David threw the string too far and it landed over the wall and on the road. Gizmo went to get the string. A car was coming. Gizmo ran onto the road.
'Stop,' shouted David.
Gizmo ran on and very luckily returned with the ball of tangled string.

A few days later, Gizmo managed to escape from the garden. He saw a man walking his dog. It was a big dog - a boxer. David just happened to be looking out of the window when he saw Gizmo approaching the big dog.
David ran out and shouted, 'Gizmo wait. Don't go near him. He is a cross man and that dog will hurt you. It is a boxer.'
Gizmo didn't listen and walked on.

The boxer pulled away.
'Dingo, come back!' shouted Mr Clip.
Gizmo turned and ran away, but it was too late. Dingo caught Gizmo and bit his leg. It was streaming with blood.

David had to take Gizmo straight to the vet. The vet said Gizmo had a broken leg - his front left. It was the eighth time Dingo had attacked and badly hurt a cat, so Dingo had to be put down.

Mr Clip was very sad and missed Dingo a lot. David felt very sorry for Mr Clip as he turned out to be a very nice man, so for Mr Clip's birthday, David bought him a cat. Gizmo became good friends with the new cat and six weeks later, when Gizmo got his cast off, he was outside running and playing with his new cat-friend, Drip.

Matthew Crooks (9)
Comber Primary School, Comber

MITZY

About a year ago, in the month of January, in a little cottage near Scrabo, lived two people called Miss Brown and Mr Hill. Sharing the house with them was a cat and a dog. The dog was called Bonnie and the cat was called Mitzy. All four of them had a normal life until Max, the mean farmer, and his bull, Bullseye, moved in beside them.

It all started one morning when Miss Brown said, 'We will have to go and see our new neighbours soon.'
Mitzy sighed.
Later on Bonnie asked, 'Why don't you want to go to the new neighbours'?'
Mitzy replied, 'I hate farms!'

Half an hour later, Mr Hill yelled, 'It's time to go out you two.'
Straight away, Bonnie said, 'Let's go to the farm.'
Mitzy yelled, 'No way!'
Bonnie was halfway there so Mitzy had to follow.
'Are we nearly there yet?' asked poor Mitzy.
Bonnie laughed.

Finally they arrived at the farm. Mitzy opened a small wooden gate.
Bonnie screamed in a high-pitched bark and yelled, 'That's a bull shed!'
Mitzy was so scared she ran into the farmer's field.
Bonnie shouted, 'Mitzy, where are you?' Suddenly Bonnie saw poor Mitzy. She had been shot in the leg. When Bonnie got closer, he said, 'Why you poor little thing. I'd better get you home.'
Miss Brown and Mr Hill were soon on the scene and had to make arrangements for Mitzy to be taken to the vet.

Bonnie, Mitzy, Mr Hill and Miss Brown did eventually recover from the whole horrible incident. Whereas Farmer Max was taken to court and fined for shooting Mitzy - and his bull was given to the Comber butchers!

Glenn Martin (9)
Comber Primary School, Comber

KITTY'S NIGHTMARE

One day last summer, in Greece, in a big city called Athens, there was a little house and in that house there was a little girl called Samantha who was playing with her cat, Kitty.
'Samantha, time to go shopping,' called her mother.
Samantha left Kitty playing with some string.

'Mum, can I go to that shop over there?' asked Samantha.
'OK, but watch the carriageway,' replied her mum.

While they were away, two nasty robbers had broken into the house. They took jewellery, the television and poor Kitty. Samantha and her mum were both horrified at the sight before them when they realised the thieves had been in the house. Next door, Mrs Beggs had heard the racket, so she went over to see what was going on. Even she couldn't believe the state of the place.
Samantha ran in shouting, 'Mum, Kitty isn't anywhere. I'm really worried.'

Meanwhile the robbers were far away.
One of them said, 'We'll get good money for her in town.'
Suddenly Kitty reached out one of her paws and scratched the robber on the face.
'Ouch!' yelled the thief. He quickly threw Kitty down who ran away as swiftly as she could.

Back home, everybody was worried about Kitty, especially Samantha. Life just wasn't the same without Kitty.

Some days later, Mrs Beggs was walking down an alleyway in Athens, when she spied a cat which looked very like Kitty. Mrs Beggs called her name and Kitty came over to her. Kitty was limping badly. Mrs Beggs took Kitty to a vet she knew. Sadly Kitty had a broken leg - her front left. Mrs Beggs had to leave Kitty with the vet but she soon hurried back home to give Samantha the news. Samantha was completely overjoyed and gave Mrs Beggs a great big hug and kiss.

It wasn't long before Kitty was allowed home and in a few weeks her leg was fine. Everyone in that area of Athens was very happy to see Kitty fit and well again.

'Purr, purr,' went Kitty as she enjoyed a saucer of milk and some fish scraps.

Sacha Ghionis (9)
Comber Primary School, Comber

POOR TESS

A few weeks ago my mum came into my bedroom and told me to get up. Tess, my cat, and Buddy, my dog, were also in my bedroom - they were playing together. I went downstairs and opened the front door to let Tess out. Buddy pushed past me and chased Tess onto the road. A car was coming. My dad went out into the street and pulled Buddy in.
'Is Tess going to be alright?' I asked.
Mum and Dad said nothing, but it was the next day before we saw Tess again. We were worried sick.

Tess arrived back limping. It looked as though she had been hit - perhaps by a car. I had to go to school.
Mum said, 'When you come home we'll take Tess to the vet.'
'OK,' I replied. I opened the door and there was Jasper, Tess' friend. He looked up at me. 'Hello,' I whispered.

At school I was so worried about Tess I couldn't concentrate properly and couldn't wait to get home.

When I arrived home we put Tess in a box and set it in the car. Tess had an X-ray and Bobby, the vet, said she had broken her front left leg. Tess had a white cast put on her leg and that night she was allowed to sleep in my room.

The following day was Saturday and Tess was carried around everywhere. I think she liked this. In a few weeks, Tess got the plaster off and she was fine.

The next day we took Buddy out for a walk and Tess followed us round the street. At dinner that night, Tess and Buddy ate off the same plate and later on that night they slept together.

Rachel Carleton (9)
Comber Primary School, Comber

THE HAUNTED HOUSE

It was the summer holidays and I was going to my uncle's house in Texas. He was rich and scary. He also lived in a huge mansion. I was 11 and I had short brown hair.

The day I arrived it was rainy and windy. As I walked through the door I got a chill down my spine.

That night I was reading in a huge library and suddenly a book fell on top of me. It was heavy and old, written in a language I couldn't understand. It looked like ancient hieroglyphics.

When I was in bed someone or something walked past but I started to get curious so I followed the thing down into the library. Then it took out the old book and started to chant something and then one of the bookcases swung open and revealed a secret lab and there were creatures. One of the creatures astounded me. It was my uncle but he was mutant. Then the creature saw me. I started to run away but it started to gain on me. It hurled the book at me and . . . *thwack!*

I woke up to find myself in some sort of tank. I had a throbbing pain in my head. Across the room, my uncle was in his tank and that thing was over at the table eating stew. I looked around the tank to see if there was a way out. I saw a latch but I needed to distract the monster. I banged the wall so it echoed into the other room. The creature got up and ran into the other room so I suddenly opened the latch and tiptoed to my room. When I saw the door I started to run. I ran into my room and bolted the door. I lay down my head to soothe the pain from the bump on it. I looked around. Then something caught my eye - a strange picture. It looked really real and then the skeleton that was in it turned its head towards me and grinned . . . I was *doomed!*

Ross Hewitt (11)
Comber Primary School, Comber

RON'S BROKEN WING

It was a cold winter's morning and the ground was covered with snow. Ron the robin was minding his own business, when, *bang*, he had hit a tree and when he opened his eyes all he could see were stars. Then he picked himself up but when he tried to fly he couldn't because of the sharp pain in his wing.

'Oh dear,' sighed Ron as a large tear rolled down his face. He went over to a rabbit's burrow and knocked on the door. A little rabbit came out. 'Hello Mr Rabbit. My name's Ron and I'm afraid I've hurt my wing. Please can you help me?'
'Certainly,' said Mr Rabbit. 'Follow me into my house and I will see what I can do for you.'

Mr Rabbit sat Ron in a chair and put a blanket over him. Just then he heard a knock on the door. He went to answer it and there was his friend, Jenny the fairy.
'Oh, hello Jenny,' said Mr Rabbit. 'Just the person I need. Ron the robin has hurt his wing. Can you fix it?'
'I'll try,' said Jenny. 'Hmm! I'm afraid it's broken.'
'Oh,' said Mr Rabbit. 'Can I help?'
'Yes,' said Jenny. 'I've got nearly all I need except a hair.'
'I'll get it,' said Mr Rabbit and off he hopped.

A little while later, Mr Rabbit found a *hare* (he thought it was the animal Jenny was looking for!) Mr Rabbit walked over to the hare and grabbed it by the tail.
'Ow!' screamed the hare. 'What do you think you're doing?'
'Jenny said she needed a hare to make Ron's wing better,' said Mr Rabbit.
'Oh, you are silly,' said the hare. 'She means a hair as in *hair*.'
'Oh,' said Mr Rabbit. 'I'm really sorry.'
'It's okay,' he said. 'You can have one from my tail.'
'Oh thanks,' replied Mr Rabbit and he hopped back home.

When he got home Ron was still in the chair. 'Here!' shouted Mr Rabbit.

Jenny came out of the kitchen with the magic drink. She put the hair in the drink and handed it to Ron. 'Here, drink this,' she said.

Ron drank it and then he felt funny. 'Oh!' said Ron.

'Try to fly,' said Jenny.

He did. All of a sudden . . . he . . . he was flying. 'This feels great!' replied Ron. 'Thanks you two!' he shouted as he reached the treetops. 'I'll visit you again!' And off he flew back home.

Lesley Bailie (10)
Comber Primary School, Comber

THE MAGIC TREE

It was a warm, sunny, summer's day and Sophie and her younger brother, Jack, went out for a walk in the forest.

Suddenly Jack saw a tree with leaves that seemed to glow. They walked over and couldn't resist the beautiful flowers.

Suddenly, everything had changed. There was snow everywhere and sweets were hanging off the trees. There were even snowmen walking around!
'Let's explore,' said Sophie.
So off they went.

In five minutes' time, Sophie and Jack saw a lake with strange plants beside it. They decided to eat the plants.
'Uuuuuuh!' screamed Jack as a pain rushed to his side. *Crack!* Huge holes appeared in Jack's side. They were gills. The children were changed into fish-like creatures. 'Let's swim,' said Jack.
They jumped into the water.
'Wheeee!' shouted Sophie as she glided through the water as gracefully as a bird.
'Look!' exclaimed Jack.
Sophie looked and saw red fish, green fish and even multicoloured fish!
'There's a cave!' said Sophie.
'Let's see where it takes us,' Jack said, but the question was . . . where?

The cave led them to a pond in a forest. They jumped out of the water onto the land.
'Jeepers!' shouted Jack. 'Look!'
There were loads of weird animals. There were blue dogs, pink bears, yellow monkeys and red birds.
Sophie suddenly saw a fairy. 'Let's follow her!' Sophie said enthusiastically.

Quickly but cautiously they went. Could this fairy be leading them into danger? The fairy led them to a purple, jelly-like place. In the blink of an eye, the fairy sprinkled gold dust on them.
'This is flying dust,' said the fairy and in a flash she disappeared.
'Let's bounce!' shouted Sophie.

They bounced higher, higher, higher and higher until they grew wings.
'I miss Mummy and Daddy,' sobbed Sophie, all of a sudden realising that they were far from home. 'Let's find the magic tree and go home.'
Swiftly they flew off towards the horizon in search of the magic tree.
'Down there!' shouted Sophie with relief.
Jack looked down and saw, glittering in the magical sun, the magic tree.
As quick as lightning they flew down to the snow-covered land.
'On the count of three we'll touch it,' said Jack.
'Okay,' agreed Sophie.
'One! Two! Three!'

In the blink of an eye, they woke up in their cosy bunk beds.
'Was it a dream?' wondered Sophie.
She then put her hand into her pocket and pulled out a lump of snow.

She looked out of the window and there, standing on the hillside was the magic tree waiting for the next children who, full of imagination, would touch its beautiful leaves and be whipped away to the land of snow!

Christopher Wallace (10)
Comber Primary School, Comber

FROSTY'S LITTLE BROTHER

One day in the land of snow, Frosty the snowman's little brother, Frost, ran up to him.

'Am I old enough yet?' he asked.

'Well I suppose so,' Frosty answered. 'A snowman's job is to stand and let children enjoy themselves,' Frosty reminded Frost. He went over to a large blue cloud and touched it in certain places. 'Go on,' Frosty said. Frost climbed onto the cloud.

'Now remember to be back before the snow melts,' said Frosty.

Slowly Frost sailed away to the world of humans. Frost landed in the middle of a large group of houses. It was night-time. He looked around. 'Pamela Way,' he read from the sign. Frost yawned, 'Go back to Snow Land, Cloud. I'm going to sleep,' and he nodded off to sleep. Oh! He was silly.

The next morning, Frost woke up to find a boy and girl throwing snowballs at each other. Their names were Briony and Ross and they were twins. Four other children came down the alleyway. Their names were Carly, Kirsty, Ellen and Aaron.

'Kirsty, go and see if Shona and Cameron are coming out,' said Carly.

Just at that moment, Shona stepped out of her house, followed by Cameron.

'Look! A snowman!' cried Aaron.

All the children (including Briony and Ross) ran over to Frost. Ross looked at the snowman and kicked it.

'Ross!' cried Briony.

'Ow!' said a voice.

'Who was that?' Ellen asked.

'Me,' said the snowman.

Everyone jumped back in surprise.

'He can talk!' said Cameron.

'Of course I can! Who do you think I am? A few balls of snow shaped like a kind of person?' exclaimed Frost.

'Yes!' said all the children together.

'Will you play with me?' asked Frost.

'Sure!' said Shona.

For the rest of the day the children played with Frost, making sure no one else was looking. They played hide-and-seek, snowballs and they even built an igloo out of snow. It was great fun.

Just as the sun was setting that evening, Briony went in for a drink. When she came back out she looked worried. 'Frost the snowman's starting to melt!' she said.
'Oh, that's okay, I'll just call on Cloud. He'll take me home. Cloud!' shouted Frost. He waited . . . and waited . . . and waited, but Cloud never came. 'Oh! Boo hoo!' cried Frost as tears rolled down his cheeks. 'I sent him home!' he said beneath his tears.
'We'll help you find your way home,' said Kirsty.
'Yeah! Where do you live? We'll take you there,' said Ross.
'Outside the second forest to the left. Oh thank you!' said Frost, and off they went.

They ran out of the estate and sneaked into the farmer's field. They trudged out of the field and paddled through the nearby river which led to the first forest. It was starting to get dark now, which made Kirsty, Cameron and Aaron scared. The forest was creepy with hardly a path except spaces between trees.

At last they walked out of the first forest. They walked up a hill before coming to the second forest.
'I'm melting! I can't go on!' cried Frost, halfway through second forest.
'I've an idea!' said Aaron, looking at the frozen lake.
'C'mon! Let's skate!' said Shona.
They ran to the lake and jumped on.
'Weeeeee!' they all said.

They jumped off the ice and went along to a clump of trees. Carly pushed the leaves away and stared at the wonderful sight before her. The rest of the children looked too. There were houses made of snow which lay under a tall mountain that glistened with snow. It was very magical.
'C'mon!' exclaimed Frost.

The children followed him to a tiny house. Frost knocked on the door. Nothing happened. Suddenly the door swung open and there stood Frosty.

'I'm home!' Frost cried.

'Well done!' said Frosty. 'I see you've made some friends.'

Kirsty stepped forward. 'How will we get home?' she asked.

'Leave it to me,' said Frosty. He waved his hand and the children fell fast asleep. Cloud came with his friends and took the children home and wrapped them in their beds. Of course, when they woke up they thought it was a dream, but trust me, they never forgot the dream adventure with Frosty's little brother.

Shona Ayre (10)
Comber Primary School, Comber

TREEHOUSE TERROR

One Saturday night, Mummy let me, Ryan, Dale and Blake sleep over in my treehouse because she said we were safe on our own, well that's what she thought at least. When we were prepared, Ryan climbed into the treehouse and we passed him our bags and then Dale, Blake and I climbed up too. At eleven o'clock we had our midnight feast and then we told ghost stories. When it was Blake's turn we heard a scrape and we saw a scratch on the window. Ryan and I got out of our sleeping bags and showed them it was only the trees and the cats. We got back into our sleeping bags and Blake started his ghost story.

'One night a boy was in bed but he woke up at midnight at the sound of a groan. He looked out the window and saw a six-eyed, five-armed and legged monster. It was green with blue stripes down its back. The creature rose out of the marsh. It let out another groan and millions more came out and followed it. In five days they had conquered the whole world.' Then Blake said, 'That's the end.'

Just then we heard a groan and another groan. We jumped out of our sleeping bags and looked out the window.
'Eh . . . I think the story is coming to life,' I said.

I was right. Out of the marsh came millions of six-eyed, five-armed and legged monsters that were green with blue stripes. And yes, they did conquer the world in five days.

Cameron Mack (8)
Fair Hill Primary School, Dromore

THE MYSTERIOUS CLOCK

One evening I was coming out my house and I saw a clock out in the middle of the field. The clock was very different from usual because it had stars on it. When I got closer to the clock it started to laugh. As I got even closer to it, another laugh came out of it. Then I picked it up and it started to shake. Suddenly it started to tremble. It jumped out of my hands and I went back in time to the 1800s.

I was in the Victorian era. It was a cold winter's night. The roads were as quiet as a mouse and I saw the clock hanging up in a tall tower. I said to myself, 'How am I going to get up there?' I turned around and I saw a sign to rent a ladder. I went to get a ladder, but I had to pay. I had no money with me so I went back to the tall tower but the clock had gone. I saw that the clock had disappeared in the distance and I went over to see the place where the clock had disappeared from. I saw nothing but a wall. I put my hand up to the wall and I saw my hand disappear, then I found myself in a warm house. Everyone was in bed. It was quiet and motionless. I saw the clock hanging up on the wall. It had a very funny look and viscous eyes. I said to it, 'Would you take me back to 2003 again?' I sat down for a minute on a chair. The clock started to talk. I got up in amazement. I looked around. The clock was gone.

Rachel McKelvey (10)
Gortin Primary School, Omagh

THE CLOCK

One night I woke up and my alarm clock had gone. I went to the police station. A policeman came up to me to ask me what had happened. This is what I told him: 'I woke up and found out that my alarm clock had gone. It had stars on the side of it. I also heard a laugh when I woke up!' The policeman said, 'Come with me in the police car to find out where your alarm clock has gone.'

I got into the police car and drove off with the policeman. The policeman crashed into a field. Where he had landed the car was bogged! The two of us got out of the car and there on the ground was the alarm clock!

The policeman rang for men to see what time the clock had been taken. When the men came they did what they were supposed to do.
They said, 'This clock must have been taken at sunset!'

I went home and put the clock on the shelf. It isn't often you have an adventure at night.

Alan Nesbitt (10)
Gortin Primary School, Omagh

MARGARET

One day, as Margaret awoke in her bed to the sound of the birds singing, she decided to go outside for a teddy bear's picnic as it was such a glorious day. She got washed and dressed and ready for action.

She got dressed in her summer dress, it was pink and looked very pretty on her. Her hair was blonde with long golden locks. She tied it up in a white bow and put on her own sandals.

Margaret lived on a farm with cows, pigs, horses, sheep and hens. She packed her picnic and got a teddy. She told her mum that she was having a teddy bear's picnic and that she would be back soon. She headed down towards the lush, green meadow, laid down a rug and sat down.

Margaret laid out their feast and brought out her teddy bear. 'Now,' she said, 'you are the king and I am the queen, now we shall have our feast, but before, we must pray and thank the Lord for our food.' Margaret prayed and began to eat her feast.

Then she and Ted packed away the picnic and went home. When they got home Dad had a surprise for her and her mum. Mum had got a puppy and she had got a pony called Daisy as well.

The next morning she got up early and washed and brushed Daisy until she shone. She plaited Daisy's hair and she did this every day from then on.

Naomi Gregg (10)
Groggan Primary School, Randalstown

THE BANSHEE

One stormy night I lay in bed sleeping. After a few moments I heard a rattling noise coming from the attic. I opened my eyes and then closed them, hoping that the noise would go away, but then I heard the noise again, so I got out of bed and shouted towards the door of the attic. I opened the door . . . inside I saw a faint person staring at me. 'Can you please keep quiet because I am trying to sleep,' I said.
The mysterious person looked crossly at me and then disappeared.

In the morning I went down for breakfast. My mum asked me why I was so pale. I said I'd had a bad night. I went upstairs to put my school uniform on for school.

That morning I walked to school because it wasn't very far away. As I passed the graveyard, the gate moved as if someone was there so I ran to school. I sat next to the window and looked out. The graveyard was quite close to my school. I suddenly remembered what had happened that morning. A shiver went up my spine.

When school was over, I ran all the way from school and past the graveyard in case anything happened. I suddenly tripped over a stone and fell flat on my face. 'Oh no!' I cried.

When I got home my mum and dad told me that we were moving house. We moved and another family moved in.
I said, 'There's a banshee in our attic.'

Linda Davison (10)
Groggan Primary School, Randalstown

CLEMENTINE

Many moons ago there was a girl called Clementine. She lived with her great, great uncle Jim who lived in the mountains. Her mother and father had died in a car crash and he was the only family member left. She hated him.

They were never friends until the day Clementine found out how much he loved her. Then they were friends until death parted them.

It happened on a lovely summer's day. The sun was shining and the birds were singing like a golden flute. Clementine was going for her morning walk. Her uncle had warned her not to because he had spotted a wolf around, but she just ignored him. She always went for walks in the forest. She was not frightened of the creatures.

She was just going round the bend when she felt she was being followed. She turned to go back but she heard something snarling. She turned around, there was a wolf. It was white and it looked hungry. Very hungry!

She started to walk backwards and then suddenly she tripped and screamed. Then there was a sound of a rifle in the air. Clementine saw the wolf dead as a dodo.

Her great, great uncle Jim stepped out of the trees with tears in his eyes and he ran over and hugged her. He sobbed, 'I love you!'

Hayley Donaldson (10)
Groggan Primary School, Randalstown

MR BENNETT

Once in Baltimore, Cork, there was a white, thatched bungalow. Alone in this bungalow lived an old man. The man's name was John Bennett.

Most of the people round-a-bouts thought Mr Bennett was a bit eccentric but the children adored him. He would play games with them and answer their questions patiently, not with a sigh like most of the adults. He was a kind man who was a widower and he loved children.

Mr Bennett's house was a small, quaint place with a grandfather clock and a range cooker in the kitchen. The only company Mr Bennett had was his collie dog, Jess.

One of the reasons that the children liked Mr Bennett was his stories. Mr Bennett told wonderful stories about his childhood during World War II. He was ten when the war started and sixteen when it ended.

Mr Bennett was also an excellent gardener and always won lots of prizes at Dublin's gardening show. He grew colourful lupins, roses and lilies, carrots, lettuces and potatoes, the best in Cork, as some people said. Everyone in Baltimore always came to Mr Bennett for help if they ever needed gardening advice.

Jess loved children as much as her master. She really enjoyed frolicking and running on the sandy beach with them.

It was said that John Bennett and Jess were inseparable and this was definitely true. Mr Bennett was rarely seen without Jess, if ever.

Everyone in Baltimore loved Mr Bennett and he always returned their love.

Sheenagh Aiken (10)
Groggan Primary School, Randalstown

A Day In The Life Of The Banshee

One fine day, Lord O'Neill was holding a large house party and decided to use my little room for some of his guests.

I was raging, fuming and ill-tempered. Lord O'Neill was going to use my room for some of his foolish, crazy and silly guests! I started moving some of the pine furniture about but the maids just kept on making the beds for the guests.

I started plotting and planning how to get rid of his posh guests. I suddenly came up with an excellent idea; I would set the house on fire. I succeeded in setting the house on fire but some said that they didn't believe that I had done it. They all thought that a big jackdaw's nest catching fire and crashing down into the house and setting it alight had started the fire. The cheek of the people who wanted to sleep in my room was terrible. Imagine people sleeping in your bed without even asking! It was just so awfully bad and insulting. Now I have to make sure somebody pays. I could try screaming or scaring somebody to death or even swooping in front of somebody. Cool.

I wonder what it would be like to be a real live person and to be able to be scared of seeing something like me. OK, got to go now, see you later. Oh you would not like to be a banshee, believe you me.

Lauren Smyth (10)
Groggan Primary School, Randalstown

WEREWOLF WARNING

One morning a boy called Richard got up at 6am. He was counting the days because he believed in werewolves.

He went downstairs to get some breakfast. Richard took a bowl and a box of cornflakes from the cupboard. Afterwards he went to meet his buddy, Leo, at the park.

Later that night he asked if Leo could stay overnight. His mum said yes.

It was 9pm when Leo got his things packed and went over to Richard's. Richard looked out the window and saw a full moon. He thought, *oh no.*

When Richard and Leo went to bed, Richard heard moaning coming from Leo. He saw hairs growing on Leo. Then he changed into a werewolf. *My friend is a werewolf,* he thought to himself. He could not believe it. He was about to scream when the werewolf woke.
He said, 'Be careful, I am your protector. I am protecting you from other werewolves,' he warned.

Suddenly another werewolf blasted in through the window. His friend protected him like he said. His friend pushed the other werewolf out the window. His mum came into the room and fainted when she saw the werewolf.

Later, Leo was turned back into a human and then they went back to sleep.

Andrew Ross (10)
Groggan Primary School, Randalstown

THE MASTER'S HOUSE GHOST

Jack and Jane were in an attic searching for things to sell when they heard a sound.

'Stop it!' said Jane crossly.

'It wasn't me,' replied Jack.

'Then who was it?'

The lights suddenly turned off. Then there was a dazzling white light and a voice said, 'Why have you disturbed me from my sleep?'

Jack and Jane ran down the attic stairs as fast as they could go. 'Dad, Dad, there is a big, white, shiny thing that said 'Why have you disturbed me from my sleep?''

'Well I'll keep an eye out for it,' said Dad.

'Oh don't keep an eye out, you might not get it in again,' said Jack who was only four and did not understand everything yet.

'I'll go up to the attic and see if anything is wrong,' said Dad.

'Time to investigate,' said Jane.

'Actually it's four o'clock,' giggled Jack.

Dad ran out of the attic waving his arms. 'It's a ghost! Help! Help!' screeched Dad.

Jane walked into the attic and Jack followed. They decided to take a torch and shine it on the ghost to see if it was real or not. They checked if it was working and it was. They shone it behind the light and saw a speaker that was making the voice. There was a giant floodlight that had been stolen from Wembley football stadium. Their mum had fooled them.

Conor McKeown (10)
Groggan Primary School, Randalstown

THE CREEPY CASTLE

One day a girl called Holly went into the forest. As Holly went deep down into the forest, she noticed it was getting darker. She turned around but couldn't find her way back, so she went on. She found a castle. There was a graveyard and Holly became scared but she went up to the door and knocked. The door opened and she went in. The door closed. There was a crack of lightning and a man was there. Holly asked the man what his name was.

The man said, 'Mark. What is your name?'

Holly said, 'My name is Holly. Can you help me?'

'Yes my dear,' said Mark. 'What's the problem?'

'I am lost,' said Holly. 'Can I stay the night?'

'Yes my dear,' said Mark.

That night, Mark went into a room and turned into a vampire. When Holly went to bed, Mark went outside to the graveyard. 'Come up,' he said and all these hands popped up. Then zombies. The zombies walked into the castle and went upstairs.

Holly heard something so she got out of bed. Holly saw the zombies and heard Mark saying come out. The ghosts came through the walls. Holly was very scared and she ran. She ran out the door and into the woods. Mark flew across the sky. He found Holly and bit her on the neck. Holly was now a vampire too.

Rebecca Nicholl (10)
Groggan Primary School, Randalstown

ABANDONED ABBY

Emily Patterson was cycling with her sister, Lucy Patterson. They were going to stop at the riverbank to have a picnic. Just as they were going past the dump they heard a cry. They left their bikes on the grass and walked into the dump. Lucy and Emily saw a pet carrier.
'There's something in there,' said Lucy.
They went closer and saw a little dog shivering. Emily took off her jumper and opened the pet carrier, then she wrapped the jumper round the dog. The dog had a collar tag which said 'Abby'. The dog was very skinny so Lucy and Emily fed it some sandwiches.

They took Abby to the river for a drink and cycled home, putting Abby in the bike basket.
'Mum, we found a dog at the dump,' shouted Emily.
'Poor thing,' said their mother, fetching blankets.
They put Abby beside the warm cooker and fed her warm milk.

Next morning she was as right as rain, running and jumping about excitedly. They fed her and let her have a run about the garden. Emily and Lucy's mum was away shopping for a lead and some dog food.
When she came back, Emily asked, 'Mum, can we keep her?'
'Yes, we can keep her,' said their mother.
'Thanks ever so much,' shouted Emily and Lucy.

Emily and Lucy were so glad they had found her. It was the best day in both their lives.

Shannon Cameron (9)
Groggan Primary School, Randalstown

MY EASTER HOLIDAYS

On my Easter holidays we had one week off. On Monday and Tuesday I stayed at my auntie's house. Later on I played with her three dogs. On Tuesday I watched 'Harry Potter And The Chamber Of Secrets'.

Later on in the week, on Wednesday, I went to Bundoran. We went to the beach and we had a picnic. My auntie and uncle brought their dog, Jack. Later on in the day we had our dinner.

The next day we went to the cinema and saw 'Johnny English'. I met my friends while I was there. When we came back from the cinema, me and my cousin went to the tennis court and played tennis. We then went for dinner. My auntie and uncle brought me back to my house.

On Friday my daddy took me down to town to get a new pair of shoes. We went for our dinner.

On Saturday my mum, dad and I went to Omagh, we got lots of stuff.

On Sunday we watched some DVDs, they were good.

During my Easter holiday I had lots of fun. I ate some of my Easter eggs and I still have some left!

I had a great Easter.

Lauren Corrigan (10)
Holy Trinity Primary School, Enniskillen

GHOSTS

One day a girl called Ciara and her friend, Kate, heard that there was a £1,000 prize for staying in Mike Myers' house for two days and one night. The ghost story begins with Joe, Sarah, Kate and Ciara.

Monday morning at 1 o'clock, everybody got together and went into the house. They went to explore and found old clothes and huge spiders on stringy cobwebs. Joe and Kate decided to go up the creaky stairs. Kate stepped on a loose step and fell. She found a secret door which led to the lab where she found the knife of Mike Myers.

Kate ran downstairs to tell Joe and the others about what she had seen. Everyone gathered together and went back to the secret room. They found bits of cloth covered in blood and pictures of his family who he had murdered. Joe thought it was cool to find all this stuff but the girls started to get scared and wanted to leave. Joe said they could go back downstairs but he wanted to stay behind to take some photos of what they'd found.

An hour after the girls went downstairs, it was getting dark and Joe had still not come back. Kate said she would go and see where he was. Kate checked the secret room but there was no sign of him. She went into the bedroom of Mike Myers. There, lying in the middle of the floor, was the knife they had found in the secret room. Kate went over to the knife and saw there was blood on it. There was a trail of blood leading over to the cupboard. Kate went over and opened the door, there she found Joe hanging, he was dead!

Kate ran back downstairs to the others but they were gone! Kate searched the house trying to find her friends. She found Ciara, she was hiding in a cupboard in the kitchen. Ciara told Kate that someone had killed Sarah and taken her away.

The two girls were hugging each other when they heard footsteps coming from upstairs. They ran outside and when they looked back they could see Mike Myers holding up his knife and looking at them through the bedroom window . . .

Lorraine Clancy (9)
Holy Trinity Primary School, Enniskillen

MY STORY

Once upon a time there lived a little boy called Callum and a little girl called Emma. They were scared of nothing and they wanted something to scare them.

One day they were watching BBC and they heard on it that they were having a competition of which team of 2 could stay a night at a haunted hotel and whichever team could stay the longest won a £500 prize. Callum and Emma phoned up the number. The woman from the BBC programme answered the phone and said they would leave at 1 o'clock the following day with 2 other people called Megan and Will.

Finally it was the next day and Callum and Emma rang a taxi and were soon dropped off at the haunted hotel and got to meet the other kids. When they all entered, they nearly changed their minds.

Soon it was bedtime and none of them wanted to go to bed as they could hear creepy noises. They stayed awake all night and talked about how scary it was, then they heard a creak, so they looked out into the hall and . . . *bang!*

I had to get up for school - it was all a dream!

Nicolle Collins (9)
Holy Trinity Primary School, Enniskillen

THE POLICE ESCORT

My story begins the night my dad went shopping! It was also Scouts' night at my local Scout hall.

Ciaran, my brother, and I were playing in the back garden as usual. Mum called for me. It was time for Scouts. Ciaran was not happy but he never is. Dad was going shopping and he took me to Scouts.
Ciaran was still not happy. 'I want to go to Scouts,' he said.
Dad drove on while Mum stayed at home and tried to calm Ciaran down. Ciaran had other things on his mind!

About ten minutes later Mum called Ciaran. She called and she called but no Ciaran. Mum looked everywhere but still no Ciaran.

When Dad came back from the shops, Mum was going ballistic! My neighbour went with Dad in the car. They looked everywhere.

In the meantime, Mum spotted a police car pulling into the drive and who was sitting on the policeman's lap? Only bold Ciaran! He had decided to stop off at the Round O to play on the swings which were a mile away. Ciaran was only three!

That night, Dad had a talk with Ciaran. He asked him to promise to never ever do that again.
Ciaran's reply was, 'No way!'

Ryan Smith (9)
Holy Trinity Primary School, Enniskillen

A DAY IN MANCHESTER

When I went to Manchester, the journey was very long but it was fun. The people who went were my dad, my brother, 3 cousins and me. I knew that Man U would win. When the day came it was so exciting and when we got to the boat . . . I nearly wet my boxers! We arrived in Manchester at 10 o'clock.

The next day came like two shakes of a lamb's tail. We went to a restaurant.
The lady said to me, 'David Beckham was sitting on that seat last night.'

The big day came! We walked for miles and then we saw the stadium. It was so exciting again. We got in and it had just started when Man U scored not 1, not 2, but 3 goals in 10 minutes. 20 minutes to the end of the game and Liverpool scored, but at full-time the score was 3-1 to Man U.

When we were coming back, there were people fighting. We stayed away. We went to Pizza Hut. I had a ham and cheese pizza. It was lovely! Then we went bowling. It was great too.

At last we walked back to the apartment and fell asleep.

Andrew Sheridan (9)
Holy Trinity Primary School, Enniskillen

A MIDNIGHT SCARE

My story starts a few years ago . . . one night during the summer holidays I was watching the late night horror movie. It had been a hot day. The window was open and I could see the moon shine bright. The smell of freshly cut grass was in the air. My family were all in bed, tired from a day at the beach. I sat alone in the room, lit only by the moonlight and the television. The film had just ended with spooky music. I switched off the set.

Standing alone with only the light of the moon, I was scared! I said to myself, 'I wish I hadn't watched that.' Quickly I ran upstairs. It was dark because the bulb had blown earlier.

In the room I got into bed. Everything looked scary. I pulled the quilt up close to my face. At the bottom of the bed I saw a ghost hovering. I was petrified. Quickly I threw a book at it. There was a clatter and a crash. I switched on the lamp. Silly me, it was my white shirt draped over the chair. Off went the lamp.

After a while I did fall asleep. I was dreaming about zombies trying to grab me. *Thud.* It landed on my tummy. I screeched, roared and bolted up like a jaguar. Lights went on, my dad first, followed by Mum, then my brother and sister came running in. Sitting on the floor, shivering with fear, was Cuddles, my little white and black dog!

Jonathan Greene (9)
Holy Trinity Primary School, Enniskillen

LOST IN THE WOODS

It was the early 1800s. The war between Britain and France was on. Beth and Annie were collecting wood in Sherwood Forest.

'Beth, I'm tired!' moaned Annie.

'Stop complaining,' replied Beth. 'We have to do it, now that Billy's gone.'

Just then a rabbit jumped out of the bushes and ran across their path.

'Oh, come back rabbit!' shouted Annie, jumping up and chasing after the rabbit.

'Annie! Get back here now!' shouted Beth.

Annie was too far ahead to hear her. When Beth eventually found her, Annie was in tears.

'They killed him!' she cried.

'Come on. Let's go home,' Beth added sympathetically.

It started raining heavily. They ran through the woods and came to a hill where they slipped because of the rain. They tumbled down and when they came to a stop, they were bleeding and crying.

They started to walk. After hours, the edge of the forest drew nearer. They started to run.

'We're almost there, Beth!' cried Annie.

They could see smoke and flames. The French army had attacked!

'No,' whispered Beth.

The colonel, Napoleon, was giving out orders whilst other soldiers were shooting men and young boys. The women and girls were being led away in trucks. A soldier looked up and spotted the girls. He took aim at them and fired. Beth was dead when Annie found her. She had escaped death.

Sarah Charity (9)
Holy Trinity Primary School, Enniskillen

A WEEK IN SLIGO

I went to Sligo with my caravan and my family. When we got there we saw a games room. Me and my brother went up to play snooker and my sister played on the scooter while my mum and dad unpacked the car and the caravan. After that, me and my mum went for a walk on the beach. When we came back it was getting dark so we went to bed.

The next day my family and I walked to the shop and got lollies. On the way back from the shop I saw an island called Coney Island. There were lots of horses on the island.

The following day I went down to the beach and I played in the sea. There was lots of seaweed and we made sandcastles. In the evening, my mum, my sister, Niamh, and I went for a long walk on the beach and we collected shells and put them into a bucket.

On Wednesday afternoon we went into Sligo town. We went to Penny's and bought some clothes and I got a pair of sandals. We had to sleep in sleeping bags in the caravan. Mummy made a fry-up for breakfast in the morning and it was very nice. I love staying in the caravan.

Michelle Flynn (9)
Holy Trinity Primary School, Enniskillen

A Day In The Life Of A Big Brother Contestant

Day 1:

10.30am
The contestants all arrive. Six girls and six boys will compete against each other to win £70,000. The names of the twelve are; Aimee from London, Sharon from Essex, Daniella from Glasglow, Sophie from Leeds, Catherine from Manchester, Me (Niamh) from Enniskillen, Darren from Yorkshire, Kevin from Dublin, Aaron from Birmingham, Ewan from Swansea, Christian from Cambridge and Paul from Ashford.

11.14am
I chat with Sophie. She seems a nice girl but is a bit boring. She bragged on to me about winning the 70 grand when we were not even there an hour! Daniella is very over-excited at being here and is always having a laugh. I must say the people are pleasant, but lots of them are very quiet. I'm just trying to be my giggly old self and I am very giddy as I am really thrilled about the whole experience.

1.25pm
Paul is cooking a sweet-smelling meal while I decide to go and have a swim with the girls and Ewan. I have a stitch in my side, but I carry on joking about. I get out and sunbathe for a while.

1.56pm
We go inside and have a delicious meal.

2.43pm
Everyone goes outside to the garden. Catherine is already narking about Ewan's accent. She's the one being annoying! Paul gets some ice cream to eat but we end up throwing it about and having an ice cream fight. It is *sooo* funny and everyone has to have a shower as ice cream is melting right past our toes.

3.26pm
Everyone is called to the 'Diary Room'. Big Brother gives us a long and hard lecture on why we shouldn't waste good food.

4.03pm
They all leave the 'Diary Room' but I stay to talk to Big Brother. I moan about Catherine being so judging, but then I cheer up and talk about what a blast I've had so far.

6.32pm
We snuggle up on the sofa and have a chat.

9.55pm
The girls get ready for bed and go to sleep.

Niamh Leonard (10)
Holy Trinity Primary School, Enniskillen

THE WALK THAT WENT HORRIBLY WRONG

I was walking peacefully along the gravel path beside the nearby river. I had just passed through the forest and was heading for home when a loud splashing sound startled me! I spun around and, to my amazement, I saw a little blue man holding a purple cane and splashing all around in a puddle (with his Wellington boots on) which nearly drowned him because he was so small. At first I thought that I was just imagining it, so I walked on a bit.

I came to a *huge* tree and I stopped to have a rest. I was leaning against this humongous oak tree when I had just heard a really loud scream for help, a loud splash and also very loud Irish music. I thought that someone was having a party, but then I thought again. What person would have a party in the middle of a dark, damp, gloomy forest? (I wouldn't!) I took my time walking back to the spot where I saw the strange man. Once I got there, there were piles of lovely, sweet, tempting foods and any kid around my age could not resist it. I started munching on the chocolate chip bun and sipping the fizzy orange juice. It was getting fairly dark and I was getting a bit scared and I had to be home before 10.30pm. I'd eaten nearly all the food on the tiny little mushroom table, but to my surprise the food kept on reappearing (which I thought was great!) My stomach started to expand and I got really, really fat. Once I had eaten that last crisp, a huge yellow beam shone down on me and a tiny grey fly came down to talk to me and tell me what to do, but I didn't know what he was talking about so I asked him.

He said in a really tough voice, 'Young Earthling, I was sent down from the planet Dancealot, it's situated far away up in the dark galaxy in the corner tucked behind Pluto. Anyway, my leader, Rabbit, told me to get you and bring you back with me. You are the chosen one. You must come with me *now!*'

I decided to go with the talking fly but the question was, how? The only way was for the fly to lift me. The fly, who went by the name of Eddy, pulled a cord from his back and out popped his muscles. As I was so heavy, Eddy told me to hold on to the fly's tiny little legs whilst he flew.

When we arrived at the planet Dancealot, there were loads of tiny shops. Eddy took me to Rabbit, the leader. He was sitting on a throne with a pink dress on. He told me that him and his people needed me. I went along with Rabbit's plan which was to . . . watch his shop while he went away to get his crown polished which was so, so stupid. Once Rabbit came back, he told the fly to take me back to Earth.

Once Eddy had taken me back, he gave me a piece of Dancealot which was green with red spots. By the time I got my belongings together it was 10.29pm and I had to be home by 10.30pm *sharp!* I ran all the way home.

My mum asked me what I had been doing but Eddy had wiped my memory and I couldn't remember what on earth had happened. I made up a story that my parents would believe. As I was walking upstairs to get ready for bed, I found the piece of rock in my pocket and smiled to myself.

Emma McGurran (11)
Holy Trinity Primary School, Enniskillen

YOU WOULDN'T BELIEVE ME IF I TOLD YOU

I was walking peacefully along the gravel path beside the nearby river. I had just come through the forest and was heading for home when I was startled by a loud splashing sound! I spun around and, to my amazement, saw a young kid had fallen from a tree and was in the river, drowning. I am a good swimmer so I did the only thing I thought I could do. I dived in and swam to him. I told him, 'Grab on to me and I'll swim you to land.' He either didn't hear me or chose not to hear me.

The next thing, I felt something like a tentacle wrap around my leg. I tried my hardest to break free and swim away but it was no use, it started to pull me down. I looked under and there was a huge mouth, half buried beneath a bed of sand, chomping its teeth ferociously. Every second I was getting closer and closer to my final resting place. It bit me on the leg and the water that surrounded me turned red. It was about to take another bite when a tranquilliser bullet hit it on what seemed to be its eye. It loosened its grip and then it was shot again and I was freed.

I was too weak to swim to the surface after losing so much blood, but I saw the shadow of someone swimming towards me before I passed out.

A few hours later I awoke on the riverbank with some strange Indian man beside me.

He said to me, 'I am the watcher. I am an un-human entity that has watched over these parts since the beginning of time. Creatures called winoes inhabited this forest until a thousand years ago when a meteor struck, wiping out all but 5 winoes. They cannot die of old age like normal humans for one reason, they don't age, so they can only be killed but no one has actually seen one because they hide away in the depths of the forest. Their plan is to use a creature called a gargantua to bite humans and turn them into winoes so that their race can grow strong again and dominate this world like they used to. The kid you saw drowning was an illusion to get you into the water so that you could get bitten. My job is to make sure that doesn't happen.'

He took me back to his hut in the forest and put stingy blue stuff on my leg to get rid of the effectiveness of the bite from the gargantua. He showed me a map of places he suspected to be winoe hideouts. After a lot of persuasion he got me to go around with him, even though I was in a rush to get home to do my homework.

We went to all of them but there was nobody about until the last one where we saw five purplish, bluish, tall, skinny creatures all talking about how they were going to have another in their race soon. They had some sort of weapons beside them so we decided to use a more strategic way of attacking them. There was a small hole to let light in on the roof which we could use to our advantage.

We climbed up onto the roof and kept waiting until they had fallen asleep for the day and then we reached down and stole their weapons. We tried them out to see what they could do and they were shrink weapons. Then we went and woke them up and threatened them with the guns. They retaliated and we shrunk them down to the size of a pea, then we stepped on them and we knew that would be the last this world would ever see of them. They had a bag of poison that we fed to the gargantua to get rid of it.

I got home just before dark and got a full inspection from my parents of where I had been and why I was soaking wet.
I said, 'You wouldn't believe me if I told you!'

Liam Mohan (11)
Holy Trinity Primary School, Enniskillen

The Beaver And The Lizard

Deep in the heart of an English forest there was a still, shallow river. In the river there was a good-natured beaver. Good-natured though the beaver was, she was still very dozy and one day she was very stupid indeed by inviting a lizard around for tea. Now as we all know, most lizards eat flies and absolutely detest fish and water. But beavers eat fish, live in water and absolutely detest flies. So as you can see it's not going to work, never in a million years, to get a beaver to eat flies and a lizard to eat fish. But this dozy old beaver had never thought of a simple solution for this - catch some flies, give them to the lizard and eat the fish herself. It would have been so simple if only this dopey old beaver had a brain, because she didn't even know that lizards ate flies. Beaver told her brother her plan.

He said to her, 'You're as dopey as dopey can get. Lizards don't eat fish. Why don't you ask him to bring his own food even though it's rude?'

'No, I'm sure Lizard would like to try some fish, after all, it's got to be tastier than flies. Yuck,' Beaver replied.

As evening approached, Beaver sat in the middle of her dam catching four huge fish. Beaver diced them up and covered them in herbs. Soon, Lizard arrived Even though he had to cross a river, the thought of a good dinner kept him going. Two plates were out and Beaver was dishing up food. Lizard climbed onto the dam and tucked in.

'These flies taste different,' Lizard said.

Suddenly the lizard burst out in purple rashes because he was allergic to fish and fell out of the dam.

'Are you going for a swim?' Beaver asked. She jumped in and started to swim.

Lizard started to crawl out of the river. He thought Beaver was playing a trick on him so Lizard invited Beaver to his house the next day.

Beaver thought they were diced up fish so she ate them quickly. Then she spat them out and ran home.

So as we can clearly see, one man's meat is another man's poison.

Dana McCusker (10)
Holy Trinity Primary School, Enniskillen

PÁIDÍ'S CHRISTENING!

On Saturday 10th of May our family gathered together for my new brother, Páidí's christening in St Michael's church. My mummy had made loads of lovely food like lasagne, salad and lots of children's food too.

We went to the church at 5.30pm and our relatives came too. There was Auntie Anne who came from Cork with her daughter Sarah, Uncle James' family, Mary my auntie, Great Auntie Annie, and Auntie Ann and her kids, Uncle Cyril and Auntie Margaret and their family, my next-door neighbour Elizabeth, her mummy and daughter and also my mum's friend Angela joined us!

Fr McGahan did the baptism! I got to read with the microphone and so did my brother, Ryan. My auntie Anne from Cork is Páidí's godmother and his godfather is Ryan, my brother. When we were finished we took lots of photographs on the altar and I got to hold Páidí in lots of them!

We then got home and had a big party! All the children went mad upstairs and made loads of noise! The adults sat and had dinner and after a few drinks they made noise too!

The kids then went outside after it dried up a bit because it had rained for hours that day! We played a football match but my cousin Sean's team won it because of my other cousin Mikey's 3 hat-tricks!

Then because Confirmation was the next day and 3 of our cousins were going, they had to leave early . . . 10.30pm!

I was really tired but I'd had a wonderful day and I was really looking forward to the next day because we had another party to go to!

Clara Love (9)
Holy Trinity Primary School, Enniskillen

ELVIS' DIARY

Today I woke up around seven o'clock because my owner was calling me. When they went to that place called school I went outside. I slept for a while because I was tired from yesterday. When I woke up I chased cats for a while.

At around quarter-past one, one of my owners came home. She tried to put me in a big box. I struggled for a while but then she got the door on. She put me in her big machine and put her hand on a circle thing.

When the machine stopped, my owner took me out and took me into a place where animals go when they're sick I think. There was a person with a big white thing on her. She had gloves as well. She kept looking at my sore paw. I think they said I had an infection or something like it in my paw. The woman kept doing things to hurt my paw. She even put a needle in it.

When I got home it was sore to walk. My owners let me straight inside. One of them gave me some milk and let me sleep for a long time. It was about eight o'clock when I woke up. My youngest owner tried to play with me but then her mother told her to leave me alone.

My two young owners went to bed about eleven o'clock. The funny thing about today was I got to stay in that night.

I like to relax.

Shauna Murphy (9)
Holy Trinity Primary School, Enniskillen

THE DIARY OF A FLEA

Monday...

Today I woke up and felt very hungry so I had my breakfast. I had a lovely bowl of dog blood. Then I felt very energetic. I climbed up a big hair of the dog that I lived on, stored up some energy in my legs and leapt onto a cat called Smokey. I got very shaken because the cat was climbing a tree. Then I looked down, I got very dizzy because I was so high up. The cat had jumped off the tree and we ended up in a very posh house. Then I saw a human with a hosepipe, the human sprayed the cat down and nearly drowned me. I managed to escape from the cat and get to my dog. Then I had my supper and went to sleep.

Tuesday...

Today I woke up and had my breakfast. I felt very bored so I invited my friend Freddy flea over for tea. Then we had a look around my dog. The dog was a shower spaniel called Homer. His owner was called Mary. Freddy and me decided to move dog. We jumped off Homer and landed very near Mary. She had a mop and bucket and, again, like yesterday we nearly drowned, but Freddy could swim. He carried me on his back up the stairs and into a room with computers all over the room. It had scary voodoo masks on the wall and a man using the computers, his name was Colin. We saw a big bottle of *flea powder!* Then Colin stood up and knocked the bottle over. We ran *very* fast, we ran back past Mary and onto Homer.
Then I said to Freddy, 'I think we are better off living on Homer.'
'You can say that again!' said Freddy.

Aidan O'Brien (9)
Holy Trinity Primary School, Enniskillen

EVACUEES

It all happened during World War II in 1939. I was only fifteen at the time. My parents were scared that I might be hurt, so I was given a small suitcase and told to take what I needed. Then later that night I was taken to the assembly hall at my school.

'What are we doing here?' I asked.

My mother replied, 'You're going away for a while, OK?'

I was frightened after that, until I'd seen my friends, Mark, Sean, Duane, Paul and the Stephen twins, they saved me some cocoa.

My parents left, then people came in.

An old lady looked at the twins' placards. 'Come on then dears,' she said.

I watched the twins walk out of the room with a complete stranger. Then, one by one, my friends disappeared until it was just me and Mark. I could hear Miss Evers and the other teachers whispering to each other. I knew something was wrong.

Then a tall, bearded man slammed open the door, 'Sorry I'm late, me damn mare foaled,' he said.

'*Sorry!* Is that all you can say?'

'Oi, look here lady, I've said sorry, what else do you want me to say? OK lads, time to go.'

I got up, Mark did the same, we walked out the door.

'Where are we going Mr?' I asked as we climbed into his Landrover.

'We're going to my farm and please don't call me Mr, call me Colin.'

A few hours later we arrived at Colin's farm, it wasn't big but I loved it.

Six years later my real parents came for me but I didn't want to go!

Justin McManus (10)
Holy Trinity Primary School, Enniskillen

HERE I AM IN DONEGAL

I woke up this morning and started barking as I wanted to go outside. My owners heard me and Aoife came downstairs and let me out. When I came back in she said something to me but I didn't understand. I wagged my tail and barked.

When everyone woke up they started rushing around packing things. What is going on here today? They put me in my little box and into the boot of the car. I sat there and waited.

We started our long, long journey. Soon the car stopped outside a small, white house. We had arrived in Donegal - my favourite place in the whole world. They took me out of the boot and all the other cases. They let me out of my box. I ran outside as fast as I could. I was very excited. I ran around the whole garden sniffing and smelling in search of food. Soon Sorcha called me inside. I wagged my tail and ran in, barking. Eadaoin gave me a big bowl of my favourite dog food. I was very hungry and gobbled it up fast.

Everyone had left the house, I was alone. I felt very lonely especially without Aoife, Eadaoin and Sorcha who play with me.

I heard a car many hours later. I jumped up onto the table to see who it was. Yes, my owners had returned. I ran and jumped on the children, barking - where have you been? Why did you leave me? I was so lonely! I barked and barked with excitement.

My owners started cooking the dinner. There was a delicious smell. If only I could jump up and eat some of the dinner. The smell was so tempting! They sat at the table eating. When they had finished, Eadaoin and Sorcha went and watched television and Aoife played with me. It was great fun. She went and hid, then called me and I had to try to find her. Where had she gone this time? I tried to pick up her scent. I found it quickly (I am a dog you see). She was hiding underneath her bed.

The three children got changed and came down to the sitting room. After a while they went to bed. Two older people stayed. I wandered around and after a while I started to jump up on them. They wouldn't let me sit on their laps and they got a bit cross, so I just lay down by the open fire and fell fast asleep.

Aoife Ní Chaoilte (9)
Holy Trinity Primary School, Enniskillen

CHILDREN DURING WORLD WAR II

A long time ago, during World War II, I was taken away from my parents during the bombing of London. I was taken to a small village in Devon with a group of children. We were set in a big hall and we waited for about one hour. Finally I was taken away to a farmer's house. His name was John Dolan and his wife was Emma Dolan.

When I got to their house I didn't like it at first but I got used to it. The first year I missed my parents very much, but as the years passed, I think I forgot them. My best friend in school also lived in the area, so I was kind of happy with him around. I only made two friends the whole time I was there. I always felt that my mum and dad died in the bombing, were captured, were starved to death or even tortured!

Thankfully they weren't because many years later they came back for me when the fighting had stopped. My mum had lost an arm and my dad had got a lot of cuts on his face. I went back with them and stayed in London for the rest of my life.

Paul McGovern (10)
Holy Trinity Primary School, Enniskillen

A DAY IN THE LIFE OF VICTORIA BECKHAM

Hi, my name is Victoria Beckham. I am 27 years old and I am married to David. He is best known for playing football with Manchester United. I am about to let you in on some secrets about a typical day in the life of Victoria Beckham.

My day starts off quite early. I usually get up when David is going training, because I have two young children, Brooklyn and Romeo. I don't always get a chance to have a lie-in. I get them dressed and then leave them to their nanny. Today is a very important day as I am promoting a new record so I have to start off with a bit of preening and pampering.

I set off to my private salon alone. My manicurist begins to transform my chewed-up nails into long strong talons. I'm getting false nails put on.

After an hour or so I head to the hairdresser's to get my new extensions put in my hair. I'm having photos later today so it is important my hair and make-up look good. It's 11 o'clock and I head off to the radio and television studios. I'm interviewed about my new song and asked to sing. I mime of course.

It's lunchtime now and I meet David for lunch in The Ivy and then go around town for a little retail therapy. We buy matching designer jackets.

Time to go home now, I will be glad to see the kids. Luckily tomorrow I'm taking a day off so I will just laze around the house and play at being a typical mum.

Hannah McDermott (9)
Holy Trinity Primary School, Enniskillen

LITTLE SISTER - BIG SISTER?

I hate the way they *boss* me about! 'Don't touch this, don't touch that!' It's so *unfair.* Can't I do anything I want just for once? 'Oh no, you can't eat that . . . it's *bad* for your teeth! Here eat this carrot stick, it's *delicious'.* Whenever I want to watch Barney or the Tweenies, it's 'You can't watch that, *I'm* watching my programme, go and annoy *Mum.* If you annoy me one more time, I'll pull the head and arms off your teddies!' *Ow!* Parents can be so selfish sometimes . . . and another thing . . . how come big sisters are so *bossy?* When she baby-minds me she makes me eat *disgusting* food, puts me to bed *early,* and always makes fun of me . . . just because she can walk and read proper. Sisters can be so *annoying* sometimes. When I grow up I want to eat chocolate 'til I *burst! Never* go to bed until morning! Watch whatever videos *I* want to watch . . . and my sister better watch out because maybe I'll be *bigger* than her when I'm older!

Beep, beep, beep. What's that? Oh, it's time to get up! *What a strange dream!* Imagine if you could eat chocolate 'til you burst! I better wake my little sister up.

I wonder, would she *like* to watch Barney or the Tweenies?

Bronagh Pye (9)
Holy Trinity Primary School, Enniskillen

A DAY IN THE LIFE OF A PERCH

I am a perch, one of the smallest fish in Ireland so it is very easy for a pike to come along and have me for dinner. I have hidden spikes on my back to give them a nasty shock if they try to eat me. I let out my spikes and in a blink of an eye there's a long 'ow' and out I come. Mr Nasty Pike, as I call him, let's just say he won't be eating anything for a while, but if he is big enough to crunch my spikes, and they normally are, I have another defence, which is swim for your life! That's what I normally do if I spot a pike 'cause it works most times.

What do you think I am, a fish superhero? Well, I'm not, so let's get back to the point. You came down here, you asked me what it's like down here, am I right or am I right? Not much if you are a fish, but if you're not and were watching a programme about fish on TV you'd be saying, 'Mummy, that fish looks funny!' and there would be boos and ehs and ohs, hey wait a minute did I say boos? I meant oohs. You'd think we're strange and dumb, but that's what we think all you people out there are. Let's get back to the point, you asked me what it's like down here, am I right or am I right? Hey stop, stall, pause, whatever you call it - I've noticed that I said something the same as I did at the start.

Now I'll tell you what it's like down here: eels twist about in knots, smaller fish like me play hide-and-seek in the reeds, bream suck the fishermen's maggots off the hooks without getting caught and of course pike play 'who can eat the most fish', roach play with the smaller fish, finally the trout just dance and at school we play football with small pebbles. I could keep going on but I have to go some time, so see ya.

Neal Beirne (9)
Holy Trinity Primary School, Enniskillen

MY CHARACTER IS BART SIMPSON

Bart Simpson is a character out of The Simpsons. He has two sisters called Lisa and Maggie and his mother and father are called Marge and Homer. Bart's best friend is called Milhouse and Bart's enemy is called Nelson.

Bart does not do well in school because he is always getting into trouble. When he is not at school he is either skateboarding, using his slingshot or playing in the treehouse with Milhouse. Besides Nelson, Principal Skinner is another one of Bart's enemies. Whenever Principal Skinner punishes Bart he always gets his own back by burning the grass or setting mice all over the school. Instead of studying he goes to the arcade and plays games for hours. Then the next day, when it is time for a test he knows nothing and asks for help but they just give him the wrong answers on purpose.

At night-time he watches films and Krusty the Klown. Bart loves Krusty the Klown because he is really funny and he loves kids. Bart loves Krusty so much that he even has a Krusty the Klown bedroom. Another programme that Bart likes is the Itchy and Scratchy show. Bart likes this because a cat and mouse kill each other.

Gavin Duffy (9)
Holy Trinity Primary School, Enniskillen

EASTER

Over the Easter week I had lots of fun. I went out to my aunt's house. My cousin, Holly, had lots of things planned for us to do. My uncle Alan was in the car rally and we had to make the sandwiches for the team. What a mess that was. Katrina went into town for more food so Holly and I made up our own recipe. It took us nearly an hour to clean the kitchen because Holly let the dogs in.

The next night we watched a video and had a midnight feast. When the weather was good we went for long walks over the fields and saw lots of flowers and birds.

I had a great week but I was glad to go home on Sunday.

Shannon Burns (9)
Holy Trinity Primary School, Enniskillen

ANOTHER DAY IN THE LIFE OF NEIL

My name is Neil and I am ten. I am paralysed from the shoulders down. I hate it. Four years ago my life was perfect, but now it's dreadful!

It all happened when I was crossing the road. I was at a zebra crossing, and thought it was okay to cross roads without looking, so, of course, I crossed without looking. I can only remember the squeaking of brakes, and then, I woke up in a place with lots of wires plugged into me. Apparently this was *hospital*.

My family are very understanding. They often have special events to raise money to pay for the care I need. We are even having a barbecue tonight.

Now it's time for the part of all journeys I hate! You see, we have a Ford Transit van, which has an old and rickety ramp on the back. I have to use this ramp every time I go on a journey.

Bump!

Down now! Don't have to go back up it for another while yet!
'Mum, now what are you doing down there?'
'Neil, your foot slipped off the foot plate so I'm just putting it back on!'
'Hello you!' shouts Ruth. She is my cousin and she has a sister, Victoria.
'Hello you two. Are you enjoying yourselves? You'll never guess what happened a few minutes ago! A lovely lady called Mrs Millar gave our family £250!'
'Wow!'
'That's amazing!'
'I know!'
'She must be very kind!' Ruth exclaimed.
'She is. Well, I'm getting hungry, are you? Let's get a hot dog!'
'Hey! Come back! One of you needs to push me!'
'Sorry!' they chorused.
'I know!' said Ruth.
'I'm getting tired now. Can you wheel me over to Mum, please.'
Ruth whizzed me over to the barbecue in a flash!

'These hot dogs are delicious!'
'I know.'
'I'm getting very tired. Would it be okay if I went to bed and left you?'
'Of course it would be. We'll get your dad now.'
'Bye Neil!'
'Bye Vicky! Bye Ruth!'
Yawn!

Now that I'm in bed, this is the end of . . . another day in the life of Neil.

Jill Mulligan (10)
Holywood Primary School, Holywood

THE BLUE LANTERN

100 miles away, in a tiny town called Pepper Pot Pine, there lived a boy and girl called Tom and Mary. They had owned a lantern for a very long time. The lantern's name was the Blue Lantern.

They lived with their grandparents. Their grandparents loved them very much. Sadly Tom and Mary's mammy had died a few years ago. When the children spoke the word *mammy* or talked about her, the Blue Lantern flickered. Even when there was danger near or about to happen it would flicker.

The children eventually found out what it was. It was their dead mother talking to them or sometimes warning them of danger. The children knew it was their mammy. They went to the library and looked up a book on the Blue Lantern. It had a few sentences stating when people die it is often the dead person speaking to you or telling you that there is danger through the Blue Lantern.

The children scampered happily home to Pepper Pot Pine. They told their grandparents what they had found out. Tom and Mary's grandparents were very happy for the children and they all had a huge party together with their friends and relatives to celebrate what they had found out. They were all very happy.

Ruth Hammond (10)
Holywood Primary School, Holywood

MY SUMMER HOLIDAY

Three years ago I went to France with my family. We were looking forward to staying two weeks in the Vendee in apartments surrounded by a lake. There was a swimming pool, a kids' club and two or three restaurants.

Right from the start my dad hated the place but I, on the other hand, liked it. We had to queue for towels and bedding. The apartment was small like a box with two small rooms, no TV and we had to walk a long way to get to anything. My dad was very angry and demanded to be moved several times but he still wasn't happy.

One night we were getting ready to go out and my dad wanted a bath before we left. He locked the door but later we heard him shouting. The lock was broken, *worse* he was only wearing a small towel. We tried to open the door but it wouldn't budge. We had to call a French handyman. When my mum told him there was someone trapped inside the French handyman thought it was a woman, he got quite a shock when he lifted the door off the hinges and spotted my angry-looking dad in a small towel, in the bathroom. The French handyman burst out laughing and my dad looked really embarrassed.

The next day my dad said that we were going to Disneyland Paris because he had had enough of this place. I was really excited and I couldn't believe I was going to Disneyland Paris for four days.

Sofie Fieldsend (10)
Holywood Primary School, Holywood

THE PHANTOM

I always love Christmas because of all the gifts you receive and I also remember all of my Christmases. I remember last Christmas the best of all.

I remember it because it was a stormy Christmas Eve and my brother Robert and I were waiting for my mum and dad to come up to bed. It seemed to take ages and ages and we found it hard to stay awake. Finally my mum and dad came upstairs and we pretended to be asleep. We waited until we could hear them snoring. We slipped out of bed trying not to make a sound. We crept silently down the stairs and into the lounge but our presents weren't there. We checked everywhere in the house and then we thought they must be in the cellar, so we crept up to the cellar door. It creaked open and we walked down the creaky steps. We were pushing over cobwebs to try and find our presents when the torch reflected off two glowing green eyes. We dropped our torches and ran, too afraid to look back and then we slammed the cellar door shut.

The next day we ran down to the cellar with our pellet guns and looked where we had seen the eyes but they were gone . . .

Oliver McCall (10)
Holywood Primary School, Holywood

OOPS! MISSED!

This year I made the hockey team. I was very excited to be chosen to be the goalkeeper. Mrs Hart arranged for extra practises in Ballykillaire Sportsplex. Mr Martin helped me to practise while Mrs Hart helped the rest of the team. First of all Mr Martin rolled hockey balls along the ground to me and I had to kick them away (with my pads of course!). The next step was for him to throw the balls at me. When I had progressed even further he hit them at me with his hockey stick. I had lots of kit to carry and wear. It took me quite a while to get ready for each practise.

Before the NI finals we had a practise match against Donaghadee PS. On my debut I felt very anxious, I paced up and down the goal line, but I managed to keep a clean sheet in our 2-0 victory. I felt very nervous about the Northern Ireland finals. I was so nervous my mouth dried up. Our group was Gibson, Ballymacash and Moorfields. As we progressed I felt less nervous. We won our group, beating Gibson 1-0, Moorfields 2-0 and Ballymacash 2-0. When I heard we were up against Strandtown in the knockout stages I felt the hairs on my back stand up, as I was more nervous than I had been at the start.

We were winning 1-0 against Strandtown until the last ten seconds, then their best player hit it past me, it hit the post and went in. I felt very angry with myself. In 'golden goal' they almost scored again, but this time I saved it. Then it went to penalty strokes. Everyone in Holywood hockey team felt terrified. In the penalty strokes it was 1-1, then it was 'sudden death'. Tension grew. Alan stepped up. Oops! Missed! It was up to me. They stepped up, shot. Oops! Missed! We were out and devastated. We tried our best and who knows, with a little bit of luck we might have gone further.

Jamie Halliday (10)
Holywood Primary School, Holywood

THE LONG ADVENTURE

On 28th July 2001 my family and I set off on a driving holiday to France and Spain for three or four weeks. I was so delighted I was going on a touring holiday for the first time. We drove down to Dublin, made one stop at a forest to have a picnic. It took us about six and a half hours. Halfway to Dublin, my sister and I had to go into the boot of our car in a sleeping bag. The boot of our car was and still is very crowded.

When we got into Dublin we had to get on a huge boat called a ferry. About one or two hours later my dad took me out to the deck and told me to hold out my arms, so I did. As I did I shouted, 'I'm on top of the world!'
My dad held out his hands and shouted, 'I'm the king of the boat!'

My dad, Nikki and I tried to find my mum and Alanna. When we found my mum and sister my mum happily said, 'Let's go for dinner.' We did so and after Alanna and I ran down to a disco that was in a hall beside the café, We danced . . . and danced . . . then after the disco there was a magic show that was really good.

We stayed in France for nine or ten days. At the end of our touring in France we had to drive some more to get to Spain which took us about two days. My family and I stayed in one caravan with two bedrooms which was crowded because my sister, brother and I were in one bedroom and my mum and dad were in the other room. In Spain my family and I only saw one family of English people. We stayed in Spain for about ten to twelve days. We went swimming in a huge swimming pool every day with our friends who we met there.

At the end of our touring in Spain we had to drive quite a lot more to get out to our boat. On the way home, we passed a sign saying, *Paris*, and I asked my dad if we could go to Paris, but he said no. When we're home my family and I had many stories to tell like when we had to drive over the mountains to get to France.

I will never forget the time my family and I drove to France and Spain.

Megan Gilbert (10)
Holywood Primary School, Holywood

THE SPECIAL DAY

One day, nine months ago, I was chosen to play the part of Jane in Babes In The Wood. I was really excited. Dean, a friend of mine, was asked to play the part of Jimmy. We had at least 40 lines to learn and actions as well, plus we had to make friends with the other principles as well as the little ones.

We had to rehearse two nights a week plus Saturday and Sunday, it was hard work every day being pushed around like slaves in a workhouse. At least we were allowed to break in the middle of the rehearsal for half an hour because the rehearsals last for three hours.

Shiela and Meta, our costume ladies made a lovely cloak from velvet curtains. She put shiny gold sequins around the edge and even put a hood on it for me for the walk down. I also wore a beautiful dress to match the cloak with green on it.

The audience found the show really amusing and enjoyed the mystery of the babes who disappeared in the woods.

Sarah-Jayne Beale (10)
Holywood Primary School, Holywood

AN HORRENDOUS HOLIDAY

One Christmas we went to Gran Canaria for a family holiday and something terrible happened.

On our third day my mum and dad decided that we would all go to a parrot show. My sister and I were very excited because we had seen some of the colourful leaflets about it in our hotel reception. When we arrived at the park we watched the parrot circus. I thought it was excellent because all the parrots were performing different tricks. One of them could ride a mini bicycle, while another was having a conversation with a man.

Then we all walked around the park looking at the parrots in large cages. My sister Hannah really liked the look of a very large African white toucan and was staring at it with great interest for ages. Hannah so badly wanted to stroke it, so she slowly squeezed her hand through the bars of the cage. However, the bird was much too quick for Hannah and it swivelled its head and bit Hannah on her thumb! Hannah was so struck with shock that she didn't even cry. My dad tried to scare the parrot into letting go of Hannah's thumb by using a twig to force its mouth open. Eventually after what seemed like a very long time his plan worked. After Dad got Hannah's thumb out a man gave Hannah some bandages to hold the top of her thumb in place.

Dad had to then drive us all down the mountain on very windy roads to find a hospital. That was a really scary drive because he was driving very fast and he didn't really know where he was going. Hannah was just so much in shock that she was just sitting shivering in the back seat. When we arrived at the hospital the doctor took Hannah into a room and started to stitch her thumb on, she was hitting him because it hurt so much.

Since then Hannah hasn't gone near a parrot or put her hand through the cage of any animal!

Emily Mills (10)
Holywood Primary School, Holywood

THING

One dark night the villagers had tucked their children into bed when they heard a scary sound at the side of the house. Just then the power went out. The husband (Sam) checked outside but just as he was coming in a black figure grabbed him. The next morning the family went looking for Sam, they found the body round the back of the house and bloody footprints leading away to the graveyard.

They entered the graveyard and found a dug up grave. At the side of the grave was a handprint and instead of fingers there were blade-like claws and even more bloody footprints leading away from the dug up grave. The family did not follow them in case they had a close encounter with the *thing* that had killed Sam. About a week later there were 11 more murders from the *thing*.

On Friday the locals formed a meeting to try and stop this *thing*. The locals created an army of 100 men, 20 rows, 5 columns. They went to the place where the last attack had been. As soon as they entered the graveyard the *thing* attacked. Suddenly a blinding light hit them. When the light died down it attacked. Screams flooded the village. Flesh was lying everywhere. The *thing* had left the villagers alone.

One night a boy was walking home when the *thing* came racing down on a horse. The boy picked up the nearest weapon, which was a stick which had one sharp end, he threw the stick which lodged into its head and kicked a bucket of water over the horse and the horse dissolved and the *thing* disappeared bit by bit. The boy ran through the village jumping and yelling with joy. But later that day there was another attack!

Christopher Uprichard (10)
Holywood Primary School, Holywood

THE TRAGEDY

When I was three I was jumping on my settee but accidentally I slipped and cracked my head open. The blood was running everywhere. My mum was shouting at my dad saying, 'Get the car out of the garage quickly.' My sister was crying. My dad carried me to the car and my mum held a towel to my head.

We arrived at the hospital, but we had to wait for hours and hours. Finally we managed to see the doctor. He removed the towel, which had turned from white to red. He connected a cotton wool bud onto a large metal stick and was trying to clear the blood. It didn't work because blood was still running everywhere so he had to call for help.

When the doctors arrived they cleaned up my head again. Once they had finished they placed cream on my hand. The cream was placed onto my hand so when the injection was inserted I could not feel any pain. Once the injection kicked in I then fell asleep. As I was sleeping they started to put stitches in my head. I couldn't feel anything. It was all over very quickly. There were 6 stitches in my head.

When we arrived home I decided to go to bed to rest. My mum was acting like a slave, because she was getting everything for me.

Emma Douglas (10)
Holywood Primary School, Holywood

DIAMONDS ARE A GIRL'S BEST FRIEND

Hollywood actress Louise Getgood was in shock after the theft of her £70,000 diamond necklace. Last night the police were called. The police have stated that Miss Getgood was having a party with her friends and neighbours. Her boyfriend, Jack Black, was in the garden. Miss Getgood and her agent, Dan Brown, were in the dining room when suddenly the lights failed. Dan Brown went to investigate when he heard a scream. Dan rushed back and by that time the lights were on.

Louise cried out that someone had snatched the necklace from around her neck and hurt her. Luckily enough Louise's neighbour, Dr Peter Murray, was attending the party. He examined her neck but could find no serious injuries. Dan accused Louise's boyfriend Jack. Jack was brought in for questioning but he denied it. On questioning Louise stated that she bought the necklace from the proceeds of her new film for £70,000 from a well-known Paris jewellers. On checking, the jewellers told the police that she bought it for £20,000.

The police returned to question her again. Louise broke down and admitted that it was a plot made up to defraud the insurance company between her agent and herself as her last film was a flop and she was heavily in debt. She was hoping to clear her debts from the claim. She told the police that she had hidden the necklace in a vase of flowers as diamonds don't shine in water and are undetectable.

Lyndsey Murray (10)
Holywood Primary School, Holywood

A Day In The Life Of A Rugby Player

To be a rugby player is hard because you always panic about whether you are going to win or lose. You have to train hard and it easily tires you out.

It also is good to be a rugby player because if you win a rugby match (tournament) you get a medal. If you win a match your coach is happy with you. If you win all your matches you receive a club shield with your name on it.

It is also good to be a rugby player because you get a free rugby kit which helps you to collect more if you enjoy collecting things.

Jordan De' Pledge (10)
Holywood Primary School, Holywood

THE BOOGIE MAN CLAN

One dark night when the owls were out catching their prey and the children of the town were in bed sleeping, there was a boogie man in Hilltops Haunted House. It just escaped and was on its way to frighten children and terrorise the town. The boogie man was tall, broad and rough-looking because of his green face. He also had a black, bushy beard about five inches long. He had already attempted murder on a little, old, plump granny and succeeded because she only had a tiny handbag for self-defence to try and hit him with.

Everyone in the town was panicking the next morning. They had heard that this happened fifty-five years ago when his evil spirits were at the peak of their power and he murdered nine people. The town gathered up men to defeat the boogie man once and for all. They also gathered all the weapons in the village they could find and started heading for the site where he was hiding.

The men marched in about twenty lines of ten, each of them holding a spear, carrying a shield or holding a heavy axe. Eventually they arrived on the site and the men threw their spears and swung their axes and the boogie man was dead in seconds.

However the next day when everyone was celebrating there was another attack. Locals think it might have reproduced but who knows. Find out in the next chapter which will soon be published.

Patrick Ellis (10)
Holywood Primary School, Holywood

DISASTER AT SEA

It was a few years ago and we had decided to go on a short holiday to Scotland. It was our last day in Scotland so we made the best of it because it was a really beautiful sunny day. We went to one of the big theme parks down in England called Alton Towers. We were having a great time and we had gone on just about every ride we all wanted to go on. One of the rides I got on was called 'Bone Shaker', I had to get back off straight away as I started to feel really sick. We went at around 3.00pm because we had to travel up to the harbour for 6.00pm. We got there about five minutes early so my sister Clare and I decided to go down onto the beach. But the tide was coming in so we had to go into the waiting room. Then it started to pour with rain and then hailstones, thunder and lightning soon followed.

The waiting room was very small and cramped. There were not enough seats for everyone so most of the people were standing, but me and my sister's feet got sore so we sat down on the damp and very cold floor. But then I took off my coat and put it on the floor so it was not so cold. The captain of the boat then announced that our boat might be delayed for about half an hour so we had to wait. Clare and I were so bored because all our games and our puzzle books were in the boot of the car. Another announcement was made. The boat would be delayed for at least another hour. I went to sleep on my mum's knee but I woke up because of all the noise. Finally after around two and a half hours we boarded the boat. Our car was one of the last cars to board because all the camper vans went on first and we were in lane six.

We all got in our seats but most of the passengers were men and some of them were very drunk which made the journey even worse. The weather conditions deteriorated but the boat still set sail. The boat left the harbour approximately three hours late. The weather was so bad that the captain said he could barely see through the front window. Some of the people were outside on the deck in the pouring rain, hailstones, thunder and lightning. One of the waitresses came around to tell us that the weather was so bad that we had to leave the shelter of the shore and head out into the open water. She advised everyone that the sea was very rough and it would be best if everyone stayed in their seats for the remainder of the journey. I was so glad that I decided to sit beside my dad because my mum was sick at least five or six times. The crossing was so bad that my sister thought that she was going to die. She was sitting on the floor with her fingers in her ears because everywhere you looked you could see people being sick. She was also praying. I was sick just once. I couldn't wait till we arrived home.

After one hour and a half hours on the boat which felt like six hours, we got to Belfast harbour. Everyone couldn't wait to get off the boat. I really needed to go to the toilet but I was not going to the ones on the boat because there was sick all over the floor and anyway the cleaners were trying to clean them. It was around 11.30pm when we eventually arrived home at our front door, what a welcome sight. Then I went straight to bed.

Emma Keegan (10)
Holywood Primary School, Holywood

THE TRIO TRIBE

One hot summer's day three children, Jessica Robins who is 15, James Roberts who is 12 and Kerrie Robins who is 7 were out collecting pine cones and leaves for their art project.

Suddenly Jessica shouted, 'Look a wishing well!'

Everyone turned and James announced, 'Isn't a wishing well where you throw coins in and wishes come true?'

No one was sure, so they all threw money in and each took a wish and hoped they would come true. Kerrie wished she could have her own teddy. Jessica wished she could win the school art competition. James, who had just finished reading 'Harry Potter and the Chamber of Secrets', wished he could go on an adventure or meet someone magical.

They waited for a while and then decided their wishes weren't going to come true so they walked on and picked up some more pine cones and acorns until they came to a big dark cave. They all wondered what a cave was doing there in the middle of the forest.

Jessica shouted, 'Come on in Kerrie and James, it will be exciting. It looks magical!'

They all walked in and saw something glowing in the corner of the cave.

Jessica saw it first and running over declared, 'Hey look what I've found, it is a pile of coins. This must be the bottom of the wishing well!'

They all grabbed a pile of coins and went to fill their pockets but were distracted when they found that the entrance in and out of the cave had been blocked by a gigantic boulder. They all looked around the cave. It no longer seemed magical. It was dark, wet, sticky and absolutely horrible.

Out of the darkness they heard a deep voice. 'Hello is anyone there?' Terrified, all the children scrambled behind a rock in the corner of the cave. They were all frightened and then to make matters worse little Kerrie started to cry because she was so scared. A man appeared. He was big as an elephant. He was as tall as a giraffe. He appeared to have a large pointed head and wore a long blue robe with yellow stars on it. The man announced loudly but very friendly, 'I am William the wizard.

Please don't be scared of me, I would never hurt a living soul especially not someone from Australia.'

The children decided to trust the man and see if he knew a way out of the cave. William declared that he did know a way out of the cave but he wouldn't tell them unless they helped him first. Short of other options, the children agreed that they would do anything to get out of the cave . . .

Anna Gilmore (10)
Holywood Primary School, Holywood

Werewolf's Play Time

One day a red-headed girl called Buffy was playing in the park. Buffy was very bright and she was kind to people. Suddenly the clock struck 3 o'clock. Buffy quickly stood up and ran all the way home as fast as her legs could carry her.

Five minutes after she was in her house, the heavens opened because it had started to rain. At 6 o'clock the sky had started to change and a full moon was out. Buffy gasped with fear and she felt her heart pounding very hard.

When Buffy had eaten her dinner she staggered up to her room. She slammed the door so hard that everything downstairs vibrated. Buffy closed her curtains very quickly and she reached out for her torch and put it on. Every few minutes she stood up and walked slowly and opened her curtains carefully. She gazed at the wood which was opposite her house and then she would close the curtains again.

She did this because when she was six her grandad told her a myth about werewolves, in which they came out of the woods at 3 o'clock. They would kill anyone they would see. Buffy has been scared ever since her grandad had told her that myth.

A few weeks later her grandad came to stay at her house. Buffy was very flabbergasted when she saw him come into her house.
'What are you doing here?' shouted Buffy.
'Do not be rude to your grandfather like that, Buffy,' her mum said harshly, 'you know he is very old.'
'Who said I was old?' said Buffy's grandad.

On the second night her grandad was staying there, he asked Buffy, 'Do you remember that story I told you when you were six?'
'Yes, I do remember that thing you told me and it scared the living daylights out of me and it still does!' she said.
Her mum came in with a tray with some tea and biscuits, then her tummy started to rumble with hunger.

The next day when her mum was out shopping Buffy's grandad came into the living room where Buffy was watching TV. He said, 'Do you remember that question I asked you yesterday about werewolves?'

'Yes,' she said in a very bad mood. 'Why do you keep asking me about werewolves?' she eagerly said.

'Well, guess what? It's true!' He suddenly jumped up from where he was sitting and changed into a werewolf!

Roisin O'Neill (10)
Holywood Primary School, Holywood

NORMAL GIRL WITH A NORMAL LIFE!

Chapter 1

Hi, my name is Julie and I am 13-years-old. I live in New York, America. I live with my mom (Dee) and my dad (Sam) and I have a cat called Tiddles. I live in a big house that is very modern. My best friend is called Lana and she has a brother called Kenny.

Six things I like about my life:

1. I'm normal, not popular.
2. I have glasses and straight hair.
3. My best friend is *not* a cheerleader (I hate cheerleaders because they think they are so cool).
4. My parents are not old-fashioned.
5. My house is modern, not 19th century like!
6. I have the fourth floor of my house *all* to myself!

I go to a mixed school called New York Girls and Boys High School. My favourite subject is art. Once I painted this picture of Lana in a cheerleading outfit and she nearly fainted because she hated it so much!

Chapter 2

When I was in maths we had a cover class. We got to talk about famous people instead! But then, something amazing happened, I found out that my mom was a famous film star!

I couldn't believe she didn't tell me! So now I have to go to these lessons to make me a 'famous little daughter'.

I have to wear loads of make-up and all these mini-skirts! Mom says that it would make me popular. As if I would want to be!

Rachel McCord (10)
Holywood Primary School, Holywood

THE GHOST CALLED CASPER

One night in a dark castle a ghost called Casper was trapped by a very bad ghost called Boo. Casper was always trying to escape but Boo was always guarding the door.

One day when Boo was guarding the door he fell asleep and Casper sneaked out. It was very bright when he got out so he hid behind a wall. A little girl called Cindy looked behind the wall because she was playing hide-and-go-seek. When Cindy saw Casper she said, 'Who are you?'
Casper said, 'I am Casper.'
The girl said, 'My name is Cindy, we can be friends.'
'That would be great,' said Casper, so they were friends forever.

Gemma Davidson (10)
Kells & Connor Primary School, Kells

A DAY IN THE LIFE OF MIKKI RIGHT

'Come on Michelle, time to get up,' shouted Isabelle, Michelle's mum. 'Mmm, why?' Michelle moaned. Michelle was stubborn and hated being called Michelle. Everyone in Midtown Secondary School called her Mikki. Some teachers even called her Mikki Mouse!

Although she didn't want to she got up anyway. She skipped breakfast and went out. Mikki thought she was lucky. She was thirteen, had lots of friends, she didn't wear school uniform and had a lot of money.

Mikki had arranged to meet Kas, Karry and Ad. They were meeting in Bill's Burger Bar.

Today was Friday, Mikki didn't want to go to school Kas, Karry, Ad and Mikki were going to Doom Dome, it was a haunted house.

Mikki's mobile phone rang on the bus. She answered it even though the bus driver didn't allow it. To Mikki's horror Kas was sick and Karry had to look after her, so it was just Ad and Mikki.

Finally, when Mikki reached Bill's she saw Karry and Ad together. Karry had lied to her. Mikki went in and told Karry to go away. Then with anger soaring through her she sat down opposite Ad and once he had explained she ran off to the river.

Once Mikki got there she saw something flying in the trees. It was too big to be a bird. It had a bow and an arrow, it was wearing a loin cloth and had a halo sitting on top of a mass of curly hair. It had a little podgy face, with a squashed up face. Its eyes were dark brown, the same as its hair. Two big, beautiful wings sprouted from its back. The very second it saw Mikki looking at it, it spoke. It was hard to understand, but Mikki heard it alright. 'Hi, Mikki, not been your day has it? You fell out with Karry and Ad.'
'Who are you?' Mikki enquired.
'How rude of me not to introduce myself. My name is Mr Cupid,' he replied.
'If you're Cupid can you get me a boyfriend then?' Mikki quizzed.
'No,' he replied.
'Then what use are you?' Mikki yelled.

Attracted by the noise a boy came over to see what was going on. He had brown hair and brown eyes. His hair was in curtains. He came over to Mikki and said, 'Hi, my name's Peter, what's yours?'

'Mikki,' she said, feeling herself turn red.

'I heard you yelling and I thought you'd fallen in. Are you OK?'

That year Peter and Mikki got together and are still going out.

Rebecca McGall (10)
Kells & Connor Primary School, Kells

TEMPER, TEMPER!

'A brat, a selfish little brat!'

'Oh, Kenneth. Don't be so hard on him, after all, he is our son.'

This is a normal conversation in the Smith family. I know they're our neighbours, but for Pete's sake would they shut up!

Sorry, suppose I can't blame them, it's the kid I should blame really, but he's a bad-tempered little . . . oops, I did it again! It all started on the kid's, or as he's called, on Basil's 5th birthday. We are going back in time . . . okay we're not, but just pretend!

As you can imagine, he had the whole house full with his friends and there were so many balloons floating about that you couldn't even see if there was a roof on the top of the house. It was the best bit of the birthday, time to open the presents. Basil was looking forward to his present from his parents the most because he had asked for a robot and had seen his mum and dad go into a robot shop about 2 days before his birthday, so for this he was very excited. As a lot of people do, Basil kept the best for last (or what he thought was best).

After opening a Batman, Action Man, Spider-Man, Pigman (don't ask me) and Barbie from a girl, he finally could open . . . *the robot!*

This was what he was waiting for, his own super-cool . . . baby's robot! It was so funny. I know I'm not supposed to laugh, but . . . ha, ha! By now the whole house was laughing at him. I felt kinda sorry for him.

If you're asking how I know this, it is because I was there. I can remember how his heart slowly broke in half at the sight of it. No wonder he turned out the way he did. How, you ask, is he a selfish little brat? He turned a babysitter to retirement, at the age of 12! He even made a babysitter commit suicide!

Back to the story. Back up to when he was 12. By now he was even worse. (I'm surprised they made it this far - his parents I mean). The dad had now gone completely bald from Basil's antics and the mum had hardly any money left! He had now been in about 250 fights at school because of his bad temper and been told about 3,001.5 times, 'Temper, temper!' and don't ask me how many times he'd had detention.

Basil had only one friend at St Walkers Primary School. No wonder, with all the fights and boasting he does. I'm surprised he has a friend. The friend was called Jack. He was a very short boy, kinda thick (in both ways). He also was very boastful and got into a lot of fights, (he just shouts at people but when they're willing to fight he would tell Basil they called him an idiot and Basil would fight them).

Now to talk about his job. I know you're saying, what job would he get? Well, you are going to be surprised about this, but . . . he turned out to be a footballer!

How did he get that job? you say. Well it was of course when he was almost 20. He had always dreamed of being a footballer and one day he had the chance of being a footie star and playing for Spurs.

He went to try-out and had to give in his record from school and achievements. Of course it mentioned his temper so in the match the goalkeeper chanted at him, 'Temper, temper, couldn't hit a rat in a barrel!' As you can guess, this set off his temper. He was so mad at the keeper that he hit the ball right at him.

You should have seen the goalie's face. He just jumped out of the way. It was a good thing he did too, the shot was so strong that it went right through the net!

At this the manager was astonished and of course picked him. Now that is what I call a bad temper!

Michael Walker (10)
Kells & Connor Primary School, Kells

THE HAUNTED HOUSE

One dark, dark night in a dark, deep, spooky forest there was a black dark house. In front of the house there were four big dogs with jaws like shark's jaws, eyes like big fat raisins and their bodies like tree trunks. Then one morning a young boy called Jimmy decided to go to the house and see the master of the house.

He set off on his adventure with a machine gun to kill the troubled dogs. You see Jimmy knew that the dogs were there because his great-grandfather had got bitten by one of the horrible dogs. Jimmy set off to the house when all of a sudden, *bang, bang!* The horrible dogs were dead.

Jimmy carried on to the door then a strange man came to the door. He looked like a butler. He was wearing a black and white suit. His eyes were as white as snow, his hair was black like a rock and his hands looked like they were shrivelled up like a bent crisp. The man had a very low voice.
He said, 'Yes, could I help you?'
Then Jimmy said, 'I-I would like to see the master of the house, please.'
The old butler said, 'Come in and stay here because my master is not here.'
Jimmy looked in the dark house.
The butler said, 'I'll turn on the lights for you and show you to your room.'

The old butler went into a room and he had his bedtime drink. His drink was Coca-Cola but that night he spilt some werewolf poison in his Coke and then turned into a werewolf and ran up the stairs.

Jimmy woke up because he heard something, then he went to the toilet. While Jimmy was in the bathroom the werewolf climbed into his bed and hid there so when Jimmy went into his bed and went to sleep the werewolf bit him. The werewolf went back into the butler's room and turned back into a man again.

Suddenly, in the morning, Jimmy was screaming.
The butler ran in and said, 'Are you all right?'

Jimmy stopped and looked at him. He looked like a 30-year-old man because he had azure eyes and short black hair and then the butler got Jimmy by the arm and took him downstairs to the master of the house. The master was home in his big armchair and said, 'What does he want, Johnson?'

The butler said, 'Look at his leg, it has been bitten by a werewolf.'

Jimmy then ran out of the door and into a cave because he was turning into a werewolf. There he saw a note that said if you picked the right cup you would turn into a human, so Jimmy picked a gold cup and then he turned into a skeleton and fell to the floor.

Two days later the butler went looking for Jimmy but he didn't find him until the third day. He saw the cave and saw that he was dead so he ran back to the house as fast as he could and when he reached the master's room he fell to the ground with a thud. The master called in the guards, but as soon as the guards went in the master was dead because someone had stabbed him. On the wall it said, 'He is dead because he made me die'.

James Porter (10)
Kells & Connor Primary School, Kells

GHOST STORY

When Mark was running down the stairs he saw a ghost and playing cards in the living room were two more ghosts. He started running and running and running and running, then stopped when there was nothing but silence . . . Mark then saw the ghosts looking in all the rooms, they looked straight at him and at that moment he couldn't move and was still.

The ghosts got closer and closer and then they vanished into thin air, Mark wondered if they would come again.

That night, after Mark had gone to bed, he heard rattling chains and screeching from downstairs. He decided that he would go and have a look and guess what? Yes, it was the ghosts, he didn't dare stay around any longer.

Mark of course was very scared and as he was running out of the room he knocked over a plate, the ghosts looked over and saw him, he was mortified. As Mark ran up the stairs a ghost appeared in front of him, he looked around and there was one behind him. What was he going to do?

Mark decided he would close his eyes, count to five and then make a run for it. He thought he had made it but at the last moment the ghost grabbed him . . .

Christopher Shaw (10)
Kells & Connor Primary School, Kells

GHOST STORY

James and Jack had just moved into Spookstown. They thought it was okay but a little strange. They had made plenty of friends and had moved into Spookstown High School.

One evening when James and Jack were in their room thunder and lightning hit the tallest building and the shock swept all over the town. The lights went out and after ten minutes the town was in darkness. James stood up and walked to the window.
'What happened?' asked Jack.
'I don't know,' said James, 'it's all gone dark.'

They both looked out of the window. They could see some big thing move by.
'It's just some cars,' remarked James.
'Get the flashlight,' declared Jack.
James walked over and got the flashlight. He walked back and shone it out of the window. Suddenly he could see huge creatures walking down the street. There was blood all over the road, blood everywhere and suddenly a head popped up. James and Jack screamed. The roof was ripped off and the door broken open. Their mum and dad walked in.
'Help,' shouted Jack.
'Ha, ha, ha!' said their mum and dad. They walked over and devoured their children.

The next day everything was back to normal. But Jack and James were never seen again. Everybody thought they had moved away. But in the garden there is a stone saying, 'RIP.'

Mark Cannon (10)
Kells & Connor Primary School, Kells

THE SPOOKY STORY!

On Friday 13th June, Emma was walking home by herself. She had just been to Jane's (her friend) house. Her house was just a couple of streets away from Jane's house. She heard footsteps so she turned around, there was a shadow but nothing else, no man or anything, just a shadow. It was moving closer and closer towards Emma, she started to run and run. The shadow was moving too. It kept on following her until she got home. She ran in quickly and slammed the door.

Later that night as she watching the news it said that many people had been seeing strange things. Emma wondered if the strange shadow had anything to do with this. She told her mum and dad.

Later that week there were several robberies. Her mum did not like living there any more so she sold their house and they moved. It was the worst day of Emma's life. She had been living in that house for eleven years. It was sad to see all her friends for the last time. She moved to Greenfield which was far away from where she used to live. Every now and then she keeps thinking of that freaky night and trying to figure out what the shadow really was.

Kathryn McCartney (10)
Kells & Connor Primary School, Kells

MAGIC MUSIC

The castle door was flung open wide, Ben and Amy hesitated, then they stepped inside. They looked around them but couldn't see anyone. There was a very steep, winding staircase and cobwebs in the corners of the ceiling. Ben and Amy stood still and didn't say a word, then eventually Amy asked Ben who could have opened the door? Ben didn't seem to care, he just wanted to go and have a good look around himself. He didn't say anything.

Finally Ben started to walk towards a room with what looked like a rather old door. 'Let's go in,' said Ben, so they stepped inside. The door gave a loud creak. There was a round old table in the middle of the room. This room seemed to be some kind of living room with old wooden chairs, the walls were covered in dark green metallic wallpaper that looked ridiculous. There were ornaments of ladies in long dresses and gloves, there was a picture of a man that looked very rich and a lady with a beautiful hat, lace gloves and a red dress with puffy shoulder pads.

Ben was a boy who never got scared but now he was when he heard a knock on the wall. Amy ran out of the room as fast as her short little legs could carry her up round and round the winding staircase. Ben ran after her, they had to be very careful going up the stairs because they could trip and that would be no laughing matter.

Amy and Ben eventually reached the top of the stairs, then ran into a room which they thought was something like a bedroom. Amy and Ben, still panting like wild dogs, ran across the room and under a bed. It was very dusty and there were a few cobwebs attached to the legs of the bed.

A few seconds later, after they calmed down and got their breath back, Ben asked if they should get out from underneath the bed and go and investigate who had knocked on the wall and how the door had flung wide open. Amy said that they were maybe just getting too worked up about things and maybe it was just a draught that blew the door open and something could have hit against the wall and made a knocking sound.

Ben didn't believe anything Amy said was true, he knew someone was there somewhere in the house. Then he told Amy to shut up and stop humming. Amy turned to him and asked him if that was what Ben called humming, someone sitting with their mouth closed and no sound coming from it at all? Ben said he was sorry but he heard a musical sound coming from somewhere. Amy did as well. They decided to get out from beneath the bed and go and see where it was coming from.

As they walked they could still hear the music so down the hallway they went and into another large room with a huge sparkling chandelier hanging from the ceiling. There was a large, black grand piano sitting beside a window. The keys were moving up and down but there was no one there to play it. They walked over to a table where a china cup was sitting half full of tea, there was a pair of glasses and a music book sitting beside it.

They then walked over to the piano and sat down on the stool. By this time the keys had stopped playing and there was no music. Then something red that looked like a waistcoat was floating in mid-air when a voice, which was not Amy's or Ben's, spoke out. A white cloud that looked like clean smoke appeared in the shape of a head, arms and long body inside the waistcoat.

Then the white shape asked, 'Who do you think you are intruding in my private castle?'

Amy and Ben stood still staring at this really weird-looking shape and didn't dare speak or move.

The voice boomed out, 'I am talking to you.'

Ben answered, 'We knocked on the door and it opened so we stepped inside.'

'You do not speak to me like that, my name is Sir Edward Matthews.' The white thing was starting to get fierce now.

Ben and Amy looked towards each other, then dived for the door, they really had to be quick. They made for the winding staircase and ran as fast as they could. They thought they were never going to reach the bottom but eventually they got there. They aimed for the front door and ran down the lane. They were halfway there when they heard *bang, bang, bang.* They stopped and looked back. The long white thing was standing hammering at the window. Their footsteps got faster and faster and in no time they were out of the lane and away up at the crossroads. They never returned to *that* castle again!

Emma Davison (10)
Kells & Connor Primary School, Kells

STANLEY THE PIGEON

Stanley Pigeon lives in a place called Beechgrove. He is a very unusual pigeon. You see Stanley was brought up by owls. He sings like an owl and he even hunts at night and sleeps during the day. This is a story of how a pigeon becomes an owl. One day as he walked down the street, (when he was still a pigeon) was the day his life changed forever.

An owl saw Stanley's mum and dad get killed in a car accident and then they decided to look after Stanley. He was taken to an old barn where his new life began. His new father taught him everything he knew. He had the rest of his life to look forward to, he learnt to hunt for mice very quickly and he even got the hang of sleeping in a nest.

Stanley is now a fully grown pigeon and he still lives in Beechgrove. After his fifth birthday his new dad (Frank) and his new mum (Catherine) told him the story of how his real mum and dad had died. Although Stanley was upset he realised how lucky he was to have been found by such nice new parents.

Catherine soon laid eggs and now he has new brothers and sisters. Stanley was happy being an owl but he never forgot his real parents.

Richard Waddell (10)
Kells & Connor Primary School, Kells

YOU'RE NOT ALONE

Once there was a man called Sid looking for a place to stay the night. He was a hungry, lonely, small man. That night he searched for miles but he still could not find a place to stay in. This man walked for a mile and a half, then the next thing he saw was a house at the end of the lane.

He ran up to this house and rang the door bell and a strange man came to the door.
The strange man said, 'What do you want?'
Sid replied, 'If it is okay with you, can I stay the night?'
The strange man said, 'You might not want to because this house is very strange here.'
The small man said, 'I don't really care, I can't stay anywhere else so I might as well stay here.'
'Come in,' said the strange man.

'Sir, you might want to have these bells,' said the strange man.
'But why? I don't need them.'
'Oh yes you will,' said the strange man. 'You will need the small bell if you want me to come up and see if you are okay, the big bell because there might be something in the room with you because as I said there is something in this house. Just to make sure you are okay I'll be in the room below you to listen.'
'Good night,' said Sid.

The strange man went into the room below the small man and waited a while before he heard the small bell. He went upstairs and then he heard the large bell, so he ran as fast as he could up the stairs. When he got there the door was locked but inside he heard screaming from Sid inside the room.

He saw a fire extinguisher, then bashed the door down with it and when he got in Sid was lying on the bed with a knife in his back. The small bell was in his hand and the large bell was six feet away from him.

Kathryn Magowan (10)
Kells & Connor Primary School, Kells

GHOST STORY

Once upon a time in a little spooky village it was Hallowe'en. Everyone was out trick or treating, except one little gang of about five people who were sitting on the kerb daring each other to do things. One boy called Darren was dared to go into the spookiest house in the street. It was called Spooksvil House. People used to say it was haunted. Nobody had lived in it for over eight years. Darren and his gang had thrown stones at the windows and they were all shattered.

The gang stopped at the gate. They all said, 'Go on Darren you were dared.'
Darren walked up to the house and saw a light flickering through the glass in the front door.

Darren put his hand out to open the door, then there was a bang and the door flew open. Darren fell back and landed hard on the concrete step. Darren heard people running. He turned around and saw his gang all running home. Darren got up again and looked into the house again. He could still see the light flickering across the hall. He began to walk across the hall and a floorboard creaked and made him jump. He stepped across the hall into a room that looked like a kitchen.

The flickering light was only a house with all the lights going. He could hear scratching that sounded like it was coming from the fridge. He opened the fridge door to see three rats eating some mouldy old blue cheese. He left the room and went upstairs.

When Darren was near the top he felt something grab his leg and try to pull him back. He turned around and saw a headless ghost. He screamed and shouted, 'Get off, get off you headless beast.'

After struggling for a few minutes he broke free and ran downstairs again. A large clock struck twelve o'clock. He should have been home an hour ago.

Running across the hall he met another ghost. *I'm getting out of here,* he thought.

With shaky legs he burst through the front door and jumped down the steps. When he hit the pavement he howled like a wild animal.

With a broken leg he limped home and said, 'I'm *never* doing that again!'

David Montgomery (10)
Kells & Connor Primary School, Kells

GRINNY

Knock! Knock! Knock! Ryan ran down the stairs to see who it was. Standing there were Steven and Justin. It was the day before Hallowe'en and everything was quiet around Brook Street except for the normal Mr Grams' door squeaking day in and out. Ryan's mum and dad watched closely as they went away, all that they could see was a very slight shadow of all three boys.

Justin was the oldest and the loudest and the bossiest, Steven was the second oldest and then Ryan. He was made to do everything that's why Justin and Steven liked him.

They ran into Jass, Laweo, Rufus, Martin and Spike. They didn't like Justin or Steven and of course not Ryan.

That night Ryan lay in bed wondering if the boys were true friends or not. The next morning it was Hallowe'en.

'A-ha, we're gonna tell ghost stories.'
'No, let's play Dare instead, I got one for you Ryan, y'know that man, what do yee call him, Mr Grals, no Mr Grass, no a-ha it's Mr Grams, yes that's it hallelujah. You have to go, well we dare you to go, trick or treating at his door, meet us back here at 8.15. *Don't be late or else!*'

Ryan went in, got his tea and went upstairs and gazed out of his bedroom window staring at Mr Grams' house and just about let a few tiny words out of his mouth. 'I'll do it.'

That night Ryan got his costume ready, he was a vampire. It was 8.10 when he left the house, he saw Justin and Steven.
'Hi,' they shouted, 'over 'ere, come on now, are you gonna do it or are you a chicken? Well.'
'I'll do it. I'm not afraid.'
'Come on then.'

Outside Mr Grams' house was a crooked old gate with a little handle and a sign which said *Beware*. Ryan was scared but he still did it. He went up the path and knocked on the door, an old man stood staring at Ryan. Ryan said, 'Um hello oops, I mean trick or treat, gimme something good to eat.'

Mr Grams said, 'Would you and your friends like to come in for a nice warm cup of tea?'

Ryan said, 'Well, okay, I might as well, thank you. Come on Justin and Steven let's go in. You have a really nice home here.'

Justin whispered, 'Not.'

They walked past a very large photo of what he said was his first wife Marree. There was something spooky about it, one minute she was grinning then she had a really sad face - how weird.

Then Mr Grams began running around like someone not wise, his head was twisting strangely and then they noticed he had another horrible head starting to grow from his chin. They all screamed loudly and tried to run but they couldn't, the doors were locked and even the picture of his wife was screaming.

'Haaahaaa, here we go I knew this would start some day or should I say some Hallowe'en.'

Ryan quickly ran out the open window leaving Justin and Steven alone in the dark. No sound, no movement just the breathing of the two boys fading away. But was it only a trick or treat?

Tammy Crawford (10)
Kells & Connor Primary School, Kells

KILLER GERM

Joe and his family were on holiday in Japan. His family were having a good time but something bad was about to happen. Joe's sister, Susan, became ill and had contracted an unknown illness.

'I'm afraid Susan has caught MBD,' To (pronounced toe) Chang, a Japanese nurse said.

'What is MBD?' Mum asked.

'Major breathing difficulties,' To Chang replied. 'It can kill. Susan's one of the first victims . . .'

'But,' Mum screamed, '*we have to go home in a few days!*'

'Mrs Tipper, you have 3 choices, go home until I call you, stay here in Japan or let her die,' To said.

'I'll go home until you call me,' Mum replied.

'It will cost 100 yen,' To said.

'Okay,' Mum said.

'The MBD virus has killed another 2 people in China and 3 people in Vietnam and so far MBD has killed 10 people across Asia,' an ITV journalist read.

'I hope Susan gets better,' said Joey, Joe's younger brother.

'So do I,' sighed Dad.

Mum, Dad, Joe and Joey waited for the news of Susan.

'If she dies, I should have said sorry to her for ripping her best Barbie doll's head off,' said Joey.

'Me too, about ruining her tea party,' said Joe.

All four were going to bed thinking about her.

The next morning, they all watched the news to check her progress. '5 people have now died in Cambodia and a further 4 in Japan. Susan Tipper, the young English girl, is said to be in a critical condition in Tokyo's hospital,' the ITV reporter read.

'Well, we've got some good news,' Joey said.

Just then the phone rang.

'Hello,' Mum said.

'Hi, it's To Chang. Good news. We have found a cure.'

'Thank you so much, bye,' Mum said quickly, as she put the phone down.

'Well?' Dad asked.

'They've found a cure!' Mum said happily. 'Next stop Japan.'

'Err . . . we need to go to the airport first. We can't just drive to Jap . . .' Joey said.

'Don't get smart now!' Mum shouted.

Joey started to cry.

'Japanese scientists have found a cure for MBD. After 1 month of 5,987 infections and 50 deaths, a cure has finally been found,' the ITV reporter said.

In the airport, Mum rang To Chang to check if Susan was hanging on.

'Of course she is. She'll be the first person to be cured,' To Chang said merrily.

The day had finally come for Susan's treatment. It would take 4 hours and it would take place just before lunchtime. While Mum, Dad, Joe and Joey had dinner Susan arrived.

'You're alive,' screamed Mum.

They all hugged each other.

When they arrived home, lots of people were waiting for them. Reporters from newspapers, TV, radio and magazines were there. The Tippers' story would make the front page of all the newspapers.

'All the people who were infected by MBD have been cured and Japanese scientists have got rid of it,' the TV reporter said.

'Just one question, Susan. How did you survive?' Mum asked.

'It was just luck,' replied Susan.

Conor Swain (9)
Kells & Connor Primary School, Kells

THE HAUNTED MANSION

It was a day like any other day for James McKenna. He was dared to enter Old Man Thompson's deserted mansion, which was said to be haunted.

That night James was at dinner with his father Rufus and he said to his father, 'Dad if someone was dared to go into a haunted house, what advice would you give them?'
'Well Son, I would tell them to follow their heart. If they're smart they shouldn't do it but if they're brave they will.'

The next day James met up with his friends, the ones who had given him the dare.
Liz said, 'So Chicken Little, are you going to go into Thompson's place, or what?'
'Yeah,' Jack interrupted. 'Are you going to do it?'
James shouted, 'I am not a chicken. I'm brave. I'll go tonight. We'll meet at the tree house at 11.30.'

It was Saturday so James could stay up late. He was watching telly by himself. At eleven o'clock he checked his rucksack - flashlight, rations, black outfit, balaclava - all there. Time to go.

He met Liz and Jack at 11.29 and they crept nearer to the mansion.
'The trees look scary,' James said. He was up against the wall.

He soon ran away when he saw Thompson's ghost and his dog. Thompson shouted, 'I'll grind your bones!'
'*Aarrghh*!' shouted James and he ran as far as he could. He ran back to the tree house to hide from Thompson.
'You had better do it tomorrow,' Liz said.

The following night they camped out at the tree house. James wondered if Liz and Jack were using him.
'Cock-a-doodle-doo,' crowed Farmer Fred's rooster.
'You'd better do it tomorrow Chicken.'
'I will. Don't worry, I will.'

That afternoon they made traps.

It was now 11.45pm and they were outside the mansion.
'Boahahahahahaha!' it was Thompson leaving.
'Go!' Liz said.

James was about to enter the mansion. It was so creepy. *Bang!* Jack and Liz slammed the door. James was trapped. Would he ever get out? Were Jack and Liz really his friends? Who knows?

William Woods (10)
Kells & Connor Primary School, Kells

When The Ghosts Attack

Samantha, Laura and Gemma were all on a school trip, when something terrible happened. The school bus crashed and they seemed to have crashed near a strange house in a dark, spooky forest.

The three friends walked silently out of the bus and quietly through the forest. Quickly and quietly they went until they got to a big door, which stood right in front of them. The three friends knocked on the door. It flew open like a flash of lightning. Samantha, Laura and Gemma jumped back.
Gemma shouted, 'Anybody home?'
Nobody answered so they walked in quickly and quietly. Then they heard a noise.
'What could it be?' asked Samantha.
'I don't know but it is very spooky indeed. What can we do?' said Gemma.
'I know, we could split up and see what the noise is all about. But we need a torch. Let's find a light,' said Laura.
'Okay,' replied the others.
'I can't find a switch,' Laura said.
Neither could the others and they said, 'We we will just have to stay together. Let's go upstairs and see what is up there!'

The three friends walked upstairs and held hands as they walked because they were very scared. Then all of a sudden they heard the noise again but even louder this time. They thought they were getting quite close but when they went into the first room they couldn't hear it anymore but it did seem like they were being watched. They heard something again and turned quickly around, but nothing was there.
'That was strange,' said Laura. 'I thought I heard someone behind me.'

They quickly carried on into the next room and as they walked in the tapping started to get louder and louder, but they couldn't see anything. Suddenly something started to appear, but what was it?

The girls ran downstairs, but as they ran three more white, blurry objects started to show up. The girls tried to dodge them but now there were thousands, popping their heads up and down from the floorboards. It was then that they thought the ghosts were attacking.

They thought and thought about what they could do. Suddenly Samantha had an idea. She thought that if they fooled the blurry objects into going out into the sunlight, they might fade away.

They got out of the door before another ghost's head popped up. They ran towards Laura's house and the sun was shining brightly. Samantha's plan had worked, the ghosts who chased them were starting to fade. 'Yeah! Great, no more ghosts,' said Laura.

The girls went back home, glad that they would never see those bad old ghosts again . . . or would they . . . !

Laura McCullough (10)
Kells & Connor Primary School, Kells

THE GHOST OF THE HAUNTED CASTLE

One day I stumbled upon a dark beach that I had never seen before. The sky was dark and gloomy. I was a little scared. The sea lay still, not a sound to be heard, not a thing to be seen. I wandered around. Then in the distance I could see an outline of a castle. I walked for a while then I could see it clearly.

I saw a rope bridge and it looked as if it couldn't hold me. I was about to turn back when I heard someone shout my name. 'Julie, Julie.'
I stopped dead and I looked back, but there was no one there. I turned back and started to walk across the rope bridge. I then noticed there was lava under me. I tried not to look down.

I got off and there was a big door in front of me. It was made of steel. The door was covered with cobwebs. The knocker was a dragon. I knocked it twice but there was no answer. I knocked once more and then again I heard, 'Julie, Julie.'
I turned the door knob and walked in.

I shouted, 'Hello, hello!' It was very dark and there was a long staircase. There were lots of knights in shining armour with axes in their hands. Where I was walking was very narrow. I was about to walk past the first knight, when its axe dropped and nearly cut off my head. I screamed then I said to myself, 'Be quiet!'

There were ten doors. Some of them were smeared with blood. The stairs were in the middle but I thought I should try the doors first. I opened the first one and lots of bats flew past my head. I looked in but the room was clear. 'The bats must stay in here,' I said to myself.

The second door was also smeared with blood, as was the third and fourth. I looked in all of them. The rooms were filled with bones and skeletons.

In the fifth there were lots of pictures and they kept looking at me. It was so spooky and I walked out.

The sixth had a sheet which looked like a ghost. This was a trick, it was only a white sheet over a chair.

The seventh had writings and drawings on the wall. I couldn't read them.

In the eighth there was a photo of me! 'How did you get this?' I shouted but there was no answer.

On the ninth door it read 'Nearly there'. I think it was written in blood.

The tenth door was locked. 'What will I do?' I said.

I left and went up the stairs. I counted them, there were 1,000. When I got to the top I was so tired. I looked and there was a door about 100 feet tall. I could just reach the handle. I opened the door and there was a man with a long beard, glasses, a rope and rings on his fingers.
He said to me, 'If you defeat me, I will give you the key to the tenth door.'
I said, 'I have no weapon.'
That second a sword was in my hand. I didn't know how to use a sword but I had to try. I really wanted to know what was in through the tenth door.

With the first strike I cut off the man's head and a table appeared from nowhere and there was the key.

I ran down the stairs like mad. I opened the door, gave it a push and there were mountains of gold and a sack. I got the sack and filled it with gold. I was about to go out of the door when I heard a roar. I ran like mad again. I looked back and it was the man whose head I had cut off. I was in the middle of the rope bridge when he came out flying. He lifted me up and was about to drop me into the lava. But would he or would he not . . . ?

Nicole Erwin (10)
Kells & Connor Primary School, Kells

SPOOKULA AND HIS GANG!

'Hello, hello, is anyone there?' shouted John, as he entered Spookula castle. After he got in the door slammed shut behind him *bang!* 'Who's there?' John ran to the door and tried to open it but . . . it would not open. *Rattle, clang,* went the chains from upstairs. A gentle breeze on the back of his neck was enough to make his hairs stand up straight.

He made his way up the stairs. *Creak,* went the floorboards and one snapped below his feet. 'Help!' he shouted and it echoed all around.

Next, a white thing floated all around him. John closed his eyes and when he opened them the thing was gone. 'I bet you that's that ghost Spookula. Spookula,' he shouted really loud. He was in for it now.

Every ghost in the building came rushing, including Spookula who asked, 'Why are you here . . . ?'
By this time John was up and away to the attic. What he didn't realise though was that all the ghosts didn't go, the old ghosts had stayed behind in the attic.
'Whooo-boo. Ahhh!'

John tried to open the window. He got it open but the ghosts pulled him down to the ground. 'H-h-help. I want my mum.'
'The baby wants his ma-ma, ugh coochie-coochie-coo. Get him boys!' shouted Spookula. 'It was your great, great, great-grandfather who killed me, so I want revenge. I was immortal but he used garlic and a shiny cross.'

John got up and ran downstairs and out of the door . . .

Kirstine Boyd (10)
Kells & Connor Primary School, Kells

MY DOG'S AN ALIEN

One day I woke up and I found that it was my birthday. When I opened my presents I found that one of them was a dog. It spoke and brought me outside and it phoned this spaceship to come down to Earth.

We went back up to his planet. He showed me around and then we went to all sorts of places. We went to a party. I never thought an alien dog would invite me to a party.

Then my dog told me how he lost his family. I thought it was a very sad story. We went looking for his family but he said it would be no use. I then heard something and I went to see if anything was there. It was his family. I told him where his family was and he ran towards them. He hugged his mum and said thank you to me.

He then brought me back to Earth and I blew out the candles.

Declan Walshe (8)
St Anne's Primary School, Belfast

THE TOWN IN THE SEA

One day a boy called John went for a walk. He found a key and when he picked it up he saw a door. He went through the door and he saw a submarine. He got into the submarine and went under the sea.

He was very far under the sea when he saw a little town. He put on goggles and flippers and went into the town. He saw people with square heads and no ears or noses. He was there for an hour and then he went home and hid the key.

The next day he went to look for the key and it was not there.

John Meli (8)
St Anne's Primary School, Belfast

PRINCE OF THE SEA

One day a mer-king was swimming in the sea enjoying himself, when suddenly a dark shadow appeared. The mer-king was determined to find out what it was.

It was a ship and something was jumping down. It was a mermaid. The mer-king swam away from her. The mer-king went to bed and when he woke up he thought it was all a bad dream.

The festival was on and all the young mermaids and mermen had come to it.

The mer-king had bad dreams about the mermaid he had seen. In his dreams he was swimming away from her. He kept on having bad dreams about the mermaid. He wished she would come back to him.

He sent out a search party to find the mermaid and he went looking too in case they found her. He wanted to marry her.

They found her and he asked her to marry him and she agreed. They lived happily ever after.

Michael McNulty (8)
St Anne's Primary School, Belfast

A Day In The Life Of My Granny

Ding-dong!
'Hello.'
'Hi.'
'You're late today, did you sleep in?'
'No.'
'What do you want?'
'Rice Krispies.'

Ding-dong
'That will be Jim.'
'Hi Mark.'
'Hi Jim.'
'Hi.'
'Rice Krispies?'
'Yes.'
'I'm going to work. See you later Mum.'
'I'm finished with my bowl, here you go.'
'Thanks.'
'Lauren get ready to go, we're late. It's 8.50, hurry up!'
'See you later.'
'Right Mark, do you want a biscuit?'
'No.'
'Do you want a drink?'
'Yes.'
'Do you want anything to eat?'
'No.'
'OK, you drink your drink and I'll read my book, and we'll play when you're finished.'

Ding-dong
'That will be Grandad.'
'Hide! Hide on Grandad!'
'He's hiding. Pretend not to see him or he might cry!'
'We're going to Curley's.'
'But we cannot go without Mark.'
'Oh is he behind the curtain?'
'No.'

'Is he behind the chair?'
'Yes, found him.'
'Right get your coat on now!'
'Right we need chips, fish and sweets for Mark.'
'The queues aren't too bad today. Have you got everything?'
'Yes.'
'OK.'
'Mark get a bowl and put your sweets in it. I'm going to collect Lauren. You can play with Mark!'
'Where did Grandad go?'
'To collect Lauren.'
'Oh.'

Lauren Cunningham (9)
St Anne's Primary School, Belfast

BEYOND THE BOOKCASE

Shannon went to the library in her house to find a book to read.

Shannon slid on a banana skin and knocked into a bookcase and it swung open to reveal a secret passage.

Shannon went through it and it led her to a forest. There she met an elf called Bingo. Shannon became friends with Bingo. He took her to his house which was a burrow underground. They played and played. For dinner Bingo made head louse soup and it tasted delicious and Shannon thanked him.

Shannon needed to go back to her home so Bingo the elf led her back to the passageway.

Anna McAllister (8)
St Anne's Primary School, Belfast

MY WONDERFUL TEACHER

It was September the third and I was going to be in Primary 4. I was so excited because my new teacher was going to be a teacher for the first time. Yes! That meant that my class would be the first pupils that she would teach.

When we saw her, she looked so nervous and the worst teacher ever. When we went into class we tried to be as quiet as we could. At break our teacher was talking to the other teachers. She wasn't so bad. She was great!

We had so much fun and when I got home my mum and dad had to slow me down before I could even speak to them.

When I was in bed that night, all I could possibly think about was what it would be like the next day at school with such a wonderful teacher!

Marie-Claire Nellis (8)
St Anne's Primary School, Belfast

THE HAUNTED HOUSE

Peter and I were on our way home from football. We took a short cut past the old church house. The sky was black as night and the wind was howling round us. Lightning struck and the old house lit up.

Suddenly there was a loud screech. I turned to Peter but he had vanished. Then I heard someone call my name. I ran towards the old house to look for Peter. All I could hear was the crashing of thunder and I was terrified.

I slowly pushed open the door. The rooms were empty except for old pictures on the walls, which were covered with cobwebs. I felt the eyes of people staring at me. Suddenly I noticed a picture of Peter staring at me. I began to tremble with fear and I ran home as fast as I could.

Eventually I was home. I opened the front door and began to walk slowly into the house. I walked into the living room and there was Peter's body lying on the floor. I heard a noise upstairs so I opened the door and started to run. I did not want to be his next victim.

Conor Compston (8)
St Anne's Primary School, Belfast

THE HAUNTED HOUSE

One day I was out with my friend. We were walking along the path which led into a dark forest. Soon we came upon a dark old house. It looked so creepy, the windows were broken and some of the tiles on the roof were missing. We climbed through a window into the living room. It smelt very damp and was full of cobwebs. We were very scared but decided to take a look around.

We went upstairs and it was very dark. As we walked past a room we could hear voices from inside. As I moved closer to the door, to listen, I knocked into an old chair. I froze, my heart was pounding and my mouth was very dry. The voices stopped and I could hear footsteps coming towards the door. Before we realised, the door flew open and there stood an old man with white hair, black teeth and long, long fingernails. He reached out to grab me but I ran as fast as I could down the stairs and out of the front door.

My friend was behind me, sweat running down his face. We kept running and running until we reached home. We made a promise never to visit the haunted house ever again!

Brendan Bennett (8)
St Anne's Primary School, Belfast

THE TOWN UNDER THE SEA

Once upon a time there was a teacher called Miss O'Carroll. Miss O'Carroll loved mermaids and one night she dreamed about mermaids. It was very exciting but while she was dreaming she was sleepwalking. She started walking to the door and then she went outside. She soon walked closer and closer to the sea. Suddenly she stopped and knelt down on the sand.

A moment later, she looked up and saw a mermaid's head upon the water. She dragged Miss O'Carroll into the sea. Miss O'Carroll couldn't believe her eyes. There, stood before her, was a mermaid and behind her was a town. The mermaid was called Mulan and she loved her name. Mulan didn't talk she could only say her name.

After that Mulan took Miss O'Carroll to see the mer-king. He was pleased that Mulan had a new friend.

At 4 o'clock Miss O'Carroll thought she had better go home. So Mulan took Miss O'Carroll to the surface of the sea to say their last goodbyes to each other. Then Miss O'Carroll swam to the sandy beach and when she stood up Mulan jumped up out of the sea and waved.

Miss O'Carroll got home safe and sound.

Rachel Dixon (7)
St Anne's Primary School, Belfast

BIONICLE ISLAND

It was the summer holidays. We were off school and James and I went to the island of Matalua. This is where Bionicles lived. Bionicles are robots.

The island is divided into six parts. It was icy, grassy, fiery, watery, stony, and rocky. James and I went to the icy part. It was cool and such fun. The Koharks and Kopaka lived here. They are Bionicles with shields and swords. Some are good and some are evil.

We were welcomed by the Kopaka and chased by the Koharks. The Koharks chased us and we nearly got caught. We ran to the beach. We found a boat and we got onto it and escaped. James said that we would not go there again.

Gerard Smyth (8)
St Anne's Primary School, Belfast

THE GRAND HIGH WITCH

It was Hallowe'en. My auntie Beth and uncle Steven were going out and I had to babysit Lauren and Rachel.

When they were gone a shining light appeared through the misty darkness. A shiver ran down our necks like a cold day. It was a ghost and it said, 'The grand high witch will kill every child unless you kill her.'

We put our coats on. I carried Rachel and took Lauren's hand and we set off for the Castle of Doom.

When we got there we went inside. We had only twenty-four hours to kill the witch. The ghosts howled as if to say, 'We're trapped and if you don't want to be trapped get out of here!'

We had only twelve hours left so we ran until we saw the witch. She sent a spell flying through the air. It hit my arm and I pretended to die. The witch cackled and was about to kill Lauren when I jumped to my feet and stuck the knife through her heart.

We then ran home hoping that Beth and Steven weren't back. We got there just in time. Just after we shut the door they came in. Beth and Steven thanked me and I winked at Lauren and she winked back at me!

Orla Frizzell (8)
St Anne's Primary School, Belfast

HALLOWE'EN NIGHT

It was Hallowe'en night and Aoife and I went trick or treating. We got loads of sweets and money. Some people were dressed up as witches and ghosts and devils and vampires. Suddenly it started to get very dark.

Aoife and I wanted to go home so we started walking. We were outside our next-door neighbour's house and there was a man walking behind us. Aoife and I ran to our house but before we could reach the door the kidnapper grabbed us. He took us to his car and pushed us in.

Finally we jumped out of his car and escaped. We ran home as fast as we could. Our mums and dads were so worried. We got lots of food and drink.

Natasha Loughran (8)
St Anne's Primary School, Belfast

THE MASKED MURDERER

The man woke annoyed. As usual he was angry but then he was always angry. He was born that way. Even as a boy he was a nasty bully. Even when he was a young man he spent his time breaking into other people's homes and stealing their stuff.

One night he broke into a house where an old man lived on his own. The sound of breaking glass woke the old man up. The old man heard footsteps on the stairs. He called out, 'Who's there?' The footsteps stopped. There was no answer so he called out again.
Suddenly the door was kicked open, 'Shut up old man,' said the masked murderer.

The old man refused to be quiet, 'Who are you and what do you want?'
'You don't know me behind this mask. I want your money,' answered the intruder.

The old man used to play hurling and lifted one of his sticks and hit the intruder on the head. Blood spurted out everywhere. The old man still wasn't safe because he tripped and the masked intruder had a knife and stuck it into the poor old man's heart. The masked murderer stole the money and left the man to die.

The police found evidence. The murderer's blood was found on the hurling stick. The police found that the DNA from the blood belonged to Alex McCoist. McCoist was arrested and he was sent to jail for life.

Eoin Fleming (8)
St Anne's Primary School, Belfast

A Day In The Life Of The Wicked Wizard

The wicked wizard was an old nasty man who had lumps all over his face. He had pointed ears, big smelly feet and long jagged fingernails. He wore a big black cloak that stank of sour milk and his pointed dark hat was all ripped and torn. His boots were silver and had holes where his big, dirty toes stuck out.

On a normal day he would wake up to the sound of a tap-dancing frog on a drum. Then he would float up out of bed and float downstairs for his breakfast. He would click his fingers and the milk would pour itself into the bowl. Then he would click his fingers again and the milk would stop pouring and float back into the fridge.

After breakfast he'd go out and look for trouble. He would find a boy and turn him into a big hairy worm. Five minutes later he'd throw frogs at old people, who were sitting on a bench outside their house.

In the afternoon he would have some fun with the traffic lights. When they were red he would change them to green and make the cars crash. He liked to set traps for people. He'd look for a window cleaner and command his bucket of water to fall on a young boy passing by.

After a busy day the wicked wizard would float into bed and fall into a deep, deep sleep.

Peter Cochrane (8)
St Anne's Primary School, Belfast

MRS LUCKY LICKS

As I walked into the corner shop, there she was standing behind the counter. Glamorous as ever, even though she was now old. Her blue eyes still twinkled as she asked me what I would like today. I asked for the usual ten pence mix and as she picked through the sweets I noticed her lovely long nails.

Mrs Lucky Licks used to work in my school. She was the most beautiful dinner lady I knew. Two years ago her husband died and she would not go out for months. Later she took sick and could not go to work. She missed her husband so much and she became very lonely. My friends and I went round to see her because she was such a sweet, kind lady.

Soon it became summer and Mrs Lucky Licks started to go out again. She went round the shops every day and one day, the man who owned the corner shop asked her if she wanted a job for a couple of hours every day. She said yes. It's great for her because she knows all the children who come into the shop and if they don't have enough money she gives them free lollies.

Yesterday I saw her in church and she had on a beautiful blue dress and hat to match. She had her hair tied up neatly and lipstick on. I was glad to see her looking so fine again.

Rebecca Rooney (8)
St Anne's Primary School, Belfast

A Day In The Life Of A Lovely Lady

Once upon a time there was a lovely lady called Miss Kindness. She was a beautiful young lady and was very kind. She had lovely soft skin and long smooth hair. She was medium-sized in height. Miss Kindness would wear lovely clothes like dresses, skirts and lovely tops with beautiful designs on them like stars and hearts. Miss Kindness was a gorgeous lady who never shouted. She had lots of friends, she gave people lots of sweets and goodies.

Miss Kindness worked in a library and was a very smart lady. She let other people play in her garden and she had things for them to play with like swings and a trampoline and slides and a climbing frame. People would go round to her house every day.

Miss Kindness would answer the door every time someone called and would say, 'Hello, would you like to play in my garden?'
The person would say, 'Yes, please, thank you.'
Miss Kindness would think, *why they are very polite.* Then she would go inside and have her dinner and go to bed.

Beth Cosgrave (8)
St Anne's Primary School, Belfast

A Day In The Life Of A Mean Girl

Rachel was a nasty girl. She always teased other people. She was the nastiest and the meanest person. She never shared anything. She always got what she wanted. Everybody thought Rachel was the ugliest girl. Everybody hated her. She always shouted. Rachel always wore baggy jeans and a top with a skeleton on it. She was always showing off.

When Rachel went to school one Monday, the teacher asked Rachel, '2+2?'
She said, '6.'
The teacher said, 'No.'
Rachel was also stupid.

The pupil that Rachel bullied the most was the cleverest person in the class. Her name was Sarah. Sarah knew all her times tables. Everyone liked Sarah but not Rachel. Rachel would call Sarah a loser because she thought she was the teacher's pet.

Rachel would also bully John, John was the best footballer. She called him a show-off, he wasn't, she was!

One day John went to Rachel and said, 'Nobody likes you and you do not have a friend and nobody likes you calling them names. If you did not call people names then you would have friends. If you did not bully people everyone might like you, so please become a better person.'

Everyone was standing around them at that moment and was shouting, 'John!' Everyone thought it was the bravest thing that someone could have said to Rachel.

So Rachel said, 'Okay' and was nice from then on and soon had lots of friends.

Joel McBrien (8)
St Anne's Primary School, Belfast

AL, THE ALIEN
(My best friend)

One ordinary school day, a new boy started in my class. He was called Al. Soon he became my best friend. The story really begins when I asked him over to my house for a sleepover. We had great fun having tea and playing football in my back garden.

As it grew dark, Al's watch made a strange beeping noise. He was getting signals from outer space. His mum and dad were phoning him on his special watch. His parents were aliens so I thought *does that make Al one?*

When they had finished talking we went up to the bedroom.
Al said, 'Okay, you saw my parents were aliens, so you probably think I am?'
'Well I do,' I said.
'Well I am morphed into human form. I came to Earth to see more of the universe and get to understand your language. Soon my time will be finished here.'

Al soon left school. 'He's left town,' the teacher said. Only I knew the truth! *Left Earth, more like,* I thought. When I was walking home my watch started beeping. Al was sending me messages!

Peter Byrne (8)
St Anne's Primary School, Belfast

THE DOPPELGANGER

One day there was a boy called James, he was seven years old. His mum had to look after his little sister so she asked James to go to the shops to get some food for dinner. It was the first time that James had gone to the shops alone, he was very nervous but he also felt very grown up because none of his friends ever went to the shops alone.

James was OK getting the food, everyone in the shop was very nice to him but on the way home he got a bit bored so he thought it would be fun to go into the huge town forest. However, when James was walking into the forest he didn't notice the sign, it said, *Warning! Dangerous! Wild animals!*

James had been walking for about half an hour before he discovered he was lost. He sat against a tree and started crying loudly. He was crying so loudly that some bears came. James ran behind a bush because he was so scared but then a little boy came up James. The little boy looked just like James; he was a doppelganger! James ran away from the bears with the doppelganger and soon he was home. The doppelganger had disappeared and it was getting dark.

James suddenly found himself in bed. Had it been a dream? James got out of bed and saw himself in the mirror; there were two reflections! Maybe it hadn't been a dream!

Sarah Toner (9)
St Anne's Primary School, Belfast

ONE DARK, COLD NIGHT

One dark, cold night in November, Jordan was lying in bed trying to get to sleep. It was impossible at first as the wind was howling and the rain was banging hard against his bedroom window.

He eventually fell fast asleep and was having lovely dreams when, suddenly, he was awoken by a loud banging noise. He jumped out of bed to see what this noise was, only to discover that his bedroom window had been blown open by the fierce wind. Jordan returned to bed but was very restless. He decided to get up and go down to the kitchen to get a drink of water.

He heard another noise whilst in the kitchen and this time he was really, really frightened. He could see dark shadows outside the kitchen door and soon realised there was someone out there. He quickly ran back up the stairs and jumped into bed. He pulled the bedclothes over his head and began to cry. He closed his eyes tightly hoping this nightmare would soon go away.

Jordan awoke the next morning only to discover that this scary experience was only a dream, or was it . . . ?

Jordan Kane (9)
St Anne's Primary School, Belfast

THE KIDNAP

One day a girl was walking home from school. She was ten years old. Once she got home she went to her bedroom. As Amy lay on her bed reading, she felt a gentle breeze from her window. She called her mother but her mother was at work.

Amy went to the bathroom. When she closed the door she saw a scary man behind it. The man put Sellotape around her mouth and carried her away.

When her mother returned from work she called, 'Amy, Amy.' There was no answer. She went upstairs but Amy wasn't there. Her mother called the police. Lieutenant Columbo came. Columbo started an investigation. Columbo found fingerprints on the window. He took them to the science laboratory. He searched for one month.

One day when he was looking at people's documents, he found a scary-looking man with the same fingerprints that were on the window. He looked up where the man lived. He lived in Castle Street.

The next day Columbo went to Castle Street to arrest the man. Columbo saw the man and beside him was a ten-year-old girl. That girl was Amy. Columbo arrested the man and took Amy home.

Amy's mummy and daddy had a massive party and everybody lived happily ever after.

Kerrie McConnell (9)
St Anne's Primary School, Belfast

THE ROBBER GRANNY

Once upon a time there was a boy called Mat who had a friend called Peter. They walked up a really steep hill and got out their slingshots and hit someone's house.

The house was a small wooden one where a granny was sitting on a rocking chair outside but when she heard the stone hit her house she chased Mat and Peter on her broomstick so they jumped into a hole beside a giant tree. She couldn't find them so she went back home.

When the boys saw the granny fly back home on her stick they ran home and had dinner then went to bed. However, that night the granny went to their houses and stole Mat and Peter and took them home to her house on her broomstick.

The granny put Mat and Peter in a sack and tied it up with rope, then she went to boil some water. While she was away Mat had an idea, he had found a nail in his pyjama pocket so he used it to cut a hole in the sack and they escaped and ran away.

Connell Morgan (9)
St Anne's Primary School, Belfast

HAUNTED HOUSE

One day a girl called Susan had just started secondary school. It was her first day. No one at all liked her. Susan told them that her house was haunted but nobody believed her, but it was true! Her house was haunted!

When she got home from school her mother and father asked her if she'd had a good time but Susan didn't answer. She got her homework out and started it. Her mother said, 'Your father and I are going out.'
Susan said, 'Okay.'

When she had finished her homework she went up to her room and lay on her bed. Suddenly the lights went out. Susan couldn't see. Something lit up her room. It was a man in an army suit. Susan was a little deaf but she could lip-read. Susan could see the man was saying something but couldn't make it out, then the man disappeared.

Susan's mother and father returned home and said, 'What's happened here?'
Susan said, 'The lights all went out,' but she didn't say anything about the ghost.

Later on that day Susan asked if her friend Mark could come for a sleepover.
Her mother said, 'Yes.'

That night the ghost came again. Susan knew what he was saying this time. She said to Mark, 'A bomb!'
Mark said, 'How do you know?'
Susan didn't answer.
'Oh, now I know,' said Mark.

Susan's father came in but the ghost had disappeared. Susan's father said, 'What was that?'
Susan told her father and they moved house!

Colleen Lear (9)
St Anne's Primary School, Belfast

THE MASKED MURDERER

Hi, I'm Matt! I was just watching one of my favourite Simpsons' episode, it's the one . . . what's this? The Simpsons have just gone blank and some boring newsflash has come up.

I changed the channel and then I was about to turn the TV off when I heard the terrifying words, 'The masked murderer's on the loose! He's already attacked most of the houses in Dunmurry Lane.'
That's my street, *'Arghh!'*
'Lock your windows,' the newsreader warned.

I ran to the window. A guy in a balaclava popped up, *'Boo!'*
'Arghh!' I screamed until I ran out of breath.
'Shut up! Someone will hear,' he said covering my mouth.
'That's the flipping point!' I shouted. He pulled me out of the window. I tried to kick him where it hurts but he grabbed my leg and stuffed me into a huge sack.
'Ow!' shouted a voice. I'd landed on somebody.
'Get off me,' a voice said.
'Who are you?' I asked.
'I'm Stephen,' said a voice. 'I got kidnapped too.'
'But you seem so calm,' I said, astonished!
'Yeah I am, well I'm scared obviously but I've been in here a while and I'm just thinking about that guy staggering about trying to carry us.'

Just then we heard sirens and we were dropped.
'Will I ever see you again?' I asked, but he was off running.

I ran home too. As I got in the door my mum came into the room, 'Bedtime!'
'But Mum I was . . .'
'No 'buts' it's half-ten.'
She never found out!

Ruairi Barr (9)
St Anne's Primary School, Belfast

THE THREE WISHING TICKETS

One day the postman came to our house. He had a parcel in his hand and said, 'This is for Jennifer.' When I heard it was for me I ran as fast as a cheetah downstairs and saw the parcel which was wrapped up in paper with shining little stars on it. It was gorgeous!

I grabbed it from my mum and said, 'Can I open it *pleeease!*'
My mum said, 'No, wait until after dinner.' After dinner I ran into the living room and opened the parcel. There were three wishing tickets inside. I wasn't really interested until I read a card which said, 'These are three wishing tickets, use them with responsibility, each one represents a wish'.

It was school the next day and I took the tickets with me. I had an enemy called Kim, she came over to me and called me names. I muttered to myself, 'I wish she would leave me alone!' The next thing I knew she left me alone.

I was in class and my teacher was shouting at my best friend, Colleen. I wished my teacher was a kangaroo and only left me one more ticket and I had to use that ticket to turn my teacher back into a teacher! After school I went home and cried up in my room.

The following day the postman came and he had a parcel. I wonder what it is . . .?

Christina Cunningham (9)
St Anne's Primary School, Belfast

THE PRESENT

Yesterday was my birthday. My grannies, grandads, aunties and uncles came to my house. Everyone gave me money and a card except my granny. She gave me a present. It was a small box wrapped with lovely shiny paper. I opened it slowly. It was a ring! I put it on my finger and it was a perfect fit.

Next day I had to go to school. I put my ring on. As soon as I got to school I had to do maths. 'I wish it was break time,' I said to myself and as soon as I said that, the bell rang. I thought, *this is pretty strange!* The same thing happened every day. Then I realised my ring was a magic ring!

The next day I went to school. 'I wish it was home time,' I said, but nothing happened. I wished again it was home time but still nothing happened. I looked at my finger and realised I'd forgotten my ring. 'Oh no!' I said. All day I kept wishing things but they never happened.

As soon as I got home I looked on my dressing table but the ring was gone. I looked all over the house until finally I found it under my bed.

The next day I put my ring on. As usual I kept wishing things but they never happened. I checked my finger but I did have my ring on. I thought of all those times I was wishing things it was not really the ring, it was just my luck!

Janice Hughes (9)
St Anne's Primary School, Belfast

WITCHES AND WARLOCKS

About 1,000,000 years ago witches and warlocks fought to the death. I will tell you a story of a warlock called Simon and a witch called Zelda who was an evil, evil witch and was planning to blow up the world, but she needed ingredients which were frogs' legs, 5 spiders, 2 bats' wings and 50 toenails.

While the witch was out, Simon went into her lair and looked at her notes. They were: 'Get ingredients, fly to space, say 'Spell' and blow up world'.
'Oh no,' said the warlock.
The witch was coming back so he took her spell book and ran away.

When he got back home at last, he said, 'What does she want to do that for?'

The witch got back to her lair and said, 'Whoever has taken my spell book will pay with their life.' She went back into her lair and put poison over the whole of it and did a spell so that she could not be poisoned.
The warlock overheard the witch and did the poison spell so that he would not die of poisoning.

Then the witch went out again and the warlock crept in. He took the ingredients and ran back to his house and built a spaceship. He took the spell book and ingredients with him and he blew up the world. He went to a different planet called Planet Zoc. He tried to blow that planet up too but didn't manage it and ended up in jail.

Jonathan Moyna (9)
St Anne's Primary School, Belfast

THE HAUNTED HOUSE

One day eight friends were playing happily in a game of skips. Their names were Caoimhe, Colleen, Christina, Jennifer, Rebecca, Deborah, Niamh and Grainne. Colleen, Christina, Jennifer and Rebecca were brave but Caoimhe, Deborah, Niamh and Grainne were always scared. They all were very careful all the time.

Then they stopped playing their game of skips and took a walk down the street. The sun was up and the street was bright. They were joking, they were laughing. They had a brilliant time.
Jennifer said, 'I can feel rain. Do you think we should turn back?'
'No!' said Caoimhe. 'We can still have fun in the rain.'
They walked on and kept on walking. Then the rain got worse. It turned into thunder and lightning. They came to a black, dull and shattered house.

Colleen, Christina, Jennifer and Rebecca went at the same time, *'Cool!'*
Then Caoimhe, Deborah, Niamh and Grainne went at the same time, *'Argh!'*

They all hid. Caoimhe hid behind Colleen, Deborah behind Christina, Niamh behind Jennifer and Grainne behind Rebecca.

They entered the house and went upstairs. They saw a shadow and they moved closer. They saw a man who got up off his chair and ran for them. They ran out of the house and went home. They told their parents the whole story and never went back to the haunted house ever again.

Karla Copeland (9)
St Anne's Primary School, Belfast

WALKING HOME

One sunny day I was allowed to take my dog to school with me and walk home with her. At the end of school I went off at a running pace because I had heard something. The clouds were looking dark and gloomy with stormy rain.

After a while I slowed down. I was already entering the wood. My dog, Susie, isn't brave and she isn't fierce but she would protect me if she could.

Well, anyway, Susie and I were walking along when Susie saw a squirrel and took off. I hated squirrels, 'Darn squirrel, hate them.' I ran to catch up with Susie. When I was running I heard strange rustling noises. I thought I had caught a glimpse of a nymph, which is a magical creature. I felt a bit scared.

Soon I found Susie, and I did get another glimpse of a nymph. Nymphs were scary creatures to me.

Anyway, Susie and I arrived home safely before the storm and we never went through the woods again.

Catherine McLaughlin (9)
St Anne's Primary School, Belfast

A Day In The Life Of A Prince

Once upon a time in a castle there lived an evil prince called Grimsey. He had a really scary face. He had always wanted a son. So one day he went down to the village and stole a baby boy. His mummy ran out and hit the prince but he threw her to the ground and rode off to the castle.

For many years he kept the young boy and taught him to be an evil young boy as he grew up. They both enjoyed going into the village and beating people up.

During one of these visits, the young boy saw some boys playing. He began to wonder why he didn't have any friends. Then he remembered that the prince didn't have any friends either.

So the young prince left the castle one night while the prince was sleeping. He met up with a young boy who was also a prince. They played football together and told ghost stories.

The young prince then went back to the castle and invited his friend to stay with him but the evil prince caught him.
The little prince said, 'If you don't let me have any friends, I will leave and you won't have a son anymore!'
The evil prince then said, 'I have always wanted a son and I don't want you to leave me so you can stay friends with him.'

The little prince was very happy he had a friend and he grew up a happy prince and had lots of friends.

Christopher McGlinchey (8)
St Anne's Primary School, Belfast

Scooby-Doo And The Lady Vampire

Scooby and the gang were in the car. Scooby and Shaggy, his best friend, were sitting at the back of the car, eating as always. They stopped the car and saw the haunted house which was on TV.
Fred said, 'Come on!'
Scooby and Shaggy were too afraid to go in. Bats flew out of the window. Fred knocked on the door.

A lady came out and said, 'Who are you? I don't know you.'
Fred said, 'That is the same question as we were going to ask you. Is this your home?'
'Yes, it is. My husband died a couple of years ago, it has been terrible without him. This house is a dump.'
Shaggy said, 'I think Scooby and I will go and have a pizza.'
Fred said, 'Alright.'

Shaggy and Scooby got their pizzas and then they saw the lady vampire footprints.
'They lead that way . . .'
'Yes, you're right, let's go that way and see what happens.'

Velma had found some footprints too. They led up to the hallway. She ran up but there was nobody there. Velma said, 'Wait a minute, it must have gone up there.' She tried to open the door but it was stuck so she tried the other way and it came open. She saw the vampire running away and then it vanished.

Shaggy and Scooby thought it was Daphne because Daphne was feeling sick. Shaggy saw the vampire going into Daphne's room but Daphne was not in her bed. She had gone down to get a drink of water.

Velma tied a knot in a rope. Scooby pulled the rope.

Scooby said, 'Okay, Velma?' Scooby pulled it and he caught it . . . it was the lady vampire.

They told the police who said, 'Well, thanks, kids.'

Before the police took her away Fred said, 'Let's take off the head to find out who it is and then they saw that it was Mrs Darke. The police took her away and there were no vampires left.

Rebecca Jackson (9)
St Anne's Primary School, Belfast

THE HAUNTED CASTLE

It was the 31st of October. My friend James and I were going trick or treating.

We found a haunted castle. We opened the door and we were very, very frightened. The door closed behind us with a bang. We were trapped!

We ran and ran and ran until we reached the top of the stairs. We went into room 1. We stood there in shock. Then we heard someone break down the door. It was my dad! He had come to save us. He ran up the stairs into room 1 and got us out. I said, 'Thanks Dad' and he said, 'No problem!'

David McCabe (8)
St Anne's Primary School, Belfast

BEYOND THE BOOKCASE

My class went to the library one day. On the way out of the library I lifted a book and suddenly a bookcase swung open. I saw a secret passageway and I went through it. At the end of the passageway I found I was in a forest.

In the forest I met an elf with big ears called Marky. He told me he was 99 years old. I went to his house which was a tree house at the top of a large oak tree. We had to climb a rope ladder to get up to it. It was very exciting. We played lots of games. I then decided I must return to school.

The elf led me back to the passageway. I walked along it back into the school library and went back to class and the teacher didn't even know I had been away.

Conor Burns (7)
St Anne's Primary School, Belfast

BEYOND THE BOOKCASE

Michael ran into the library at home to find a book. He leant on an old bookcase. The next thing he knew the bookcase opened to reveal a dark secret passageway. There were cobwebs all over the place. Michael walked into it and he tripped over a dead bat and fainted.

When he woke up he felt a remote box so he pressed one of the buttons and he seemed to go back to the 60s decade. Michael recognised his dad from old photographs. He was boogieing on the dance floor surrounded by lots of girls. When Michael went onto the dance floor nobody saw him because he was invisible.

Then Michael saw the remote box again so he went over and pressed the button below the one he touched before and Michael went into the 70s decade. In this decade people wore different clothes because it was all punk.

When he pressed the button below again, he went into the 80s and he went to a Michael Jackson concert. It was amazing!

After this Michael pressed the button below again and went to the 90s. He saw his mum and dad get married. He got quite emotional at this special occasion.

Then he pressed the button below and he went to a millennium party. When the party was over, he pressed the last button and this button put him back in the present.

Michael Gorman (8)
St Anne's Primary School, Belfast

BEYOND THE BOOKCASE

I was walking down the street one night and I saw the haunted house everyone had been talking about, so I decided to spend the night there to prove it was not haunted. I went home and got a few things I might need for the night.

I broke the glass window of the haunted house and climbed in. When I switched on my torch I found out that I was in a library. I was walking out of the room and I slipped over a dead rat and hit my head against a bookcase. It opened up and a secret passage was revealed. I went inside and there were lots of spiderwebs touching my mouth.

As I walked down the passageway I heard voices but I could not see anyone. I kept on walking until I reached the end of the passageway. I came to a battlefield. I saw lots of people dying and there were tanks and helicopters and planes everywhere. Bombs were being dropped.

The next thing I heard was my daddy saying, 'You are having a nightmare, Brian. Everything is OK now.'

Brian Óg Smyth (8)
St Anne's Primary School, Belfast

THE TREASURE CHEST

One day a boy and girl called Jack and Jill went on holiday to Galway. They went to the beach. They had so much fun, then Jack noticed a sign. He took Jill with him to see what it said, *Keep Out!*

Jill spotted a very dark hole in the cliff so they went in. Jill didn't want to go in but she had to. Then they heard a little voice from outside the cave. It was their mum calling for them to go home but they went on through the cave.

There were lots of crabs and bats inside the cave. They found a chest so Jack thought it must be a pirate's cave. He opened the chest and there was lots of money, diamonds and other precious things.

The children were so rich finding this treasure that they never spoke about the jewels again.

Niall Devlin (8)
St Anne's Primary School, Belfast

BEYOND THE BOOKCASE

Jack went to the library and was taking a book from a shelf when a door swung open. He was pulled into a secret passageway. It was full of cobwebs and bats flying around.

Jack was frightened but he walked down the passageway and then saw an unfriendly ghost in a forest. Jack was very cold because it was wintertime. He started to run around to try and keep warm but he fell into a trap.

Jack saw a door and he opened it very quickly as the ghost started chasing him. When he went through the door he saw he was back in the passageway. He started to run again so the ghost couldn't catch him. When he reached the end of the passageway he ran through the door quickly and closed it very quickly. And he never heard of the ghost again.

Fiona Hartley (8)
St Anne's Primary School, Belfast

BEYOND THE BOOKCASE

Yasmine went to the library with her class. When she lifted a book from off the shelf, the bookcase opened to reveal a secret passage. The passageway was very, very dark. It had cobwebs everywhere. Then she tumbled down the stairs and stopped in front of a mirror. It forced her to walk into it even though she tried not to.

The mirror made Yasmine go back in time. She met Queen Victoria when she told her guards to take her down to the dungeon. In the smelly dark dungeon she escaped through a window. She ran through the mirror into the passageway and ended up back in the library.

She said to herself, 'I will never go near that bookcase again!'

Hannah McGlinchey (8)
St Anne's Primary School, Belfast

THE RESCUE

One summer day there was a fisherman fishing and a little girl called Emma was walking nearby. She never went to school because she kept getting bullied. She decided to go for a walk along the side of the bridge. A car was coming so she jumped onto the bridge wall and fell into the river.

A fisherman heard a splash. He hadn't spotted the girl until her head popped up from the water. As soon as the fisherman noticed her, he dived into the water to save her. He brought her to shore, she was unconscious so he had to give her mouth-to-mouth resuscitation, then he asked her where she lived. The little girl told him she lived nearby and the fisherman carried her home.

The little girl told her parents about this man. Then the town mayor rewarded the fisherman by saving the little girl's life by rewarding him with a brand new fishing net.

Gareth Doyle (8)
St Anne's Primary School, Belfast

BEYOND THE BOOKCASE

Sophie went to the woods to visit her granny. She loved to explore her granny's house. She went upstairs into the library and she got a book out. Then suddenly the bookcase opened and she saw a secret passage. She went down the steps and she came to a playroom. She met two elves and they showed Sophie around the place. She stayed overnight.

She woke up the next morning in her own bed. 'They brought me back home,' said Sophie.
Mum said, 'What are you talking about?' Sophie explained about going behind the bookcase in Granny's house yesterday and meeting the two elves. Mum said 'It must have been a dream as you weren't at your granny's yesterday!'

Sophie Webb (8)
St Anne's Primary School, Belfast

BEYOND THE BOOKCASE

It was Saturday. I had just moved into my new house. I loved the old library. I went to lift a book. The bookcase swung open. There were stone steps leading down to a dark secret tunnel. I walked down the steps feeling very scared but excited.

The end of the passageway seemed to take me back in time. I was in a palace. I heard someone coming so I hid. It was Bloody Mary, who my cousin had told me about. I fell backwards in shock and she saw me.

I ran for my life but I ran into two guards, somehow I got away from them. They chased me but I hid behind a bush to get my breath back. Then Bloody Mary came up behind me and grabbed me. I started screaming!

I then woke up with my mum saying that it was only a dream.

Sinead Molloy (8)
St Anne's Primary School, Belfast

A DAY IN THE LIFE OF A BALLERINA

I was walking to my classes. Ballet classes. Yes, I go to ballet classes. I'm good at it. My name's Jessica but everyone calls me Jess. My mum's called Sarah. My dad's called Jon. I have an older brother called John. We live in a bungalow. My room's painted light purple with photos, pictures, posters of ballerinas.

Well, anyway, I was walking to ballet classes. I was excited because there was going to be a surprise, Miss McCooe had told us last Thursday. My friends and I had been talking about it ever since. I quickly got dressed and ran out. Miss McCooe told us that a ballet company was in town and were going to pick a few of us for Corps de Ballet. I was really excited.

When I got home I told Mum all about it. 'Do you think they'll pick me?' I asked.
'I don't know,' my mum said.

Next Thursday, they were there. They were holding auditions. 'Everyone gets a chance,' they said. Finally my name got called, 'Jessica Blair,' they called.

I was nervous but I went. I started my performance. I talked to myself, 'Keep that leg straight! Keep smiling! Don't worry!' They said it was brilliant. I told Mum all about it. She said it didn't matter really.

I went back the following Thursday. They said they had a list and would read it out later. At the end of class they read out the list of names of those who would go through, 'Rebecca Richards and Jessica Blair!' they said.

I was in the Corps de Ballet!

Catherine McFall (9)
St Anne's Primary School, Belfast

A DAY IN THE LIFE OF MY FRIEND, SARAH

One day when Sarah was doing maths, she asked me what to do.
I said, 'Go and ask the teacher what to do.'
So Sarah went up and asked the teacher what to do. The teacher said to go and sit down and he would do another sum on the board. Sarah sat down and Mr McCooe did a sum on the board. The sum was 2.7+1.3. Mr McCooe asked Sarah to go up and do the sum on the board. Once Sarah got the answer, everyone clapped because they knew she'd got the right answer. Mr McCooe asked Sarah if she knew what to do then. Sarah said, 'Yes.' Sarah sat down and did her work for 15 minutes.

Once the bell rang for break time everyone went out and played 'chase'. Sarah was 'it' and chased everyone. The first one she caught was Ross. Ross then chased everyone but then he started chasing after me but just before he got me the bell rang, then he caught me.

Once we got into class Sarah got out her custard creams for her break. Once she had finished her break she got straight to work. In five minutes Sarah had her maths done. Sarah went up and asked Mr McCooe if he would mark her work. Sarah gave Mr McCooe her maths book. Mr McCooe told Sarah to sit down until he had finished marking it. Sarah sat down and did some religion because everyone else was doing it. Sarah had done 2 minutes of religion when Mr McCooe called her up to get her book back.

After 5 minutes Sarah felt suddenly sick so she told Mr McCooe who rang Sarah's mum and she came and took her home.

Tara Rouse (9)
St Anne's Primary School, Belfast

A DAY IN THE LIFE OF . . .

A day in the life of Bilbo Baggins . . . he is a hobbit - a very small creature. They are only about three feet 10 inches tall, have curly hair and pointy ears. They don't wear shoes. They have big hairy feet which are not flesh, they are made of leather. They live in a hole. Not a wet, smelly hole with worms and beetles in. The holes they live in are their homes. Their homes are a bit like ours, only their doors and doorways are round and they have far more rooms - at least two living rooms, two bedrooms, two kitchens and one study room.

A day in the life of Bilbo Baggins would be peaceful, walking about the lovely Shire, smoking a pipe.

I think it would be like this - I got up at about 8.30, got dressed then went into the kitchen, made bacon and eggs, had a cup of tea and some buns.

After breakfast I went outside and sat reading the newspaper after looking at the sights.

After reading the newspaper I went walking about the lovely hills of he Shire. I could see other hobbits playing. I could see the trees blowing I the wind. I went to the edge of Hobbitton and sat, taking a break.

Then I got up, walked over to the bridge into Hardbottle and had a smoke of my pipe (using the tobacco in my pocket.) I walked through Hardbottle feeling the lovely spring air blowing in my face. I looked and saw people planting, farming, drinking and playing chess.

I went back to the house, sat on the sofa looking at my map from the hobbit story.

After looking at it I put down and fell asleep. When I woke up it was supper time. I put on the kettle and made some toast. After that I went to sleep again.

And that is a day in the life of Bilbo Baggins.

Thomas McKeown (9)
St Anne's Primary School, Belfast

A DAY IN THE LIFE OF DAVID BECKHAM

My name is David Beckham, also known as Golden Balls. In a match there is only one thing on my mind, to hit the target and to have power in it. In the summer most of all I worry about being transferred. It is very hard this year because there are a lot of good teams that want me like AC Milan, Real Madrid, Barcelona - all of those are good teams.

My wife Victoria, also known as Posh Spice, says, 'I want to go to the sun!' Most of the time she is sitting in the rain watching me playing a game of football, but if I was to move to Italy or Spain she would always be in the sun or sitting in a romantic restaurant watching me playing on a TV. If I was to move to a Spanish or an Italian team, my ambition would be to have the number seven shirt but I would never be able to take Luis Figo's place.

I change my hairstyle nearly every month. I like my Mohican because I was always very warm in a World Cup match - it kept me very cool. I liked it when it was longer because it usually rained in England.

My second favourite bit of my house is what is in the garage - my beast, the Ferrari. It is hardly ever driven but it is nice to have it to show off to people that come round to my house. My gym is the best thing in my house. I work-out there to pump up my muscles.

It is time for my bed now. Night-night, sleep tight. Don't let bugs bite.

Brendan Haughey (9)
St Anne's Primary School, Belfast

A Day In The Life Of A Victorian Girl

'Wake up Molly,' the housemaid snaps.

Well, we have visitors, what a surprise! Today is a most exciting day, but first let me introduce myself. My name is Molly Crochet and I'm 10 today. I have a brother called Edward who is 12 and who I adore.

Let me tell you where I live. I live in a most splendid house by the park and during the first few weeks of holidays, which starts today, we go to our holiday house by the seaside.

Today we are going to piano at 2 o'clock and dance class at 6 o'clock. We are also going to our holiday house at 7 o'clock this evening.

Now it's time for breakfast. Cookie has made a beautiful fry-up with toast, boiled eggs, a piece of bacon and a glass of milk.
'Out of the house right this minute!' the housekeeper roars. 'Come on Edward. Hurry up.'

Just around half-past 12, Edward and I meet our best friends at the park. Our best friends are so wonderful, their names are Laura and Louise. I like Louise more.

First we went to the old tyre and have lots of fun.
'Oh, I've got to go to piano lesson at 2 o'clock, bye.'
'Come on, get inside or the dogs will get you,' Nanny says sharply.

'How was piano children?' Mother calls.
'Great Mother, but Molly got her fingers closed in the piano lid.'
'Oh darling, are you alright?'
'Yes Mama!'

Later on we go to dance class which is okay. I do the tango with Tommy Brown, my dream boy!

I'm so excited. We are going to the holiday house by the seaside in five minutes. We will pack our bags and jump into the carriage and in two hours we will be there.

'Molly, Edward, wake up, we're here!' Papa whispers.

So the young Victorian had the best 10th birthday ever!

Deirbhile Carson (9)
St Anne's Primary School, Belfast

MY FATHER GOT KIDNAPPED

James was washing the dishes. It was nine o'clock. He was going upstairs when he heard a knock on the door. He looked through the peephole and saw 15 men. He knew what the men wanted. James had a map, it showed you where to find gold. James was planning to go and dig for it, so he did not answer the door. Soon they got fed up and busted down the door. They found James and his map. They brought him to the castle and locked him in the dungeon.

The Next Day

James's son, aged 23, was going to visit his father. When he arrived he saw the smashed windows and there was also a note saying, *Help! I am a prisoner. I am in the top of the castle.*

Alex went to the castle and saw two guards and asked them if he could talk to the king. However, they knew he was trying to save James, so they pulled a lever and he fell through a trapdoor. He then felt himself fall into the dungeon. He saw his father in the dungeon, but they discovered a way out, got the map back and escaped home.

The next day they dug for gold.

James Smyth (8)
St Anne's Primary School, Belfast

HALLOWE'EN NIGHT

One night me and my friend, Amy, went out trick or treating on Hallowe'en. We were going to call on all our neighbours in the street. We dressed up as two princesses. Each house gave us sweets or money. Some bad boys dressed up as monsters and started to chase us.

Then the fireworks started. We were scared by the loud noises. We started running. We saw a big ghost hanging outside a door. We started screaming. We thought someone was still following us but there was nobody there. The boys were gone.

We started to laugh. When we got home we counted our money and ate our sweets. We'd had a great night.

Caoimhe McLaughlin (7)
St Anne's Primary School, Belfast

THE CONCERT

It was Saturday 22nd June 2002. This was the day of the Westlife concert. My mum had bought tickets ages ago. I was very excited. I went to the concert with my best friend, Clare, by taxi. The taxi came to my house and took me and Clare to the Odyssey Arena. Westlife are my favourite pop group.

Before the concert started. We bought Westlife T-shirts, Westlife hats and light-up wands. We even bought popcorn. Then we sat down in our seats. We were in the very front row. We had a great view.

When the lights went off everyone cheered. We put on our light-up wands and waved them in the darkness. After the support bands had finished Westlife came on. The Westlife fellows looked cute in their costumes. We sang along to all their songs. We loved the concert - Westlife were class.

When we got home we thought it was the best day of our life.

Aoife McGettigan (8)
St Anne's Primary School, Belfast

THE SECRET CAVE

Sam and Aoife Henderson moved to an old, abandoned house. It was near Black Beach. Their mum and dad were busy unpacking. Aoife and Sam took Ben, their dog, for a walk along the beach. They spent all morning exploring and they found a secret cave.

In the cave Ben began to bark. The children ran over. They found torches and what looked like treasure. They ran home and told their mum and dad who called the police.

When the children went to bed, the police caught the thieves.

The next day Sam and Aoife got a reward. Ben got some doggy treats and they got their photograph in the paper. They were heroes!

Donal Rooney (8)
St Anne's Primary School, Belfast

THE SECRET TREASURE

One day my friends David, Matthew and I were out for a walk on a beach. We decided to go and find some shells for our collection. *Suddenly* we all disappeared. We fell into a great dark hole.

After a while our eyes got used to the dark and I found a path. It led to a door. In a corner we saw three skulls. David thought we should turn back, but we couldn't, it was the only way out.
'But we just have to go on,' said Matthew.

We went into the room that the door led to. It was very quiet. Then a huge scorpion jumped up from the ground and threw three swords at us - we just missed them. Matthew sliced its legs off with a big whack. David cut its arms off and I threw my sword at its neck.

After we killed it, two lights appeared and made a chest appear with some type of power. A key was floating above it. We opened the chest. There was bright, shining gold. The treasure glittered in our eyes. David stepped on a switch that made stairs come up underground. The stairs led us out of the cavern. We were all gobsmacked and rich!

Conor Pelan (8)
St Anne's Primary School, Belfast

ABOUT A BOY

One cold winter's day Oliver's mum and dad went out. The door opened and a dark figure came in. It was his babysitter. His babysitter treated him like a slave. Oliver thought to himself, *I wish mum and dad were here.*

One night he got his chance. He jumped out the window. 'I'm free,' he said. Oliver headed into town. It was a few miles away. He caught a lift on a truck full of cabbages. Oliver jumped off in the centre of London. He found a friend, Brian.

Oliver and Brian became good friends. They went to visit the Prime Minister, Tony Blair. Oliver and Brian walked quite far. It started to snow. Brian and Oliver ran for shelter. Do you know who he saw? His mum and dad! They went home and threw the babysitter out.

Clare Crossan (8)
St Anne's Primary School, Belfast

UNICORN ISLAND

'Unicorn Island is real!'
'No it isn't.'
'It is too Deborah!'

Alex and Deborah were sisters. They had a fight over nearly every single thing that there was to fight about. Alex had claimed Unicorn Island, her fantasy world, was real.

Soon they forgot all about it and went out for their picnic. The minute they sat on the rug it zoomed into the air. When it landed Alex and Deborah were in another world. 'We're at Unicorn Island,' said Alex.
'Don't be ridiculous.' But they were on Unicorn Island. 'It is true. This is really here,' said Deborah.
'What's that?' said Alex.
A unicorn had just raced through the trees. It was a white and silver unicorn.
'It's so beautiful,' said Alex.
'I agree,' said Deborah.

Bang!
'What?' said Alex. She was home in bed, but in her hand she held a silver horn.

'It was true,' said Alex. 'Unicorn Island, I was there.'

Sarah Morgan (8)
St Anne's Primary School, Belfast

My Great Idea

I was walking in town when I passed a Timeshifter factory. It was a newly constructed factory and it had a large poster advertising Trocaire on the side. I felt very sad knowing that the children in the poor countries were hungry and thirsty. Then I remembered the Timeshifter Change.

All Timeshifters are born from fertilised eggs. They each have their own special power. The Timeshifter Change has the power to shoot money out of his back when fed with spaghetti and is shaped like a purse.

I walked into the factory and bought the Timeshifter Change, as I had some money in my pocket. I brought Change home and fed him lunch, and lots of money shot out of his back. I donated the money to Trocaire. It had been a good day.

Eoghan Ryan (8)
St Anne's Primary School, Belfast

Jaws

Once upon a time there was a little girl called Jenny and a little boy called Eric, they were twins. One day they asked their dad if they could go fishing in their new raft boat. 'Yes, when do you want to go?' said their dad happily.

'Can we go now?' said the twins.

'Yes,' he said. So they went out in their new raft boat.

'This is amazing,' they said.

'Then we will get it out in the water,' Dad said.

They set off. They sailed the boat into the distance and took the fishing rod out.

A few minutes later the rod was getting heavier and heavier. Suddenly their dad was falling off the boat. He shouted, 'Pull my legs up!' So they pulled their dad's legs up, but they started to fall as well. Everything was seriously getting out of hand. They were falling even more.

Suddenly the raft boat tumbled over. The next minute they were in the water. Their dad was still holding onto the rod. He saw that there was a shark with sharp white teeth - it didn't look friendly at all. They swam as fast as they could but they couldn't get to shore. The shark was getting closer and closer and *snap!* They were dead and the water was the colour of Red Riding Hood's cape.

Natalie Press (9)
St Anne's Primary School, Belfast

THE MAGIC BASKETBALL SNEAKERS

Once there was an orphanage in Belfast. There were 20 children in the orphanage. Some of the children were good and some were bullies. There were three good children, Daniel, Hugh and Chris. Sometimes clothes were sent into the nuns for the children.

One day a coat was brought in. Hugh tried it on. Suddenly a pair of sneakers fell out of the pocket. The sneakers were white with red lines on each side. On the tongue it said MJ. Daniel said, 'Hugh, Chris, do you know who MJ is? Michael Jordan. It can't be Michael Jordan.'

A gang of bullies came by. One of them was called Tom. Tom tried to take the sneakers from him and then Tom got them. He threw the sneakers up onto the electricity line but they got caught on the line.

Later that night Daniel, Hugh and Chris went back out but it was raining. They put on their coats and their welly boots and went out into the rain. When they arrived back at the house the boys could hear the distant rumbling sound of thunder. Daniel climbed the tree closest to the sneakers. There was a sudden flash of lightning. Daniel could see the lightning dance around the sneakers as Chris and Hugh shouted. Daniel found himself flat on his back on the ground. Beside him were the sneakers.

The next day Daniel was sitting on the bench during PE. They were playing basketball when Tom the bully slipped and fell. The teacher called to Daniel, 'Put on your sneakers and come and play for Tom.' Daniel put on the sneakers and had a great game. His team won by 15 points and guess what? Daniel scored them all!

Daniel Lavery (9)
St Anne's Primary School, Belfast

GOING THROUGH THE MIRROR

One morning a girl called Anna woke from her sleep. She got out of bed and pulled on her odd socks and weird jumper. Just as Anna finished dressing, she noticed she couldn't see her reflection in the mirror, but she saw a small town surrounded by creepy woods. Anna put her hand through the mirror and was pulled in. She walked through this strange new world until she came to a small town.

As she walked into the town she noticed people looking at her suspiciously, but one small boy walked towards her. He said, 'Don't go into the woods.' Reluctantly she had to, to get home. Anna walked into the woods. The sun was setting and she was very sleepy. She looked around to see if there was a den to sleep in.

The next morning when she woke she heard crying. There she saw a thing that had frightened everyone - it was a wolf. Anna felt sorry for him. She said, 'Come back to the people, there is nothing to be frightened about.' As they walked towards the town a worm hole opened. Anna thought this might take her home but she didn't want to leave the wolf alone. She asked him to go with her. They jumped into the worm hole. It led them to the land of dragons. They approached a baby dragon who turned into a king dragon. It trapped Anna and put her in a dungeon.

Watch this space for the sequel!

Niamh McDermott (9)
St Anne's Primary School, Belfast

BEYOND THE BOOKCASE

Clara Rosa lived in a cottage in the town. Clara's best friend was called Daisy and she was very, very rich. Daisy rang Clara and invited her to come over. ' Yes,' Clara said.

So Clara set off to Daisy's house. They played hide and seek and Clare was on it. 'I can't find her anywhere,' Clara said, fed up with looking in this large house, so she thought she would read a book. But as she was taking a book out of the bookcase, the bookcase swung open and a secret passage was revealed. There were cobwebs and stone steps in it. Beyond, there was darkness so Clara just went in. As she walked on the stone steps she felt a cold breeze. *It's really dark down here,* she thought. Suddenly in front of her was a mirror. *What is a mirror doing down here?* she thought. Out of the mirror came lightning and forced her into the mirror. She came in another place and she hoped she was back at her home. 'Where am I?' she said.

Boom! She was in a battlefield. 'I think I'm in World War II!' said Clara.'

As she walked on and on she became more and more afraid. She saw lots of bombs falling and suddenly one fell on top of her.

Clara woke up with Mrs June, Mr June and Daisy. 'Are you OK?' said Daisy.
'I am dead,' said Clara.
'You are not dead. The bookcase fell on top of you when you were looking for me,' said Daisy.
'What, I am not really dead?' said Clara.

Christina Sturgeon (7)
St Anne's Primary School, Belfast

BEYOND THE BOOKCASE

Jack was in the library with his class browsing at the books. When they had selected a book everyone lined up. Jack was at the end of the line. He tripped and knocked into the bookcase. It opened and there was a dark passageway full of cobwebs. He walked in and fell on a few steps. He got up and walked down the rest of the passageway.

When he got to the bottom he heard voices and he felt a cold breeze. He saw a ghost and he thought, *oh no, where will I go?*
The ghost said, 'Will you come and play with my friend and me?'
Jack said, 'Yes, I will play with you and your friends.'

They had lots of fun playing games in the Land of Ghosts. They played tag, hide and go seek, and lots of other fun games.

Jack soon realised that it was time to go so he said goodbye and left the Land of Ghosts.

He went up the passageway. He saw a lot of bats and mice on the way. When he got back to the library he saw a calendar and it showed the 18th August 2010. Jack said, 'But I left in 2003 not 2010! But I don't look any different.'

He went out of the library and went to his classroom. His class wasn't there, it was a different class and a different teacher. He went over to a boy and said hello, but he didn't say anything, so he put his hand on the table. His hand went through the table. Then he realised that he had been in the Land of Ghosts for too long and the ghosts had turned him into a ghost, so he decided never to go there again.

Amy Hayes (8)
St Anne's Primary School, Belfast

BEYOND THE BOOKCASE

My class and I were looking forward to going to the Argory. When we got there we went on a tour of the house. I really loved the library. When no one was looking I went to get a book. I saw the one I would like. This book was about a witch and I hoped I would see as real witch so I took the book out and I started to read it. Then I saw a button and I pressed it. The bookcase opened. I looked down and then fell down into an old house where a witch lived. The witch was friendly and she asked me did I want some soup? I said yes and she gave me some of her soup to eat. After that I went back up the passage and out of the bookcase.

When I arrived back in the library my class had gone. I then walked downstairs and is saw my teacher. She said, 'I have been looking for you. Where have you been?'

On the way home on the bus I told her about my adventure.

Sarah Donnelly (8)
St Anne's Primary School, Belfast

THE RESCUE

On a hot summer's day a little girl came home from school early. She was called Eimer. She was unhappy because she got bullied at school. She ran to the bridge and sat on the edge. She saw a man fishing. It was her daddy's friend.

She was looking at her reflection. A car was going very, very fast. She didn't notice and lost her balance and she fell off the bridge.

The man heard a splash in the water and he ran under the bridge. He saw her floating down the river and he dived into the water and saved her. He swam to the bank and took her home.

Her mum and dad were very happy to see her. He got a prize for being a hero.

Ciara Marsden (8)
St Anne's Primary School, Belfast

FLOPPY GETS SAVED

One day it was raining and Floppy the dog fell in the mud and he slipped into the river. There was a plank of wood near so he jumped onto it. The raft sailed down the river. Tom and Sarah were his owners and they were playing guns and pretending to shoot Floppy, but Floppy got scared. Tom and Sarah shouted to Floppy to get off. He headed off towards the waterfall. The wind blew him fast down the river. A fisherman was fishing and Floppy fell into his net. The fisherman said, 'I caught a fish dog.'

The children saw the fisherman with Floppy and the children ran up and thanked the fisherman for saving Floppy.

Clodagh Cooke (8)
St Anne's Primary School, Belfast

BEYOND THE BOOKCASE

I called for my friend on a rainy day and no one answered, so I walked on and I saw a haunted house. The door was locked so I climbed through a window into the library. I lifted a book from the library and the bookcase came flying back. I saw that there was a secret passage.

There were cobwebs and stone steps and there was darkness. I walked in and I met a scary ghost, but he wasn't really that scary, in fact he was a friendly ghost. We talked a lot and played. I was very happy with my new friend, but I said to him that I must go home. I went back up the passageway and pushed the bookcase open.

I left the haunted house and as I walked home I saw a newspaper blowing. I lifted it and the date on it was Monday 2nd May 2003. I said, 'This can't happen because it was only 1st March 1993 yesterday.' I ran into my street but no one knew me and I knew no one.

Marc Gillen (8)
St Anne's Primary School, Belfast

THE FAMILY NEXT DOOR

Do you know about the family that used to live next door? People said they moved but I know what really happened.

It was a dark, cold night and it was raining. The family had been watching a horror movie. When they were going to bed they could hear weird sounds and in the bathroom mirror they could see a ghostly person. The family thought they were seeing things (but they weren't.)

In the middle of the night the family awoke when they heard an eerie sound. On the stairs there stood a ghostly figure of a boy holding a dagger.

The family started to panic and ran into one of the bedrooms. They closed the door and locked it. Meanwhile the ghost was floating towards it with the dagger in his hand. When he reached the bedroom door he floated through it but his dagger could not pass through. The family were petrified and tried to run past the ghost and out the door.

The ghost grabbed the dagger and threw it at the family. The dagger floated towards the family and one by one it stabbed them to death, and as the dagger passed through each member of the family they disintegrated leaving only a pile of dust. It was as if they had never existed.

I know what you are thinking, *how do I know?* I know because I was there, I am the ghost who killed them!

Rouchelle Magee (10)
St Anne's Primary School, Belfast

BEYOND THE BOOKCASE

Catherine, an 18-year-old girl, decided to go to Finaghy Library one day. She arrived near closing time. She was in a hurry and she fell into a bookcase. Catherine saw a secret passage. She decided to go in. Catherine was excited. There were cobwebs and spiders. At the end of the passageway was a forest.

Catherine heard a man crying. She was scared. The man was called Frank. Catherine said, 'What is the matter?'
Frank said, 'I have no friends, I've been here a long time.' He was very sad.
Catherine said, 'You can be my friend.'
Frank said, 'How will we get out?'
Catherine said, 'We will go back through the bookcase and we'll be back in Finaghy Library.'

They were together for a long time. They both fell in love and got married. They had four very noisy children. Catherine and Frank named them Joseph, Megan, Lucy and Jack. They were very happy, but when the children were noisy they were not so happy.

Megan O'Neill (8)
St Anne's Primary School, Belfast

A FOOTBALL MATCH

One glorious day I was walking into a football pitch where Liverpool were playing Arsenal. I'd got free tickets.

Michael Owen got the first goal in the tenth minute. Robert Pires had a great chance but the keeper, Jerzy Dudek, saved it. They then had another chance with Thierry Henry. He hit the post and then Patrick Viera hit it wide. As Emile Heskey was going to take a shot he was fouled and he hurt his shin. He was taken off and replaced by Milan Baros. Danny Murphy stepped up to take the free kick and scored. The final whistle blew and the final score was 2-0 to Liverpool.

Then I went home and got my dinner. After I went out to play football.

Michael White (9)
St Anne's Primary School, Belfast

LACY MACY

A girl called Lacy Macy was at her friend Jennifer's sleepover. There were three girls and three boys. They were getting quite bored so they all decided to play dares. Suddenly they all looked at Lacy. They all decided to dare Lacy to go into the haunted house. Lacy said, 'That house isn't haunted,' and went off feeling fine.

As she entered the haunted house she walked around looking at all the pictures. She finally came to one picture which had a man on a bicycle. He was riding his bicycle in the haunted house. She then got frightened.

Lacy Macy ran back to her friend Jennifer's house as fast as she could and told all of her friends she was frightened. She even told them about the man on the bicycle, but all of her friends said, 'Too bad!'

She sadly walked back to the haunted house in tears of anger. As she entered the haunted house, she walked back to the picture of the man on the bicycle. Everywhere she moved the man looked at her. She lay down and fell asleep. Her friends entered the haunted house The next morning, Lacy's friends heard a loud *bang!*

They looked around and came to one picture which had Lacy on the bicycle. Her friends were feeling really bad with themselves.

Everyone ended up talking about her. Lacy's mum never ever talked to the children again!

Niamh McAuley (9)
St Anne's Primary School, Belfast

THE DARK HOUSE

There was once a girl called Linda. One day Linda went past the dark house. Then she saw something move, but she didn't care what it was. Then, that night when she went in, she saw something come out behind her. The man was in black. Six people followed him around the corner. The next morning Linda went outside and she went into the dark house.

It was dark, but something moved behind her and the door closed. She went further in. There were spider webs on her and bugs. Then she heard a noise. It said, 'Come closer, Linda.' So then she went closer. It had weird drawings on the walls and dead people. She found a book and it said how to bring the dead back to life. It was scary.

So she read it all. Everything started to move, then Linda ran back to the door, but it was stuck. She could hear the dead. They were coming closer, so Linda burst down the door. They got her and Linda was gone. Linda's mum and dad called the police. Linda's mum was scared and she started to cry and thought how the people in the black house had killed Linda.

So never go near the dark house 804, or else they will get you.

Deborah Magee (9)
St Anne's Primary School, Belfast

THE BIG MATCH

One day I entered a competition. I won the competition. The prizes were two tickets to see Liverpool Vs Manchester United.

It was at Anfield, Liverpool's stadium. When we got there, we went in and then got our seats. The match began. It had just started and Liverpool scored within 10 seconds into the match. The crowd went wild.

It stayed like that for the rest of the match. At the end I got Jerzy Dudek. I met other players like Sami Hyypia, Steven Gerrard and Milan Baros. Me and my dad really enjoyed it. My team won.

When I got home, I showed my mum and sister. After that I went round to my friend's house. We started playing football. I showed them where the players had signed.

The next day I told all my friends in school. they were amazed. It was the best day of my life.

Gavin Walshe (8)
St Anne's Primary School, Belfast

A DAY IN THE LIFE OF JOHN

Once, there lived a boy called John. He was nine years old and he had black hair. He had blue eyes and he had big feet and he had big ears. His was really small and had a small nose as well. He was stupid, but he was very sneaky and sly, but most of all he was very nosy about other people's business, because he was always asking, 'Where is he going?' and, 'What is she doing?'

John was also very sly, because once he called for some of his friends and only let a few of them play in the game. John was also disobedient. Once, he did not go in when his mum told him to. He was a bully to people that were younger than him and he said that he was the best footballer in the street and if anyone said they were better, then he would hit them.

When John was angry he would bite his lip and if anyone saw him biting his lip, they would run away, because if anyone stayed they would get very badly hurt. He expected people to laugh, even when he was not funny.

It was a pity that John was like that, because he had no friends. If he was a much nicer person, he would have had lots of friends. Maybe he wouldn't have looked so grumpy then.

Tiarnán McKenna (8)
St Anne's Primary School, Belfast

THE CAT'S ADVENTURE

Once upon a time, there lived a woman called Amy. She had a bird table in her garden where her two favourite birds came to eat every day.

A stray cat saw the birds eating as he peeked over the hedge. He sneaked over to the birds, but Amy was washing the dishes and saw the stray cat. She ran into the house, snapped up her broom and chased the cat away.

Jack McFeely
St Anne's Primary School, Belfast

THE RESCUE

On a summer day, a little girl was walking along a bridge. A robber came along, driving a stolen car. He was driving so fast, that the little girl fell into the river.

A fisherman fishing in the river dived in and saved her. He carried her out of the water and brought her home. Her mummy and daddy were very happy, so they told the mayor. The mayor rewarded him with a fishing rod.

Niall Flynn (8)
St Anne's Primary School, Belfast

A MAGIC SURPRISE

There was once a girl called Christina. She woke up one morning and went downstairs. When Christina got downstairs the postman came. The postman knocked on the door. He had a big present for Christina. Christina answered the door and the postman gave Christina the present.

When Christina took the present, she looked at it. It had a wrapper on it. The wrapper was light blue like her eyes and with yellow stars on it.

The corner of the wrapper had Christina's name on it. Christina was really excited when she saw her name.

She opened the present as fast as she could. When she was opening the present, her hands were shaking. Christina opened the present and shouted, *'It's a magic wand!'*
She shouted so loud, that she woke the whole house up.

Two weeks later . . .
Christina told her mummy that her wand wouldn't work, so Christina shouted, *'I want my wand back!'*
Christina's mum said, 'You never will.'

Jennifer McMahon (9)
St Anne's Primary School, Belfast

THE DEATH DAY

One day, my friends Grainne, Christina, Karla and I went to the park. We are all best friends. Christina had a goldfish, Karla had a cat. I had a budgie. We were all 10 years old. Grainne was coming over to my house and I was so excited. We always went to the park after our homework, but this day was different. This day was the Death Day!

After half an hour of fun, we all went home. Grainne was, of course, coming with me. We baked buns and then we took three of them to the cinema to see 'Seeing Double' from S Club. It was great. then we went home and had a pizza. Then we played with my budgie, Bluebell. We phoned Karla and Christina, but nobody answered, so we assumed that they were out.

Me and Grainne went to the park, while my mummy went out shopping and my daddy was at work. Suddenly, Grainne got a phone call on her mobile. It was her mummy calling to tell Grainne that her little sister, Ruby, had died!

Grainne started to cry, so we went home. As soon as we got home, we got a phone call from Karla, calling to tell us that her cat and Christina's goldfish were dead! I ran to see if my budgie was dead and he was! I ran to my room crying, because I was so upset and Grainne was trailing behind me.

Caoimhe Bradley (9)
St Anne's Primary School, Belfast

THE HORRIBLE GHOST

One night, some boys named Gary, Dennis and twins named George and Henry, were all at a camp for boys. Every night Dennis told ghost stories, but the one he told that night was different, because it came true. The story was about a ghost. As I said, it came true and the ghost just appeared right in front of their eyes. The ghost looked weak, but was very powerful. No one ran away, because they were not afraid.

Gary spoke, 'You must be weaker than a baby.'
The ghost started laughing and said, 'Yeah, right! I'm more powerful than the strongest man in the world!'
Swish! The ghost vanished in mid-air.

The next morning . . .
'Arrgghh!' Henry screamed.
All their noses were gone!
'Oh no!' George cried, shivering, 'Gary shouldn't have said that ghost was weak. I think the ghost did this to us!'
'That ghost is powerful! Gary, look what you've done to us!' cried Dennis.
'Well, it wouldn't have happened if you hadn't told that story,' shouted Gary.
They spend the whole day arguing.

The next morning, their noses were back, but the ghost was waiting there for them to wake up. Then, when they woke up they were afraid this time, because they knew the ghost was powerful.
Gary said, 'I'm sorry I called you weak, really I am.'
'*Hmm,*' the ghost murmured, 'tell you what, if you be friends with me, I'll leave you alone.'
The boys decided they would be friends.

John-James Loughran (9)
St Anne's Primary School, Belfast

The Woods

One day, there were two children called Dean and Claire. They went to the dark woods. The children saw trees moving in the dark shadows. Dean and Claire heard lots of rustling in the trees. They walked fast, but they tripped over a thick log. They were very frightened. Then the two children tried to find a way to get out of the dark woods.

Dean and Claire saw bright sunshine and they walked towards the sunshine and got out of the shadowy and dark woods. They went home and told their parents all about it and they never went into the woods again.

Dean and Claire found out what was in the trees. It was three little kittens.

Niamh Parker (8)
St Anne's Primary School, Belfast

ME IN AN ALIEN WORLD

One day, I was out having a water fight with my friends. I went in to get changed, by myself. My mum was away on holiday. The house seemed strange. I opened a cupboard and got pulled in. I was spinning around in a big pool. It was not summer, it was winter and it was cold and blustery. I heard something bleeping. It was a big green alien.

He came over and said, 'What are you doing here? You are not an alien. You are not a pupil.'
I said, 'I know. Don't hurt me.'

I opened my cupboard and got pulled in. Then I saw a huge green door, covered in slime. I opened it and to my relief I was back in my room, safe and sound, or was I?

What was that bleeping sound underneath my bed?

Gemma Dempster (9)
St Anne's Primary School, Belfast

UNDER THE SEA

There was once a beautiful young girl, with long blonde hair, called Amy. For as long as she could remember, she had wanted to be the best swimmer in the world. As a baby, her mum said that every time she had a bath, she would try and swim under the water.

One time, Amy and her family went on holiday to Portugal. On a nice sunny day, they came across a wonderful, white, sandy beach and a lovely, clear, blue sea. Her mum and dad sunbathed and her young brother made huge sandcastles, while Amy went for a swim. It wasn't long before she noticed something shiny at the bottom.

As she swam deeper, the light got brighter and there, in front of her, were millions of sea creatures, of all different shapes, sizes and colours. There were sea horses, starfish, dolphins, sea urchins, sharks and beautiful mermaids and lots of colourful, tropical fish.

Time passed, when she noticed a strange shadow behind her, she turned around and saw this ugly-looking creature with two heads, twenty legs and one eye.

She swam to the surface to get away. She popped her head out of the water and called her family, but she noticed that the beach was clear. The creature grabbed her leg and started pulling her back into the water, as she screamed, she felt someone shake her. She woke suddenly and realised it was all a dream, because she was still in her bed.

Hannah Hughes (9)
St Anne's Primary School, Belfast

A GHOSTLY GIRL

One hot summer's day, a girl was playing outside my garden. I ran out to say, 'Hi,' because I haven't got many friends. She seemed very nice and offered to be my friend.

Next day at school, she was with another group of girls. They were looking at me strangely. When I got home, she came to my garden again. I told my parents about her going off and leaving me.

My mum came to the door to find out what was going on, but when she came out, she couldn't see her. I could see her, but she couldn't.
'Now Andrea, are you making this up for some attention, because I'm not cross with you?'
'No Mum, there she is. Can you not see her?'

When I went to bed that night, I realised it was a doppelgänger.

Rachel Rogan (9)
St Anne's Primary School, Belfast

THE HOUSE OF DOOM

One spooky night, there was a young girl walking her dog. The girl was called Hannah and her dog was called Spotty. She decided that she should go for a walk in the woods for a change. There were lots of scary noises in the woods. Spotty stayed very close to Hannah, because he was scared, but Hannah wasn't.

After she had walked through the woods, she saw a very old house. She had never seen the house before in her life. So she went into the old house. When she walked in, the door slammed shut behind her. She ran to the door and pulled the handle, but it would not open. She was trapped.

Suddenly, she saw a shining figure coming towards her - it was a knife floating in mid-air and it was chasing her! The she ran to the kitchen door and locked it. When she turned around, she saw a werewolf standing there, his mouth dribbling with hunger.

She picked Spotty up and ran out the door and did not stop running until she got home. When she got home, she told her mum the whole story.

Kerri Magee (9)
St Anne's Primary School, Belfast

The Shadowy Gunman

One day, Alex McCluskey from Mortemor Street, was walking home from school. It was hailstoning hard. Alex thought Friday afternoon wouldn't have been such bad weather. When Alex got home, he couldn't find his mum or his sister.

Alex went into the front room and started to watch TV. Suddenly, he was taken aback by the man who had just stepped out of the shadows, accentuating his words with a Swedish accent, he said, 'Hello, vould you like to come vis me?'
Then he shot Alex with a stun dart.

When Alex woke up, he was lying down on a wooden board, in what seemed like a completely sealed room, but then, when he looked up, he found a trapdoor leading up the way. the room was so big, that even if he stood on his bed, he wouldn't be able to reach the trapdoor.

Just then, he noticed there were two other beds in the room, one with his sister, who was 13 and one with his mum, but he didn't know what age she was. Alex jumped down and went to wake them up, but they were already awake. The both stood up simultaneously and made a plan.

Alex's plan seemed to be the best idea, so they used it. They all started to pile the chairs up on top of each other. When they were finished, Alex climbed to the top of them and popped the trapdoor open, he climbed out. Freedom!

Donal Murray (9)
St Anne's Primary School, Belfast

A Day In The Life Of Mungo

Once upon a time, there lived a monster, but not like any other kind of monster. This monster was small and skinny. He had green hair and blue-coloured skin. He had three purple eyes and six arms. His name was Mungo the Monster.

Mungo was a very happy monster, he was very cheerful and always smiling and he was kind and caring to other monsters. But other monsters were not kind or caring to Mungo. None of the other monsters would play with Mungo.

At monster school, Mrs Honey was a lovely teacher, who felt sad for Mungo. She kept trying to make other monsters like Mungo, but they just called him a baby monster, as he cried every time they would not let him play in their games.

A new girl joined the class and she was called Muffy. Muffy was only a very teeny weeny monster and she was only able to catch up with Mungo, at any of the games. Muffy and Mungo became close chums and they began to have lots of fun time together. All the other monsters began talking to them and soon Muffy and Mungo had lots of friends in their school, High Hill Primary School.

Meadhbh Walsh (8)
St Anne's Primary School, Belfast

A Day In A Life Of A Witch

Once upon a time, there was a witch and she was called the Queen of Ugliness. She was mean and nasty and horrible. She had loads of enemies. Most of her enemies were beautiful and kind and gentle. She hated those people the most. There was one person that the witch despised, and her name was Miss Perfect. Everyone loved Miss Perfect. Everyone except the Queen of Ugliness.

The Queen of Ugliness was in her ugly castle, sitting in her ugly chair. The Queen of Ugliness said in a not so pleasant voice, 'How can I annoy Miss Perfect? I know, I'll give her the chickenpox. No. That's not a good idea. I know. I'll cast an evil spell on her.'

The next day, when Miss Perfect woke up, she was butt-ugly! 'Oh no! What's happened to me? I have to go to the police.'
When Miss Perfect told the police, they looked and they said, 'We know, it was the Queen of Ugliness, she did this to you. Let's go to her spooky castle.'

When they got there, they knocked at the big door.
'Who's there?'
'It's us, the police.'
'Come in. Have a seat.'
The policemen looked at each other and they said, 'You're under arrest for turning this beautiful woman into a witch.'

Then the police put the witch in jail and Miss Perfect bought the castle and turned it into a dream palace. And she lived happily ever after.

Melissa McComish (8)
St Anne's Primary School, Belfast

BEYOND THE BOOKCASE

I had just moved to a new house, but it was an old house, In this house, there stood a bookcase in the library. I went into the library and threw a ball against the bookcase and suddenly, it swung open. It revealed a secret passageway. I decided to go down it. It was very dark down the tunnel, but there was a bit of light at the bottom. When I arrived at the bottom, I was in a battlefield.

There were lots of noisy helicopters and bombs dropping and people getting shot. I felt frightened. I saw a shelter, so I went into it. I saw a door, so I walked over to it, but a man shouted,
'Stop! You're a spy!'
He put a gun to my head.
I shouted, 'Please, please, don't shoot me, I don't want to die.'

I woke up screaming. My mum put her hand on my head and said, 'It's OK, it was just a nightmare.'

James McComish (8)
St Anne's Primary School, Belfast

THE FRIENDLY GHOST

Once upon a time, there was a boy called Tom, who was nine-years-old and his sister called Mary, who was seven-years-old. They were moving house with their mum and dad, to a big mansion in the country. The mansion is very, very old and sat on top of a hill, in its own land. There were no neighbours for miles around.

When they arrived at the mansion, Tom and Mary looked at the house and said to each other, 'Oh my goodness! What a big house, what a very big house, we could get lost in that house!'

On the first night they stayed in the house, they were sent to bed quite late. It was very dark and spooky. There were allowed to stay in the same room, because they were a little scared. As they lay in bed, they heard a little voice saying, 'Will you be my friend?'
Mary and Tom both went screaming into their mum and dad's bedroom. They said, 'Don't be silly children, you must have been dreaming, go back to bed.'

Tom and Mary went back to their bedroom, but they were not dreaming. They both got into Tom's bed and held each other's hand.
Again the voice said, 'Can I be your friend? Don't be frightened.'
Tom said, 'Who are you? What are you doing in our new house?'
The little voice said, 'I am Jasper, the friendly ghost. I would really like to have some friends to play with, will you be my new friends?'
They looked at each other and said, 'Yes.'

Mark Fitzsimmons (9)
St Anne's Primary School, Belfast

ALIENS

On Earth, there are lots of people who want to go to Pluto. On Pluto, there are lots of aliens who want to go to Earth. This story is about space.

One day, there was a girl called Becky. On Pluto, there was an alien called Zark. They both wanted to make spaceships and they did.

Becky was filling up her spaceship with fuel. Zark was filling his spaceship with fuel too. They both got into their spaceships and took off to Pluto and Earth.

When they were half-way there, they both crashed. Both children were floating in outer space and very slowly, they disappeared.

Caitilin Greig (9)
St Anne's Primary School, Belfast

LOST MEN I

One day, two men were in the jungle. They saw something moving in the bushes. They followed it deeper and deeper into the jungle, crossing rivers and trees, until it disappeared. Daniel decided to set up camp.

'Good idea,' said AJ, 'I'll get the food and you get the water.'

They split up to find what they needed. AJ took a rifle and walked stealthily, like a cat stalking its prey. AJ saw something moving. He crept up, he pulled back the green leaves, but it was a lizard. Then something struck his back at great speed. He was getting up, when he came face to face with a wild boar. It went for another strike, but AJ dodged it. Quickly he ran for his rifle, the boar dived at him, but he shot it in the heart.

AJ trailed the wild boar back to camp, then he heard Daniel shouting for help.

Niall Gallagher (9)
St Anne's Primary School, Belfast

Bob the Fish

My name is Bob the fish. I live in a big blue ocean. I swim with my friends every day. My best friends are Jimmy the jellyfish and Sally the seahorse. We sometimes play hide-and-seek. I always hide in the seaweed.

One day a big boat sailed by and caught me in a net. I was taken on board the boat and put inside a big glass bowl. Every day children would come and have a look at me, as I swam round and round. They fed me fish food and I didn't like it. I would rather be out in the deep blue sea with all my friends. Maybe the captain will throw me overboard and I will be free to swim back to my family.

Declan Ferguson (9)
St Anne's Primary School, Belfast

CAUGHT IN AN AIR RAID

I can hear wailing sirens as I run down the street. Deadly bombers fly overhead, I jump into a bunker to find my family, wounded. They are sitting in a corner, weeping mournfully. I can hear the killer bombers fly past and then a dangerous explosion very near and I think it hit the old church.

The sounds of rushing uncontrollable fire engines are in my ears. Frightened people are screaming helplessly on the streets, yelling, 'The bombers are coming this way!'
I look around me, frightened people sit listening tensely to the sounds in the streets and sky.

All of a sudden, it became quiet, people cheered as the all clear rang. They cheered as they emerged from the bunkers; as soon as they saw the streets, it went quiet. There were people lying on the streets, dead. Almost every building was on fire. Fire engines were doing their best to fight the blazing fires. The people immediately started to help bring out water from the houses that had not been touched. The water was still running. The people were suffering from shock and depression, to see their family's dead and some wounded. Most of the buildings were totally ruined.

Four terrible weeks later, they were still not finished rebuilding, when those feared sirens rang. Again . . .

Paul Mogey (11)
St Anne's Primary School, Belfast

THE FIGHT OF ALEX AND JESS

Alex and me have been best friends ever since I can remember, but one day we had a *massive* fight. I had borrowed Alex's notebook without asking, but it was really her *diary!* (There was some rude stuff, like bad words, so I won't write it.)

I was walking up the street when Alex stopped me.
'Oh look,' she said, 'the diary reader! What *will* she read next?'
'I didn't know it was your diary,' I replied, 'if I did, I wouldn't have read it!'
'Right,' Alex said, sarcastically, 'you just happened to find my book, thinking it was okay to take it! Why do you think it had a lock?'

Oops, the piece I didn't tell you. The lock.
'But . . .' I said, 'I had the same key as yours. And I read something. You wrote that you want to be Tracy's best friend. Do you hate me?'
'Now I do!' shouted Alex, 'And you, Jess, I shan't be your best friend anymore!'
My eyes went watery, but I never cry . . . I'm as tough as old boots! I'll show her!
'See if I care!' I shouted back, 'But you don't have a best friend! Who will it be?'
'Tracy!' said Alex, 'And I bet *she* won't read this!'

I wish I could rewind time, but I can't. I don't even like Tracy, so why should I care? But I *do* care. I like Alex, I want her to be my friend, not Tracy's!

So Alex walked off, leaving me standing there, alone.

Fionnuala McCartan (11)
St Anne's Primary School, Belfast

AN EXTRAORDINARY DAY IN THE LIFE
OF AN ORDINARY FAMILY

Once, there lived a quite ordinary family. Nothing unusual had ever happened to them. They lived out in the country, in an ordinary house, surrounded by an ordinary garden. In the middle of this garden, stood a solitary apple tree. One of the children, John, happened to be playing in the garden one afternoon. Something made him look up at the lower branches of the apple tree. What he saw there, made him stand still in horror. Hanging from a branch, was a huge bag-like spiders' nest, with many hundreds of spiders crawling around it.

'Dad!' screamed John, as he ran towards the house. Moments later, John and his dad, who was carrying a net, came running towards the tree. John's dad was surprised to see such a huge nest so late in the year. 'They probably won't survive the winter. It's best just to leave them alone,' said John's dad.

But the spiders had other ideas. When John's sister, Susan, went to bed that night, she got the shock of her life when she pulled back the bed cover, to see at least 20 huge, glowing tarantulas, crawling about. She used her full lung power to let out an enormous scream. She ran about, pinching herself and throwing bottled water over her face, just to make sure that she wasn't dreaming.

Unfortunately, it wasn't a nightmare. Her scream had alerted her mum and dad, who quickly burst into the room. Her dad gasped and her mum fainted, when they saw the spiders. When her dad touched one of the spiders, it faded away. Quickly, he touched the others, only to see them fade away too.
'This must have something to do with the nest in the apple tree,' said Dad.

Armed with a stick and a torch, he raced to the apple tree, but the bag-like nest was gone.

'Well I never! Ghost spiders,' said Dad.

Suddenly, he felt something crawling up his leg, *inside* his trousers!

Olivia Campbell (8)
St Anne's Primary School, Belfast

THE MOST HAUNTED HOUSE IN AUSTRALIA

My name is Charlie and I am seven-years-old. I have an older brother and two older sisters. We live with our parents in Sydney, Australia.

In the area where we live, I know all the different kinds of birds and wild animals, such as the kangaroos and the koalas, who only eat the leaves from the eucalyptus trees which grow everywhere. There is danger from the red-backed spider, which can hide in your shoe and give you a very nasty bite.

To every child in my neighbourhood, the most terrifying sight is not a dangerous, wild animal, but an old run-down house that no one has lived in as far back as I can remember. Its garden is full of thistles and long grass. The back garden looks more like a forest, with eucalyptus trees growing everywhere. The house itself is really old looking. The windows are cracked. Broken shutters hang down. The paintwork is peeling everywhere.

Why should an old house be so frightening? I have heard stories of people running out of this house, screaming their heads off in complete terror. Stories of a headless man and a crying woman or banshee being seen in the dead of night, are well known in the neighbourhood. The most scary of all the stories, to me anyway, are of two wild-looking horses, with bleeding cuts and flecks of sweat all over their bodies, charging wildly down from the house to the beach. Just as they reach the water, they disappear.

In two days time, I will be eight. I have made a decision to go into the old house on my birthday. I need to know its secret. I will be prepared for anything!

Megan Murphy (8)
St Anne's Primary School, Belfast

A GHOST STORY - THE PIANO

'Kerry! Get up out of bed. We are moving house today,' called her mother, Angela. Her dad, John and her younger sister, Anne, were already up and having breakfast downstairs. Kerry was nine years old and her little sister, only eight months.

Kerry eventually slid down the stairs and sat herself in her usual chair at the breakfast table.

Conversation soon turned to the new home that they would be moving to that day. Kerry had never been to the new house, but she had seen pictures of it. She fired questions at her parents about its rooms - especially hers. She asked about the size of the garden, where she would play.

Soon after breakfast, the removal van arrived and everything was soon loaded up. Last of all, Kerry carried her big box of toys to the back of the van and pushed them in. Now it was time to go!

When they arrived, Kerry was not exactly impressed with what she saw. It certainly wasn't her dream house. It didn't look as pleasing as it did in the photographs that her dad had showed her. It looked much older and . . . strange. But Kerry accepted it. Dad told her that her room was the first room at the top of the stairs.

She hurried up the stairs, but when she got halfway, she suddenly stopped. The sound of a piano came from her room. She moved forward, but much more cautiously. Maybe it had just been her imagination. But no! The sound of the piano was now louder as she approached the door. Fear now gripped her, but she just had to go on.

She twisted the handle on the bedroom door and pushed. Just as the door opened, the music stopped and cold air wafted over her. She didn't see anyone, but she knew that she would be sharing her room with someone else! An invisible friend, or enemy?

Molly Rice (8)
St Anne's Primary School, Belfast

CAUGHT IN AN AIR RAID

July 17th 1944 was the day it all began. It started off as a gloomy day, it was cold and misty. I heard loud planes, then I heard a long siren going through the city, very loudly and clearly. My baby sister came into the bedroom and said, 'We have to get out of here!'
'How?' I asked. 'No, we have to wait for Mum and Dad to come back!' My sister said, 'No, we can't wait for them. We have to get supplies and go to the shelters.'

We ran outside, still hearing the sirens while we were running away. We also heard the sounds of planes flying overhead, dropping bombs quickly and dangerously.

Blood was flowing down the street drains. People were running fast and screaming loudly. Suddenly, I heard and saw buildings falling down on top of people. People were hiding in small shelters, cautiously. They feared losing members of their families and the destruction of their families. Families were hiding underground.

We heard the troops running by, firing bullets at the planes. At that point a second siren rang and we knew it was all over.

Aoife McDonald (11)
St Anne's Primary School, Belfast

THE GHOST

One day, I was walking home with Nathaniel. Nathaniel went to the shop, while I was left behind, walking home by myself.

As I was walking home, taking very small strides, I noticed a very old house, which I had never seen before.

I decided to cross the road to look at it. As I got to the house, I saw a large, snake-like handle which sent a shiver down my spine. I went into the garden, after the side effect from the shiver down my spine was wearing off.

I went into the house's patio and saw an old man running around the back. I called out, 'Who's there?' but nobody answered. I was wondering what the man was doing in this house.

I thought this was enough for one day, so I went home to do my homework, because it was Tuesday.

The next day, Nathaniel set off for school without me. As I was walking along I looked for the house, but it was nowhere to be seen, so I followed my footsteps to where I had come out of the house before, but it wasn't there. In its place, was a big mansion as wide as the length of a bus and taller than a skyscraper.

As I was walking, I was itching to know why it hadn't been there before. I saw the house and I definitely saw a ghost up at the window. I had seen a ghost. I told Nathaniel.

Simon Sweeney (9)
St Anne's Primary School, Belfast

ONE SCARY WALK

When I was walking home from school one day, I heard this noise in the bushes. I was scared and frightened and I walked faster and didn't look back. The noise started to get louder. I was running when it had faded in the spooky woods. Finally, I got to my house feeling frightened and out of breath. I told my mum and dad what had happened and they were shocked.

The next morning I got up from bed and asked my dad if I could have some money for the bus. I'd decided to take the bus from now on.

Just to be safe!

Eamon Parker (9)
St Anne's Primary School, Belfast

A Monster Called Mavis

There once was a monster called Mavis. Now Mavis is not a very pretty monster, well most monsters aren't pretty but even in the monster world Mavis isn't a sight to see. Even her mother who loved her dearly would not say she was a great beauty.

One day Mavis was on the monster website when she came across a poster that dazzled her. It looked something like this.

Mavis read the poster very quickly but the word *talent* sparkled in Mavis's mind. Mavis had signed into the school without informing her mother first.

The next day a parcel arrived for Mavis containing two pink dancing shoes, a tutu and a navy cloak. Mavis squeezed into the tutu, gave up on the shoes and put on the navy cloak for her first day.

When Mavis arrived at the school she stood in line with some other girls.

For the next few days Mavis was a bit of trouble, with a capital T. The teacher was a short-sighted old lady and often asked Mavis why she was wearing flippers in the hall. Mavis was picked to be in a play called The Swan Princess. All the other girls were swans, but Mavis was a flamingo (because of her tallness.)

On the day of the play 200 proud mothers sat in the audience and waited for the music. 'Music please,' shouted the principal. The music started. Mavis pranced onto the stage. 200 mothers headed towards the exit. Mavis tried to pull the curtain but it fell out onto the orchestra. Mavis sighed dramatically. 'I think I'll be a better movie star!'

Grainne McKinney (8)
St Anne's Primary School, Belfast

THE EMPTY ROOM

When I was alive this is what happened. I found myself sitting there on a grey stone beach in dark, dull room. I was starting at a barred window. I had been staring at it for ages so I looked down at the white floor and saw a shadow. Then I heard a scream so I turned my head swiftly and saw a doorway. I stood up and walked slowly towards it. I stopped at the doorway, stuck out my foot and turned into a big grey hall.

All that was there was a door on the right about four or five yards down. I started walking faster than usual down the hall. When I got to the door on the right I found out it was barred up. It was misty when I looked into the room but I heard a whip and someone say, 'Get out while you can!' This time I ran as fast as I could. I saw a high barred up window so there must be an exit but it was a dead end. I heard a footstep coming closer.

My eyes were open but everything was black. I suddenly woke up and I was getting tortured *so get out while you can!*

This is what I wrote just before I died!

Ruari Mulvenna (9)
St Anne's Primary School, Belfast

VICKY, JADE AND THE SHOPPING MALL

Vicky and Jade loved to shop. They would go seven days a week but Vicky only got her money on a Friday so did Jade. One Friday they went to the mall. Vicky saw the top of her dreams. She ran to get it but the shop was closed. 'Oh darn!' shouted Vicky. the top was red with sparkles and a butterfly.

The next day was Saturday. She ran to the mall. The shop was opened. She ran to it but to her surprise the top wasn't there. She ran out and went to Jade's house. She knocked on the door. Jade opened the door. 'Oh Jade,' said Vicky nearly crying, but to her surprise Jade was wearing the top. 'Where did you get that?' said Vicky, a bit angry.
'I got it today in the mall,' Jade said, twirling around to let the whole world see. 'Isn't it fab?' Vicky just walked away. Jade shouted, 'What's the matter?'

On Sunday Vicky went to the shop (a clothes shop.) Vicky saw the top in the glass window. Vicky's eyes lit up. She ran in and bought it. Vicky called for Jade. They said sorry and went to a school disco in their new tops.

Shannon Foster (9)
St Anne's Primary School, Belfast

259

A DAY IN THE LIFE OF POOH BEAR

In the trunk of a very, very tall oak tree there lived a chubby, yellow bear called Winnie the Pooh who had some friends called Tigger, Piglet, Eeyore, Rabbit and Owl.

One day, on the first day of autumn, Pooh Bear got out of bed and went to the window. There he saw a massive pile of leaves at the front door. As he went to dive into the leaves he landed on something very hard. As he cleared away the leaves he found a honey pot. He opened the honey pot and started to eat the sweet, golden honey.

As he ate he noticed a note on the honey pot but since he couldn't read he went to Piglet. Piglet was cooking breakfast and didn't know how to read either, so Pooh Bear went to see Rabbit because he knew he was very, very clever.

On the way to Rabbit's, Pooh Bear met Tigger. Pooh asked Tigger if he could read, so Tigger started to read, this is what he said, 'Boo Pooh, slimy wimey ha ha ha!'
'What does it mean?' asked Pooh.
'I don't know,' said Tigger.
'Let's go to Rabbit.'
Rabbit went the same way as Tigger. This is what he said, 'Boom, boom, ha ha ha.'
'I know who to go to,' said Tigger.
'Who?' said Pooh.
'Owl of course.'
'Owl is the smartest in the world,' said Rabbit.

They went to owl. Owl read the note properly. This is what it said, 'Dear Pooh, I just want to say that I'm moving house. From Eeyore.'

Aisling McLaughlin (9)
St Anne's Primary School, Belfast

A Day In The Life Of Jennifer Lopez

Beep, beep, beep! Beep, beep, beep! I woke up. *Aarrgh!* 6.30, I'm so tired.

'Come on Jenny, wake up, you're shooting your video today!' Sarah said (she's my make-up stylist.) I completely forgot about the video. I'm shooting my new single 'I'm Glad'. I am glad, it's going to be fun. The video is based on the film 'Flashdance'. Katie quickly came into my room to do a quick run over of what I'm doing. Katie is my dance choreographer. She just went over all the hard bits in it. I had to go with Jacqueline to get my clothes ready for the first scene, but when we got there the clothes were gone!

Jacqueline got the other clothes. She was always worrying about things going missing and for once something did go missing. I couldn't believe this, but when I got to the stage the background was gone! 'What's going on Jacqueline?' I asked.
'I know as much as you know Jenny.'

This was getting quite freaky. Well there wasn't any extra backgrounds. They had to cancel the video till Monday - two days from now. couldn't wait that long!

Well Monday arrived . . .

They had found out who had taken the stuff but they wouldn't tell me until after the video.

The video was great. I didn't forget any of the dance moves, Katie had taught me so well.

I couldn't help myself laughing when I heard who had taken the stuff - *Britney Spears.*

Niamh O'Kane (9)
St Anne's Primary School, Belfast

A Day In The Life Of Milan Baros

Milan Baros is a professional footballer who plays for Liverpool. He joined Liverpool in 2002. He is excited because he is playing a match today. He went to a restaurant with the rest of the team. They are playing against Manchester City. Milan Baros is always nervous.

The kick-off is at 3pm at Anfield. He starts as a sub. He is not very happy with Gerard Houllier's decision. The match has started, the crowd cheer with happiness. The half-time score is Manchester City 2, Liverpool 0. Baros is still not happy.

In the second half he is coming on for Emille Heskey. Gerrard lays it on from a corner kick, gets it through to Baros and he scores. The crowd go mad. Liverpool have pulled one back. It's now 2-1 to City. They're coming back. Murphy curls in the free kick. Oh, Joey Barton has fouled Baros. It's a penalty to Liverpool and Joey Barton has got a straight red card, and City are down to ten men. Baros to take, he scores and runs up to the crowd. It's now 2-2.

Now Houllier is happy because he brought Baros on. There is twenty minutes remaining. Manchester City have a corner now. Hyypia has hand-balled it. It's a penalty to City. Dudek has saved it - it was a lovely save. Gerrard has passed to Baros. He's kicked one, now two, three and he's scored. It's a hat-trick for Milan Baros. The referee has blown his whistle. It's all over. Man of the Match, Milan Baros. He will never leave Liverpool now.

Darragh Loughlin (9)
St Anne's Primary School, Belfast

A DAY IN THE LIFE OF SHERLOCK HOLMES

It all began in a forest where a man was walking down the path. Suddenly he got stabbed and died. Later that morning a man called Sherlock Holmes was walking down that same path and saw the dead body and there was something beside it, a gold pin. At nine o'clock he walked to his friend Watson's house and showed him what he'd seen.

Hours later they went to the station and showed the police the pin. They scanned it for fingerprints but there was nothing.

As Sherlock and Watson were walking out of the station the inspector called them back and said there had been a murder. Sherlock and Watson went straight to the scene. It was a dark alleyway outside a main road. At the very back was the victim. As Sherlock looked around he saw a comb and there was a blonde hair in it.

Watson and Sherlock went back to Baker Street to discuss the crime.
Holmes said, 'I must see the wives of those men.'
Watson said, 'I'm right on it.'

Some time later Watson returned and said these men were recently divorced and Holmes said, 'I still need to talk to their wives.'
Watson said, 'They were both married to the same woman . . . !'

They went to the woman's house and banged on the door. A woman answered and her hair matched the blonde hair on the comb. Her earring matched the gold pin, so they arrested her for murder and as they searched her house they found a knife. She was put in jail. Watson and Holmes went back to Baker Street. Watson said, 'Another job well done.'
Sherlock said, 'It's elementary Watson.'

Daniel Barr (9)
St Anne's Primary School, Belfast

A Day In The Life Of ... Mitch

The day I met my owner Sean Webb I was so happy because I had been behind those bars for ages. He took me out quite carefully because I am very young and I get nervous quite a lot. I started to lick him very slowly. He took me to meet his family. Oh, I am really scared, I don't really know what to do.

There they are. They are coming. They are running and charging at me like mad, so big and tall, but soon I found out they're not so bad. I fell asleep in my master's sister Caoimhe's arms. She has such lovely, warm, soft hands. I could really, really get used to this you know. Caoimhe set me down in my small little cage to sleep. Oh yes, so soft and cuddly. By the way, my name is Mitch. If you want to know how I got my name just ask. In fact, I will tell you how. I got my name by Sean's dad because he used to have loads of Jack Russells and he had one which was always left out and his name was Mitch.

OK, well this bed is so soft and I thought I was the cuddly one. Wait a minute, yawn yawn, *snore, snore, snore, boom!* What was that? Oh it's OK, it's just the door. These really strange people came through the kitchen door. Soon I found out they were my cousins and guess what, they have a dog too, but I bet she's not as cute as me.

Well Lucy, my cousin, says that she loves animals but says dogs are the best. She said that I was so cute and wanted to hold me. Caoimhe and Lucy went out to walk me, well it was sort of carrying me. It was a really nice night and we had a lovely breeze going on our faces and once again I fell asleep - asleep dreaming of the days when I am going to have with my family and cousins. Well that was me asleep for the night.

Lucy Torney (9)
St Anne's Primary School, Belfast

A DAY IN THE LIFE OF TWEETY AND JOEY

When Sarah and her family bought me I was very scared. When we were going somewhere it was like an earthquake. When we got home it wasn't so bad because Sarah had bought another bird. I thought she was beautiful. She had yellow feathers with white ones around her mouth, but she wouldn't like me, I am just plain green with some yellow and purple.

The next day I heard Sarah saying to her dad that Tweety was in love with another bird. By the way, my name is Joey. I didn't understand my name at first. I really like Tweety as a name but I couldn't have that name as I am a boy. Anyway, I will tell you a story about what happened to Tweety and me last night.

When Sarah's brother David was playing football outside he kicked the ball too high and hit the cage. The door flew open and the cage hit the ground and now I have a broken wing and it is *very sore* but Tweety will keep me safe because she is very nice to me. Every day Sarah comes to me and talks to me but sometimes she gets angry because I tweet a lot. Her sister gets really angry when she is trying to study and I always tweet and I get shouted at and I squeal, 'No!' although they don't know what I am saying, yippee.

Sarah Maguire (9)
St Anne's Primary School, Belfast

A DAY IN THE LIFE OF MY CAT SOX

I'm in the Dunnganon Cat shop waiting for someone to come and take me away from this horrible place. Suddenly someone comes in. It is a little girl and her mum. They say that they would like a kitten, so the woman takes the lady and the child over to all the other kittens who get the attention and I don't get any.

The little girl is coming towards me. Oh please take me, please. The girl is saying she likes me and wants me. The woman takes me out of the cage and hands me to the girl. She says that she wants me. As she turns around I stick my tongue out at all the other cats and they start purring. I cost £40. I am taken home in a big, big car in a cage. I can't wait till I get home.

A few minutes later we are home. They let me out of my cage and I run to the litter tray to do what I've got to do. I thought I knew the little girl's name, I called her Richel. I felt proud of myself. Richel thought I would like to rest in the chair beside the heat, so I come inside and see a chair with a cushion on it just for me. There is a bowl of food and drink of milk. I lie down and rest. I can't wait till tomorrow morning.

Rachael Flanagan (9)
St Anne's Primary School, Belfast

A Day In The Life Of Sabrina

Hi, my name is Sabrina. I'm a teenage witch but I live with normal people. I love being a witch, well most of the time. My best friend is Valerie and I've got another friend called Harvey. They're really good friends! I live with my two aunts, they're called Helda and Zelda. I love living in the normal world, but there's one girl who is my worst enemy. That's when I love being a witch. Once I turned her into a goat!

My friends Valerie and Harvey don't know that I am a witch. I'm going to tell you a bit more about being a witch. I am trying to get my driving licence, but I have to figure out the family secret before I get it. I forget to say that I am half-mortal and half-witch. I can make my magic do anything I want it to. Sometimes I use my magic to help others or sometimes I use my magic to do bad things like remember I told you about turning that girl into a goat.

The next day I could not get my locker open so I used my magic. The bad thing about it was that my friends saw me and dared me to use it, so I did and we all got zapped into another world. I did not know how to get back so I took my friends to a fair. We had lots of fun, we got on rides and bought some balloons. But then suddenly we got zapped back to my house. I don't know how it happened. My friends said they had a very good time, but the next day they had forgotten about it.

Katie Wallace (9)
St Anne's Primary School, Belfast

THE BOY WHO WANTED A DOG

There was once a boy called Henry who wanted a dog, but his mum said no! He had been asking her for months. She said, 'What's the point of getting a dog if you're at school and we are at work? There would be no one here to mind him. I will not tell you again, no!' Henry gave a sigh then walked to his room.

His mum and dad were talking about this dog. Then they thought, *we could get him a dog and when he's at school and we are at work Peter could mind him.* They made up their mind and were going to take Henry to the pet shop as a surprise

They set off the next day and Henry asked, 'Where are we going?'
His mum and dad said, 'We are going to Uncle Peter's house.' Then they told him at last, 'You're getting a dog.'
Henry froze in shock, then at last he said, 'We're not?' He jumped up and down. 'Thank you so much.'

The next day the dog went to Uncle Peter's house. While Peter was sleeping Spot ran away to Henry's school. When Henry came out of school everyone laughed and he said, 'Where did you come from?'

Sarah McCabe (9)
St Anne's Primary School, Belfast

THE RETURN OF MELIFICENT

Once there was a princess called Emma who lived with her aunt Grace because an evil witch called Melificent killed her parents. Melificent was the family's enemy because she was the servant Penelope's sister, but there was one thing Emma didn't know that she had a sister who worked for Melificent. When Emma was eleven she heard how her parents had died.

One day Emma opened a trapdoor and found photos of her and her sister Fiona. Emma took one of the photos and brought it to Grace. 'Who's that?' asked Emma puzzled.
'That's your sister Fiona,' replied Grace. 'Where did you get this?'
'Under the trapdoor,' replied Emma. 'Em, could I go for a walk? I'll be back before dinner.'
'OK, but be careful,' said Grace.

Emma knew where to find Fiona and shouted, 'Help!'
Penelope heard and shouted, 'I'm coming Emma.'
'Help!' shouted Emma and Fiona.
'Nobody's gonna save ya,' snarled Melificent, but Penelope put up a fight, grabbed the keys and freed the sisters and they lived happily ever after together.

Kate Lundy (9)
St Anne's Primary School, Belfast

MY FRIEND'S SLEEPOVER

One day Shannon invited me and my friends Rachel, Janice, Grainne and Caitlin up to her house for her birthday and for a sleepover. We had a good laugh first. We went out to play and took turns on Shannon's bike. Then we went in and she opened the presents that she had received. We played some games, had some dinner and some sweets, then we went upstairs watched a video and made some necklaces. Shannon's mum brought us up some sweets and a drink. Then we messed about for the rest of the day.

When we turned off the light we all went, 'Woo,' and Grainne got scared. She's scared of the dark, so we left the light on for the rest of the night, but the rest of us couldn't sleep so we stayed up all night.

Next morning we woke up at about 9 o'clock and went down to get breakfast. We went upstairs, got changed and went down the stairs. We watched TV for about half an hour and took some sweets, watched a video then had more sweets. We went out to play for a while and then went home at about 3 o'clock.

I told my mum about what had happened and showed her my necklace which we made for friendship and went out to play for an hour. Then I went in and watched TV and told my brother Kevin about what happened, showing him the necklace as well. I went out and showed my friends the necklace.

Alanna Morgan (9)
St Anne's Primary School, Belfast

THE PHANTOM

One Sunday two very nice children called Bill and Mary went for a walk down the street. It was about 9 o'clock and the night was stormy and cold. They heard a very weird and scary sound coming from the dark, dark end of the street with no street lights. The children walked slowly towards the noise and saw the phantom lurking behind a large tree. He was the ugliest creature they had ever seen. He had one black eye in the middle of his twisted head. The phantom said, 'If you do not find the pot of gold and silver I will kill you.' Then he hypnotised them and made them his slaves.

They were frightened and shivering with fear. They searched until midnight and went home and searched their garden but with no luck. Bill and Mary had a restless night and had nightmares. They went to the phantom and confessed, 'We cannot find any gold and silver.'
Again the phantom said, 'Then I will kill you tomorrow.'
Bill and Mary searched and searched.

The next evening the phantom caught them as they were trying to sneak home. He killed them both and left them lying at the dark end of the street. Their parents found them and with sad hearts arranged their funerals.

Fifty years later the very same thing happened to two other children and the strange thing was they were also called Bill and Mary. It happened in the same street on a cold, stormy Sunday night.

Michael McCamley (9)
St Anne's Primary School, Belfast

MONIQUEA THE MERMAID

Once upon a time there was a mermaid called Moniquea. She was beautiful and very friendly. The king was called Ronald. He was very greedy and jealous. He always got his own way but one day he didn't.

He wanted to marry Moniquea. Moniquea didn't want to marry him because she knew what kind of man he was. She was a maid in the castle. In the castle were two sharks called Tim and Tom. They were mean sharks. Tim and Tom were shark guards. They stood at the door in case robbers came. There was a goldfish called John. No one saw him after he said to the king that you had to be married to be the king. No one saw him because Tim and Tom had him for dinner that night.

Moniquea's best friend Andrea's boyfriend Christopher always told the truth and was very kind.

One day Moniquea was at the market when suddenly out of nowhere two sharks came and kidnapped her. There was only two sharks in the sea, Tim and Tom. Luckily Moniquea saw that there was a hole. She had long nails so began picking at it. The bag broke and she got out. Tim and Tom began chasing her. She arrived home and as soon as she was settled down there was a knock on the door. It was three octopuses. They barged in and took valuable things and left. She chased them and fought with the robbers and managed to retrieve her good.

Emma Marsden (9)
St Anne's Primary School, Belfast

A DAY IN THE LIFE OF A GUINEA PIG

I sometimes wonder what it would be like to be a guinea pig. I know it would be boring being locked up in a cage but what if you escaped. Well, this story is about three guinea pigs, how they escaped and what they did.

It was early in the morning, Munchy, Crunchy and Starksky went out for their breakfast. It was a lovely, sunny day and the sun was shining through the chicken wire at one side of the cage. Their owner came out with carrots and apples. Starksky's favourite were apples. Moniquea, their owner, opened the door of the hutch and took Starksky out. Moniquea put lots of carrot and apple in for all three. She said she had to go to school. Oh no, is it that time?

Suddenly Moniquea left in a flash. Munchy decided that they would have a day out too. Fortunately the door was unlocked and the guinea pigs escaped. They knew there was a dog next door, so they decided to stay in their own garden. It was now 25 past 12 so they started eating dandelion leaves. The grass was quite wet as it had been raining for the last few weeks. Once they had finished they were quite fat. They could hardly walk back to their hutch, Eventually they waddled back and talked about their fabulous adventure.

Laura Toland (9)
St Anne's Primary School, Belfast

A Day In The Life Of A Witch

If I could be a witch I would love to fly. I could get all the mums and dads to turn into little sweets. I could have a party, then I could turn the babies into flies. I would go on my broomstick to paradise and meet some boys with a boat. They would try to take me away but I would have magic teeth and bite the chains. When the boys came down to feed me I would slice them with my knife and get my broomstick free. Me and my broomstick would find my pet cat and we would leave. We would go home and have another party. I would invite my friends, Emma and Andrea. We would party all night and give people frights.

Emma and Andrea would stay in my house and we'd stay up till 7.00 in the morning. We would go to the sweet shop. I would turn Emma and Andrea into witches. We then would get on our broomsticks and go to see our mums and dads. My dad is called Peter and my mum is called Maria. Then me, my mum and dad would go to Spain to have fun on the beaches. We have a house over there. Then we'd come back to my house and my cat would have kittens.

Moniquea Doherty (9)
St Anne's Primary School, Belfast

A DAY IN THE LIFE OF ROMANS

Romans are very interesting, or so I think. I love them for their style and beliefs. Now I will tell you about the Romans.

The Romans had a very good army and conquered many lands. You had to be loyal to be a member of the army. The army was a brilliant job if you didn't get killed and if you were loyal you could get promotion. You would have to be skilled to be a member of the army. You needed skills such as cooking and building. The men would sign up for 20-25 years.

Romans had a very bad sense of style, or so my teacher would say. I think it was fascinating. They wore togas, women wore several layers of apparel and robes made of wool. The men wore knee-length togas.

The Romans made baths and pumps. They had a bath every nine days (they must have been smelly!) A Roman's life was extremely different. I would have loved to be a Roman because I would have been in the army.

Declan McAlister (9)
St Anne's Primary School, Belfast

THE DEATHS

Louise Woods was a normal girl - blonde hair, blue eyes, the usual. She moved to a new school called Saint Gemma's. Her old school was Rockwell High. Louise was a bit shy at first but she made friends called Virginia, Laura and Naimh.

On Monday Virginia didn't come in, nor for the next three days. On Friday Miss Collins made an announcement. She looked nervous. 'Virginia has been murdered.' There was complete silence. 'Her body was found last night on her bed. Her heart was taken out of her body and placed beside her bed.' That night Louise couldn't stop thinking about poor Virginia.

On Monday Laura never came in, nor for the next three days. Suddenly there was a scream from the corridor. It was Lucy Rooks, a primary 1. Louise ran out to the corridor to see what had happened. There was Laura on the floor - dead! Louise couldn't get over it.

On Monday Louise walked to school, but didn't meet Naimh. Naimh was ill. She was screaming, 'I am dying.' It was a terrible sight. The next day Naimh died. That night there was a phone call. Louise answered it. 'I will kill you like the rest of your friends.' He hung up.

Louise went to school the next morning, but she never came back. The following morning a teacher heard a banging noise against the store room door. She opened the door there was Louise in her blue school uniform with a rope around her neck swinging back and forth. She was dead.

Ellen McLean (9)
St Anne's Primary School, Belfast

THE OLD HOUSE

A long time ago, around 1890, there stood an old house on the top of a hill. Nobody ever went near this house. It was said anyone who entered would die or be cursed for life. *And so the story begins.*

In 1890 two girls were accused of being witches so as a punishment they were sent into the old haunted house. The girls were called Miranda and Anna. The village people followed the girls up to the old house. The girls were put inside. The door was slammed shut and locked. The girls stood in the house shivering. The house creaked, they jumped and screamed.

If they were going to find a way out they would have to be fast. Suddenly they heard a scream. Something appeared in front of them. They ran back to the door banging it and screaming. The figure came closer. *Bang!* Another two witches appeared. The witches were called Moniquea, Andrea and Emma. The girls were terrified. It went dark. There was another scream and a loud bang. The witches were gone.

Miranda opened her eyes to find Anna on the floor with her arm covered in blood. Anna had fainted during her terrible ordeal. Miranda banged even harder. The door was still locked. There was no way out. The girls were trapped there forever.

Now if you pass the old, haunted house you can hear the girls scream. *Ha! Ha! Ha!*

Andrea Lees (9)
St Anne's Primary School, Belfast

THE HAUNTED HOUSE

One day there was a banshee chasing after two children called Jacqueline and John. The banshee found them picking apples in the woods. She went over to them and said, 'Would you like to come to my house for dinner?'

'Yes,' said Jacqueline and John.

Jacqueline and John followed her but they did not know she was a banshee. When they arrived at the house the banshee asked them their names. 'We are Jacqueline and John,' replied Jacqueline.

'What is your name?' asked John.

The banshee said, 'My name is Enid the banshee.'

Jacqueline and John spoke together. 'Enid the banshee?'

'Yes,' she said. Then the banshee caught them and threw them in the dungeon and shouted, 'I will kill you tomorrow.'

Jacqueline and John began to cry. The banshee heard them. Suddenly the banshee went into the dungeon. She saw a hole in the wall where Jacqueline and John had escaped. The banshee saw them running away and darted after them. The banshee clocked them going into the woods and followed them. All three were suddenly lost. They all started to walk about and eventually banged into each other.

Suddenly the children found there was a way out of the woods. They recognised the tree in front of them. It was the only tree in the wood with no leaves on it. They followed the path out of the woods and escaped from the banshee. They arrived home safely from their most awful adventure ever.

Donal Brady (9)
St Anne's Primary School, Belfast

THE HAUNTED HOUSE

It was the 26th of April when the Laverys moved house. There were five in the Lavery family. There was Chris, Pat, Ryan, Mum and Dad. Chris was six, Pat was nine, Ryan was 12. Chris did not want to move but Pat and Ryan did. It was about 10 o'clock. The Laverys were getting very excited.

The next morning the van came to take their stuff from their house to their new home. It was a tall and dark house. Mum opened the door with a squeak. There was a great big room. Chris was getting scared and felt like screaming, but he didn't. Pat and Ryan wanted to go up the stairs and pick their rooms, but Chris stayed downstairs.

When they went into one of the rooms there was a skeleton hanging on the door. Then they came running down the stairs screaming. The doors and windows started to open and close and the whole family started to scream.
Mum said, 'A walk might calm us down.'
'OK,' said Chris, Pat, Ryan and Dad.

When they were walking away from the house Pat saw a ghost that had a hat on his head. Everyone ran away. Suddenly something tapped Ryan on the back and made him jump.

The next morning they moved back into their old house.

Christopher Murphy (9)
St Anne's Primary School, Belfast

THE HAUNTED HOUSE

One day, in 1678, a boy called James had to go on a school trip to visit a haunted house. They all went in and never came out!

In 2003 another class were asked to go on a tour and they agreed. They went with their bags tightly packed and a pair of extra clothes because they were going for two days.

When they got there, they knocked on the door at which it replied with a scream. When they heard it, they all wanted to go back to school.
'Can we go, please, oh please can we?'
'No! We're staying,' the teacher howled.
We all agreed on it, we were staying.

Soon the doors opened and let them go through. They went in and that night they all slept with the doors open. A cloud of smoke which was a spirit came in. It turned into James. He had a knife and he stabbed the teacher.
He said, 'One down, twenty to go, *ha, ha, ha.*'

The next morning all of the children went to wake the teacher but they saw she had been stabbed in the heart. Jerry went outside and the spirit attacked him. They didn't see him again. It was time to go and all of the other children got in the bus and when they were nearly at school they crashed and died!

Ryan Graham (9)
St Anne's Primary School, Belfast

THE HAUNTED HOUSE

One day there was a boy called Peter and his mum and dad were called Sheila and Paul. They were going on a holiday to France. Peter was really excited. They were leaving the next day. They were going on a plane.

The next morning Peter got up, got ready and left without his breakfast. When he got to France he went to a hotel in Lyon. When he got in he went to bed.

The next day Peter went to a museum and he saw a headless skeleton but he thought it was a fake. When he got home it was night and he went to bed. When he was asleep the skeleton came back and woke him up. Peter got very scared and tried to get away but he got caught.

The skeleton took him away and brought him to a haunted house. Peter got really scared and climbed out of the window and ran home. The next night it happened again, and the next, and the next. But one night it didn't happen, so Peter went to the haunted house to see if the skeleton was still there. He was and there were a lot of other skeletons as well - lots more. Then Peter got really scared but he couldn't get away.

Eventually he got away but still they followed him everywhere. Peter tried to get away but he got caught again, they locked him away in the haunted house, closed all the windows and went away.

Later they came back and let him out. They tried to cut his arms off but he got away and never saw them again!

David Fitzpatrick (9)
St Anne's Primary School, Belfast

GHOST STORY

'Alright, time to get up,' whispered Steve to his friends. 'Everyone's asleep now.'

Steve, Greta, Raquel and Jack sneaked out of their tent and made the campfire. They were on a weekend camping trip and stayed up to tell ghost stories.

'I've got a good story, listen,' said Raquel. 'It all started in a small village called Peterstown, the Jones family were going on a camping trip, like ours, to a Canadian forest. Brook, the child of the family, was always embarrassed when she went with her father on these trips because her father hunted werewolves . . .'

'Why did you stop?' asked Greta.

'I don't know but it feels like something's watching us,' Raquel replied.

In the distance a fierce-sounding wolf howled.

'Ignore it,' Jack told them. 'Continue the story.'

'OK. So the Jones family had arrived at their campsite not knowing that werewolves killed people in there.'

The wolf howled again.

'This is getting too creepy now. I'm asking Mum what's up with that wolf,' Steve said quietly.

Steve and his friends entered his mum's tent. They found a half-eaten corpse and a trail of blood leading from a massive hole in the back! They turned around and screamed!

'Is that a . . .' Jack couldn't finish his sentence. His head had been ripped off!

The rest started to run but they couldn't outrun the werewolf chasing them! Then they died, painfully.

The werewolf growled, it had been here fifty years, many people go to see it . . . but nobody comes back.

Denika Leonard (11)
St Columban's Primary School, Belcoo

DAVID BECKHAM FOR A DAY

I have just been to the hairdresser's and am making my way to Old Trafford for the Champions League Final. The teams are Man United against Bayern Munich. I am just ready to go out on the pitch. I am now shaking hands with the other players. Now Man United have kicked off and storming down the pitch is Ruud van Nistelrooy. He is just outside the penalty area and is tripped. I am taking the free kick and I score.

Right now I have a fifty-fifty ball with another player and he hits me on my ankle and I go down in real pain. I think I have broken my foot. A stretcher comes to pick me up from the ground and is taking me to an ambulance which transports me to a hospital.

Later on I am X-rayed and then I am told the news. I am shocked to find I have a broken ankle. I am not fit to play for four months. I am so disappointed.

The good news for the ladies however is that now I can spend more time in the hairdresser's and concentrate on my modelling career!

Conor McAleer (9)
St Joseph's Primary School, Cookstown

THE HAUNTED HOUSE

It was a thundery night and the air was spicy, warm and still. I was following the moon. I saw a gate, opened it and went inside. I saw a very old house that was pitch-black with a long, windy, narrow road up to it. I walked slowly; the leaves from the trees kept falling down on my head. I could hardly see the door as it was covered with cobwebs and streaming ivy. I knocked on the door but nobody answered. I pushed it open with some force and it creaked loudly.

As the door closed behind me, I looked around the room. I was in what looked like a living room but nobody had lived there for some time. The dust made me choke. The walls were a deep red colour and there were some old broken furniture hiding in a large stone fireplace. As I walked through the room I could feel someone watching me.

I walked into the old kitchen, which had a stone flagged floor. It would probably have looked nice if it were brushed. A mouse crossed the top of my shoes and as I looked down I could see bloodstains on the stone floor. It really frightened me. Had someone died here? I wasn't waiting to find out.

I still felt there were eyes watching me and as I ran I could hear a door slam in another room. I ran for the front door but I couldn't get it open. I tried again and again and finally it opened.

As I ran down the long, winding path my heart kept beating faster and faster, it felt like it was going to jump out of my body. I kept thinking I could hear footsteps and as I reached the bottom of the path someone put their hand on my shoulder and I nearly jumped out of my skin. I kept running and running. At this stage it was very dark and there was very little street lighting. I hid behind a hedge and I peeked out. I saw a figure coming towards me. I was so scared. I felt like screaming but I knew I would be found if I did.

Hold on! It's the movie director, Steven Spielberg. As he got closer I hid deeper in the hedge. He pulled me out of the hedge and said that the haunted house was the set of his latest movie and he wanted me to star in it. I'm going to be famous!

Aoibheann McAleer (9)
St Joseph's Primary School, Cookstown

The Castle Of Doom!

It was a dark, stormy and spooky night in the month of October and a vampire called Spiky lived in the castle of doom. The Lupari family moved in from Italy and they had garlic with *every* meal. Spiky hated garlic (he was a vampire after all) and he decided to make up a plan to get rid of them.

He tried to frighten them at night but he couldn't get close to them because they reeked so much of garlic. He tried dancing in a white sheet like a ghost on the kitchen roof but they loved the idea of living in a haunted castle, so this didn't work.

He was so fed up so he went to get his friends called Sparky, Lizzy and Gazar. They landed at the castle of doom and Sparky had a brilliant idea to get rid of them.
'We will destroy all of the garlic so that we can get close to them and then we will really scare the life out of the family.'
So that's what they did.

After their hair-raising night, the Lupari family were so terrified that they packed their bags and left for Italy straight away.

This meant that Spiky could have as many parties as he wanted with Sparky, Lizzy and Gazar, his friends. But there definitely would be no food with *garlic* served in the Castle of Doom again!

Megan McNally (8)
St Joseph's Primary School, Cookstown

AN ENCHANTING PLACE

Once, long ago, there was a strange place and it was a very mystifying place in which there were colossal trees with branches that looked like immense long fingers pointing at you. The mysterious place had a big mountain and right in the middle of it was a dark, hollow cave. It was as black as coal inside. Behind that were other mountains which pointed like icicles upside down. On the mountainside there was a round face with staring eyes with a pointy witch nose. The sky was a bright florescent orange with yellow mixed in to make it look like a sunset. The cave in the middle looked like a big mouth ready to gobble you up or something mysterious would just jump out at you.

Down the side of the mountain, flowing so gently, there was the waterfall. It was so clear and sparkling with fairy dust that at the bottom it looked like a wishing well. The roots of the trees looked like long, skinny legs with pointy toes at the end. Birds were flying high in the sky, swooping down to catch their prey. The tops of the trees looked like a face with a really large nose that was going to sniff you out and eat you with its enormous dark, black, cave mouth. In a spooky and enchanting place you never knew what would happen.

Emma Campbell (9)
St Macnissis Primary School, Larne

THE MAGIC KINGDOM

As I approached what appeared to be the bark of a large oak tree, to the right of the tree the branches seemed very witch-like with long, clawing fingers. Over to the left there were icy mountains which were as white as snow. There was a waterfall that looked as clean as a whistle and flowed as fast as lightning. The grass at the front of the tree was so spring-like with snowdrops darted here and there. I almost could imagine a family of bunny rabbits hopping in and out of the waterfall. High up in the bark of the tree an owl was curled up fast asleep, resting for night watch.

At the opening of the bottom of the tree it appeared very dark, almost like the entrance to a cave. As I ventured closer, music struck my ears. Curiously it drew me inside the cave and very much to my surprise I did not enter a spooky room. In fact I had entered an underground cave. It was lit up with little houses, little plastic rabbits, little frogs and lots of wood creatures singing and dancing merrily. For a split second I felt I was in the magic kingdom.

Rachel McIlgorm (9)
St Macnissis Primary School, Larne

THE HAUNTED HOUSE

My friends and I went on a camping trip with the cubs one weekend in the old forest. On the first night we sneaked off through the forest and came across an old rundown house. My friends were too scared, so I entered the house on my own with only a torch to guide me. The wind blew through the house and the floorboards were creaky. I could also hear strange noises, like people talking from a room upstairs.

I went up the stairs, tripping on the last step causing me to drop the torch. It went out. I opened the door of the room and entered. I could hear scratching on the floorboards and strange noises above me, but I could not see without the light from the torch. I could feel something at my feet and something touching my head. Feeling very afraid I turned to run from the room but I tripped over something and fell to the floor. My torch hit the ground with a bang, causing the light to come on. I grabbed the torch, pointing it to the floor and then the ceiling. All around me on the floor were rats with long tails and on the ceiling were bats with sharp red eyes and large wings. In the corner of the room I could also see a dark shadow which looked like an old man. I screamed and ran from the room, making my way down the stairs and out of the front door.

I ran through the forest screaming for help but soon realised that I was lost. The forest was very dark and I could hear lots of noises which made me very scared.

Suddenly I could hear voices in the distance and lots of shadows appeared between the trees. As they got closer I recognised that it was my friends and the other people from the camp. I ran over to meet them and knew that I was now safe. After getting told off by my leaders we returned to camp.

Lauren Brown (9)
St Macnissis Primary School, Larne

THE OLD MILL

Forkhill is the nicest village. There is a church, chip shop, supermarket, some houses and an old mill. It is the creepiest, weirdest and scariest place in Forkhill. The name of the mill is 'Brooks' and it was previously a grinding mill. My dad said that his dad went down there with oats and corn every week to get it ground into flour. Children say that a man died in the mill by falling onto the machinery and that it is haunted. The buildings are covered in ivy and trees. There are about five buildings down there. One of them is a pig house, another is the mill. It is over two hundred years old.

People say that they hear strange noises like banging and squeaks, but I have only been down there three times with my friends. At the rear end of the mill there is a wheel which water turned to keep the mill going. Water turned the wheel and the engine started working. The sound of the river is a bit scary because the water is lapping off the rocks in the river. Some people store their goods in one of the houses and we think they are stolen because they are covered in white blankets. That frightens us and my friends go down to see the goods sometimes.

I think we are taking a risk because there might be robbers using the place as a hidey-hole and they might get violent if they were found out.

Lisa Black (11)
St Oliver Plunkett's Primary School, Forkhill

A SPOOKY STORY

There is a very interesting place in Forkhill. It is a deserted old mill and it is very, very scary down there. When you go down there you will nearly go to the toilet in your trousers. Once, Christine, Gemma, Darren and me went down to the mill to look. It was our first time being down there but Tomas, Paudie, Ryan and Stephen were already down there. They heard us coming so they hid to scare us. They went into a shed and we went into the same shed. When they jumped out and shouted *boo* I nearly jumped out of my skin. We ended up in fits of laughter.

People say that the rich man who owned the old mill fell into the spinning machine and it automatically turned on and his head got chopped off. Horrifying, isn't it?

One day Shannon and me were walking down the lane when all of a sudden Shannon screamed. We started running. When we got to our house she looked very shocked.
'What's wrong?' I asked. 'Calm down! What happened? Did a wasp sting you?'
She said, 'I saw a man with a knife in his hand! He was so scary. He was in the mill window.'
'Are you all right? Do you want a drink of water? So what did the man look like?'
'He was as white as a ghost.'

When I got her calmed down we went up to the shop and got some sweets. Then we went down to the park and stared at the mill window, swinging back and forth for ages. Believe me, we will never ever go down there again!

Penny McGovern (10)
St Oliver Plunkett's Primary School, Forkhill

THE HAUNTED HOUSE

In this story I'll tell you about a spooky, old, dark and dreary house that is built close to me. It is covered with ivy and surrounded by trees. A lot of people, including me, think that it is haunted. Now and again you would hear noises coming from it, but you wouldn't pass any remarks on it. At midnight, on the 30th October 2000, different kinds of noises were coming from it. It was really scaring me, it had my whole family awake. This wasn't normal and it was strange to hear them only on a spooky Hallowe'en night.

We decided to leave it for a few more hours but the noises didn't stop. We all gazed out the windows of our house to see what was happening. We saw ghosts flying in and out of the house, smoke coming out of the chimneys and the lights turning on and off. We left it until the morning and then decided to go to the house, but didn't find any clues of evidence as to what had happened. It really freaked us out. We went to our neighbours and asked them if they had heard anything. They said they had.

We think of it every time we go past the house and it scares us. Every Hallowe'en night we try to stay up all night to see if the same thing will happen again but so far it hasn't. The mystery still lies with us!

Nichola Byrnes
St Oliver Plunkett's Primary School, Forkhill

SCARY STORY . . . GRANDA'S MEMORIES

When my granda was about sixteen he was sent to an old man's house to see if he had recovered from his illness. When he finally got to the house he was surprised to find that there were three men (one being the old man who lived there) telling some really scary ghost stories. When he went into the house he started listening to the stories and then he ran out of the house. He was really shaken.

When he got out of the house he met up with his mates. They were having a good chat when my granda dared one of his mates to go into the top room in a spooky house that they were walking past. The house was old and supposed to be haunted and it looked even creepier in the light of the bright moon. He took up the dare and got his stuff to prove that he went up to the top room. He got a hammer, a nail and two matches. One match was so he could see where he was going when he was going up the stairs and the other one was for him to see where he was hammering the nail. Anyway he started to walk towards the house and as soon as he went in the door, Granda and the other mate wandered back to my granda's house.

When there was no sign of the other mate they got their torches and went back up to the house to see if he was OK. When they got there they found that he was dead from a heart attack. He had nailed his coat to the ground and thought that the ghost wouldn't let him out of the house!

Cathal Adams (11)
St Oliver Plunkett's Primary School, Forkhill

THE MILL

Our village is very small, although it has a coffee shop and Spar supermarket. It also has two mills, but one of the mills has been knocked down. The mill that is left is an old and dirty place. I heard that a man got caught in a machine down there and was killed. My granny's brother, Jim, used to work there. All the local farmers brought their corn to get it ground into flour. Someone told me that the mill was haunted. Once I was in it and I heard noises and footsteps. I was told that there were lots of car alloys hidden behind the mill. Some people put tyres in the water and sat on them to float down the river. The old mill is now a part of the farm. There was a skull beside the mill but it was not a human skull.

Many years ago a wee girl was playing beside the river. She fell in and drowned. The water took her away down the river where her body was rescued.

When I was inside the mill a plank broke and a step broke. It frightened me so much and left me feeling scared, so I quickly left.

The mill is a stone building with a big wheel for powering the machinery inside the mill.

Stephen Coleman (11)
St Oliver Plunkett's Primary School, Forkhill